Kline

"Did you see that f... night's report?" ... at the menu. "The mugg... shoes."

Mendoza grinned. "Maybe he just needed some new shoes, Art."

"The witness said he was a lot bigger than the victim. I wonder if they fit him."

"One of life's little mysteries," said Mendoza. "We'll never know."

———————— ★ ————————

Blood Count

SHANNON DELL

Blood Count

WORLDWIDE®

TORONTO · NEW YORK · LONDON · PARIS
AMSTERDAM · STOCKHOLM · HAMBURG
ATHENS · MILAN · TOKYO · SYDNEY

BLOOD COUNT

A Worldwide Mystery/July 1988

First published by William Morrow and Company, Inc.

ISBN 0-373-26006-7

Printed in U.S.A.

This one is for
RINEHART POTTS

"It matters not what man assumes to be;
Or good, or bad, they are but what they are."

—PHILIP JAMES BAILEY
Festus

ONE

"I JUST FIGURED you'd want to know how it happened I was there," said Bill Cassidy. "Like I say, I run that station out on Pico. My night man, Ted Smith, he comes on at six, only last night he was late. It was the dog, see." Cassidy was about forty-five, with an earnest bulldog face and scanty sandy hair. "It's a cute little dog, Sergeant Hackett."

"Yes, yes," said Hackett. Witnesses were either too taciturn or too voluble.

"See, he was just about to leave when the dog got hold of something poisonous and got awful sick, and they had to rush him to the vet. Ted and his wife, they're just crazy about that dog. So Ted called me from the vet's, said he didn't know when he'd get to work. But they pumped out the dog's stomach or something and he's goin' to be okay, but Ted didn't get to the station until eight o'clock, so that's how come I was just on my way home. At that intersection there, Olympic and Alvarado. It was about eight-thirty. My God, that was a terrible thing to see happen—just terrible. That poor little girl."

"Yes," said Hackett again, patiently. Luis Mendoza was half-sitting on a corner of the desk, smoking and listening in silence. "Could you tell us—"

"I saw the whole thing," said Cassidy. "My God. There wasn't much traffic that time of night, or many people in the street."

At that hour on a Friday night—last night—there wouldn't have been. At about eight-thirty Mrs. Marion Crane and her eight-year-old daughter Alice had been on their way home from the library on Olympic Boulevard, which they visited every Friday night; both of them had a small bag of borrowed books. As they crossed the intersection with the light, to wait at the corner for the bus to take them home to Benton Way, a car had run the light and plowed into them squarely, and without braking had vanished down Alvarado at a high rate of speed. The little girl had been killed instantly, and Mrs. Crane was in the hospital with a fractured pelvis and various other injuries, still unconscious with concussion.

"They were the only ones crossing the street," said Cassidy. "Like I told you, I was sittin' in my car right across, headed up Alvarado, and I saw the whole thing. This damn car never slowed up at all, just ran the light—goin' maybe forty-five, fifty—and I think maybe the driver was drunk, it was weavin' all over between lanes before that. And I can tell you what it was—it sounds crazy, but it was an old Model A Ford."

"You don't say," said Hackett. "I'll be damned."

Cassidy nodded vigorously. "That's what it was. Once in a while you do see 'em, still running pretty good. My God, fifty-five, fifty-six years old—but I understand it was a pretty damn reliable car, and some guys make it like a hobby, sort of, these vintage cars like they call them. And it was a sedan, not a coupe—a four-door. And I'll tell you something else, it was fresh painted."

"Shiny," suggested Hackett.

"Right under the arc lights," said Cassidy. "Sure. Like it had just had a coat of paint. You know all those old jobs were painted black—well, so was this one, but it was new paint. All glossy and shiny."

"I'll be damned," said Hackett again. "Well, we'd like you to sign a statement about this, Mr. Cassidy. It'll just take a minute to type it up."

"Sure."

Jason Grace was talking to the other witness at his desk across the big communal office at Robbery-Homicide. When Bob Schenke of the night watch had covered this last night, he had talked to only one other witness, and what he had said now backed up Cassidy. He was a teenage boy, and he had told Schenke, "Gee, that car—all I can say is, it was a real oldie, it looked sort of like those cars the gangsters used to drive, in the old movies, you know."

"That poor little girl. These damn fool drunks," said Cassidy. Hackett typed up a brief statement and he signed it. "I sure hope you catch up to him. But even if you do, and put him in jail, it won't help the little girl or her mama. Oh, I'm just glad I could tell you something, just hope it'll help you catch him." He went out, following on the heels of the other witness, and Jason Grace came to perch a hip on the corner of Hackett's desk.

"Anything useful from that one?" asked Mendoza.

"Mr. Neil Cushing," said Grace. "Something definite anyway." His chocolate-brown face wore a thoughtful expression; he brushed his narrow moustache absently. "Retired widower waiting for a bus on his way home. He'd been out to dinner and went to see an old western at one of the rerun houses. They took his driver's license away last year—he's eighty-two—but he's driven all his life and knows cars. He says, of all things, the car was an old Model A Ford, a sedan."

"Definite," said Mendoza. "We've just heard the same thing. But, as Cassidy says, you do see them occasionally. Still perking along after all this time." He grinned mirthlessly. "Which is probably more than you can expect of anything getting manufactured these days. As the saying goes, they don't build them the way they used to."

"Well, it gives us a place to look," said Grace. "Ask Sacramento about all of those on file."

None of them made any immediate move to do that. The office was quiet, empty except for themselves; it was Galeano's day off and everybody else was out on something. In this second week of November, Robbery-Homicide, headquarters, was not quite as busy as usual: a couple of still-unidentified bodies, the normal number of heists to work, a couple of suicides with the paperwork getting cleared away.

Pat Calhoun came drifting in, sat down at his desk, and lit a cigarette. "So what's the new corpse look like?" asked Mendoza.

Calhoun sat back and shut his eyes. He was the latest addition to the team, one of the bright boys making rank early, a big handsome wide-shouldered fellow barely thirty, but he had put in four years as a detective at the Seventy-Seventh Street station and knew his job. "Nothing very interesting, and nowhere much to go on it." The latest corpse had been spotted by a patrolman just after midnight last night, on the sidewalk outside a bar on Temple Street. "You saw Conway's report. He asked at the bar but nobody claimed to recognize him, and it's the kind of place where they get a lot of transient trade. Also a fairly noisy place, and it's entirely possible that the man was shot right there and nobody inside heard the shot. Anyway, he was shot—in the head, looked like a fairly big gun, the lab will tell us. I went over to the coroner's office and had a look at him, at the clothes. Nothing very distinctive about him—about forty-five, medium size, shabby old suit needing cleaning, ditto old shirt and underclothes. There was some I.D. on him, a lapsed driver's license and Social Security card. He was one Joseph Naysmith, and the address on the license was up in Hollywood. It's a rundown apartment building on Berendo, no manager on the premises, and nobody there remembered him—I chased down all the tenants who weren't home, but the license was four years out of date."

"So, dead end," said Mendoza. "Unless he's in our records and we get a handle there."

Calhoun agreed amiably. "There's just one thing that did strike me. Funny little thing."

"Oh?"

"His hands. A beautiful manicure job—might be professional. Nails buffed to a gloss, white pencil run under them, cuticle all neatly trimmed."

Mendoza sat up. "Funny isn't the word," he said interestedly. "Otherwise looking like a run-of-the-mill down and out? Not quite a skid row bum, but definitely not in the money." His nose twitched; Mendoza was always intrigued by anything slightly offbeat.

"That's right. Tell you one thing," said Calhoun thoughtfully. "He'd never used those hands at anything like manual labor. Nice soft, white, ladylike hands."

"Extraño," said Mendoza. "I take it you passed his prints on to R. and I.?"

"Naturally. We ought to hear something from them any time."

Higgins and Palliser came in together. It was coming up to the end of the day shift. They were both looking tired. "Do any good on anything?" asked Hackett.

Higgins just grunted, settling his bulk into the desk chair and lighting a cigarette. "Don't ask," said Palliser. "The heisters are a dime a dozen, all over the place. Half the time only a vague general description, and even if the victim picks a picture out of the books, we know what eyewitnesses are worth. The only thing we can say definitely—the one on the liquor store Wednesday night is probably the same one who hit that market last week, by the description. Big and husky, but not young. Dirty sports clothes, a big gun, tattoo of some kind on his left arm. Which is helpful. Tom didn't come up with anything on that other heist. We just ran into him downstairs, he looked beat and said he was taking off early." That one was even vaguer, the holdup of an independent pharmacy last Tuesday night; Tom Landers and Nick Galeano had been working it, but the description they had from the pharmacist was a handful of nothing—"Just a young fellow, thin, dark, sort of a pale face—no, I didn't see a gun, he had the gun in his pocket—" And after pouring over the mug shots he hadn't made any.

Wanda Larsen came in and said, "I won't even sit down, I'm going home and thank goodness tomorrow's my day off." A fairly pretty blonde, she was now looking tired and subdued. "We've just about got this juvenile thing cleared away, just some more paperwork to do." The only reason Robbery-Homicide had gotten involved was that the juveniles—a pair of teenage boys high on angel dust—had killed an adult in the process of robbing him, an inoffensive pawnbroker who had just refused to take a tape recorder from them, suspecting it was stolen, which it had been.

Mendoza yawned and stood up. "Saturday night—there'll probably be some new business coming up. Maybe I'll take off early too."

"Business a little slow?" The voice from the door was cheerful and brisk. They all looked around and Hackett uttered a little groan.

"And what the hell are you doing here?"

"Got something to hand over to you. Could be a kind of funny thing." Jeff MacDonald came in, pulled up the chair from Landers' desk, and sat down. He plunked down a woman's handbag on the desk and pulled a Manila envelope from his breast pocket. MacDonald was one of the investigators for the coroner's office, a stocky, dark, youngish fellow with a luxuriant handlebar moustache.

"So what now?" asked Mendoza resignedly.

"Well, it didn't look like anything for you, to start with." MacDonald was filling an old brier pipe. "Accident, pure and simple. Or an O.D. of some kind. Patrolman came across the car about twelve-thirty A.M. this morning, on Fourteenth just off Sepulveda. The car was rammed into a light pole at the curb, and a woman dead behind the wheel. Not a mark on her, and the car wasn't damaged much. It's a rented car, by the way—Hertz. Two-door Ford. She could have had a heart attack, whatever, lost control of the car. Anyway, the patrolman didn't think it was anything for the detectives, and called us. One of our night watch went out, took some pictures, brought the body in. The car's in your garage. Nothing looked unusual until Dr. Cox did an autopsy this afternoon."

"So what did the lady die of?" asked Hackett. "Any I.D.?"

"Oh, sure, there's this and that in her handbag. Well, I was sitting in on the autopsy, and when Cox got into it, it looked like something more than an accident. Of whatever kind. You'll get the full autopsy report sometime tomorrow, probably, but to go on with—she wasn't drunk or high on anything else. What killed her was a depressed skull fracture—a pretty bad one—right here," and MacDonald illustrated on his own head. "Right behind the left ear. Skin not broken, no external bleeding. In fact, our old friend the blunt instrument, as the old mystery writers used to say."

"So she didn't hit anything in the car," said Mendoza.

"Pretty obviously not. Not much in the car could have caused that kind of blow—the dashboard, the top of a door—but if that was the case, somebody moved her afterward, put her right behind the wheel. Cox says she was unconscious from the time she was hit, couldn't have moved. And there she was draped over the wheel as if she'd been driving, rammed the car into the pole herself."

"I see," said Mendoza. "So you dump it in our laps—I suppose that's her bag, and a dozen of your boys have plastered their prints all over it, and the car."

"Now, Lieutenant," said MacDonald reproachfully, "we know better than that. You may find a couple of mine on the bag—we had to look for I.D., naturally—but we haven't started any investigation, that's your job now. I've got the pictures of the scene for you—"

"And since you've been through the handbag, I suppose we needn't delay a look while it's printed. Hell."

"It's all yours," said MacDonald. "There's next of kin to notify—we haven't done anything about that. She's a Louise Cannaday—evidently lived in Indianapolis, by the I.D. She was registered at the Sheraton Plaza, by that card in the bag—we haven't verified that either."

"Thank you so much," said Hackett.

"All in a day's work. Hope you can find out what happened to her." MacDonald knocked out his pipe in the ashtray on the desk and stood up. "You'll be getting the autopsy report. You'll let us know whatever you find out."

"If anything."

They watched him out rather glumly. Grace yawned and said, "That Model A Ford. I'll get on the wire to Sacramento, and then call it a day." Wanda was just leaving, Higgins and Palliser reaching for their coats. Mendoza stabbed out his cigarette in Hackett's ashtray and said somnolently, "And tomorrow is also a day. See you in the morning, Arturo." He went back to his office for hat and coat and went out after Higgins and Palliser. Calhoun, yawning, stood up and started for the door. The phone rang on Hackett's desk and he picked it up.

"These prints," said Horder up in the lab. "Calhoun handed them in this morning. Said they belonged to a Joseph Naysmith. We don't know them, they're not on file with us. I passed them on to the Feds."

"Okay, thanks," said Hackett. He beckoned to Calhoun at the door and passed that on. Calhoun flipped a hand at him and went out.

It was ten minutes of six. Hackett eyed the handbag on his desk. Next of kin, he thought. One of the thankless jobs they came in for. It was a handsome, expensive-looking bag, black pigskin-grained leather, square, with double handles and a single snap catch. Gingerly he opened the catch and upended the bag on his desk.

The wallet was newish-looking too, blue leather with a double coin purse and behind that a range of plastic slots. In the coin purse was a little wad of bills and change, amounting to thirty-seven dollars and fifty-eight cents. The first plastic slot held a driver's license for Mrs. Louise Cannaday, an address in Indianapolis. It had been issued less than a year ago and was valid for four years. He looked at the photograph with some interest. Whoever she had been, Louise Cannaday had been a good-looking woman. Not young—her age was given as fifty-five—but not looking her age: she must have been something of a beauty as a young woman. It was a triangular face with high cheekbones, a wide generous-looking mouth, her most striking feature the thick dark hair with a broad streak of white through a heavy wave sweeping up from the forehead. She had intelligent dark eyes, a straight nose, rather sharply arched brows. The description said Caucasian, five-five, a hundred and thirty, eyes brown, hair black. He leafed through the other slots. A Visa card. Library card. Medical insurance card. A hand-printed slip of paper, notify in case of emergency, Dr. James Cannaday, another address in Indianapolis, a phone number. Hackett sighed and reached for the phone. Get it over with and have it done. It would make him a few minutes late. He couldn't remember the time difference between California and Indiana: two hours, three? It didn't matter.

He got, after an interval, Dr. Cannaday, who sounded fairly young and, on hearing the news, incredulous and shaken. He said, and his voice went high and shocked, "*Mother!* But I don't understand—what happened? You said police—Mother's *dead*? Dead—an accident—but I don't understand, she's a very good driver—what happened?"

"We don't know much about it yet, I'm sorry. It happened last night, and apparently it wasn't an accident, doctor. We'll be investigating. You understand we'll want to know the answers to some questions—she was just visiting here, apparently—" Hackett edged a card from under the wallet with one forefinger. It was a square pink-toned card, with a line of elegant italic script at its bottom: *THE SHERATON PLAZA FLORIST SHOP.* At the top was another line of printing, *To welcome you*, and below a single written name: *Adele.*

"Yes—yes—she was flying home tomorrow—and then I had a wire from her last night, she was staying over a couple of days, I don't know why—she said Tuesday, she'd be coming home Tuesday—but my God, what could have happened? How could she be—oh, my God, don't call Sue! My sister—I'll have to call her—oh, my God, I'd better come—there'll be all the arrangements, she'd want to be here with Dad in the family plot—" And now he was nearly crying, incoherent and stunned. "I'll have to come—call Sue and tell her—somehow—but I don't understand what could have happened—it's nothing that *can* have happened, Mother dead—oh, my God, we'd all been so happy about the baby—oh, God, I don't know how to tell Sue—I'd better come—"

He wasn't in any state to answer questions. Hackett said, "Will you let us know when you'll be getting in, please, doctor? Sergeant Hackett, Robbery-Homicide, L.A.P.D. headquarters."

"Yes, of course—I'll have to see—reservations—and call Sue, but she mustn't come—I'd better talk to Dan first—" He was numb now. "I'll come—as soon as I can—but I don't understand what can have happened—"

Hackett put the phone down. The night watch was coming in—Matt Piggott, Bob Schenke, Rich Conway—all on, on Saturday night when there was usually new business showing up. He collected his coat and started home, fifteen minutes late, and when he got out to the parking lot found it had begun to rain. It was the second storm they'd had since the start of the season; maybe they were due for a wet winter for a change. At any rate, it was coming down hard and slowed the tedious drive on the freeway up to Altadena, to the sprawling old house on the dead-end street. Angel had dinner nearly ready for the table and was firm with the children. "Now, Mark, let your father have a peaceful drink before dinner, he'll look at your homework later. He'll read to you before bed, Sheila, don't bother him now. Tough day, Art?"

"Not bad," said Hackett. "Just more of the same." Generally they all got used to shelving the various cases on hand when they left the office, but there was some faint curiosity at the back of his mind about this one. What had happened to Louise Cannaday? Staying at the Sheraton Plaza—one of the classier hotels—so, very solvent; and the son sounded like a nice ordinary fellow. And he thought, damnation, he should have told the lab to have a look at that rented car in the police garage.

MENDOZA WASN'T harboring much curiosity about any of the cases on hand, except very faintly for the corpse with the well-manicured hands. It was very seldom that any kind of interesting mystery or anything unusual turned up for Robbery-Homicide to work; monotonously, they were dealing most of the time with the results of that old devil human nature, the crudities and stupidities and violence. It was a slow drive home up the freeway through the solid sheets of rain, and it was nearly seven o'clock when he turned up the hill above Burbank and the tall wrought-iron gates swung politely open to admit the Ferrari. It was pitch dark below, but there were welcoming lights in the big Spanish house at the top of the hill. He wondered briefly how the Five Graces were faring in the downpour—the sheep installed to keep the underbrush eaten down—but Ken Kearney, their man of all work, had built a shelter for them beyond the stable and corral.

He ran the car into the garage beside Alison's and went in the back door. Their surrogate grandmother Mairí Mac-Taggart was busy at the stove. "Well, and it's time you were getting home."

"Rain," said Mendoza. "Everything all serene?"

"As much as you could expect with all these noisy children about. That pair can always think up something new to fret Alison, but what I say is you just have to thole it. Only they come by the stubbornness just natural, her mother having been a McCann."

Mendoza laughed, shrugging off the trench coat and dropping the Homburg onto the nearest chair. "If you can't lick 'em, join 'em, that's what it comes to." He opened the cupboard over the sink, took down the bottle of rye, and before he reached for a glass the alcoholic half-Siamese El Señor arrived at top speed and slid half the length of the counter, demanding his share in a raucous voice. "You're a disgraceful drunk," said Mendoza, and poured him half an ounce in a saucer. He wandered down the hall to the big living room. The other three cats, Bast, Nefertite, and Sheba, were cozily tangled together on the couch, and Cedric, the Old English Sheepdog, was sound asleep in front of a blazing fire on the hearth. *"¿Qué nuevas, mi cielo?"*

"Need you ask?" Alison was sitting in her big armchair, nursing the new one; the firelight made a flaming nimbus of her red hair. He bent to kiss her. The new one—the very unexpected one—and, as Alison said firmly, the last one—had arrived peacefully and with no fuss just over two weeks ago, a rather diminutive but quite healthy female with a full head of black hair. "Nothing new at all," said Alison, "more's the pity. That pair of little hellions—"

The twins, hearing the sounds of his arrival, erupted down the stairs to greet him exuberantly. With the advent of chillier weather they had temporarily forgotten the issue of the swimming pool, but of course they had a new interest these days.

Greetings over, Johnny hung fondly over one side of the armchair and Terry over the other. "She's still so awful little," said Johnny, "but she's awful pretty. She's a lot prettier than Luisa." Baby Luisa—now no more the baby—would be tucked up in bed now instead of under everyone's feet. Johnny patted the new one. "Pretty Sissy."

"Sissy's not prettier, she's just different," said Terry. "Luisa's just as pretty—"

"No!" said Alison despairingly. "If I have to tell you a million times, you two, her name is Cecelia! I will not have her saddled with such an inane nickname!"

"But Mama, it's an awful long name when she's so little, and you kept saying, she's baby sister—Luisa used to be baby sister but now she's big baby sister, and this one's little Sissy—"

"It's a good name for her when she's just new," said Terry.

Alison shut her eyes. "All the trouble, deciding on a really nice name—Cecelia Anna—and you two have to dream up something so silly—I won't have it. She's Cecelia. You'd just better practice saying it."

Mendoza sipped rye, sitting in the opposite chair, and laughed at all of them. "I don't think you're getting anywhere, *mi vida*."

"I simply won't have it," said Alison. "She's such a darling, and to land her with such a silly—" Cecelia suddenly uttered a loud belch.

"Oh, she burped all by herself," said Terry proudly.

"Sissy's awful smart," said Johnny.

THE NIGHT WATCH didn't get a call until ten-thirty, when a dispatcher relayed a mugging out on Third. Rich Conway went out to look at it, and found the patrolman—Gibson—still there, with the victim and a witness.

The victim was Bob Oakley, and he'd had a bad knock on the head and a couple of bruises where he'd fallen on the blacktop of the parking lot, but he didn't want to go to the hospital. "I'm okay, just shook up a little. And I couldn't give you any idea what the bastard looked like, he come up behind me, I never got a look at him at all—I was nearly up to my car, had my keys out, when he jumped me—thank God I didn't have much on me, only about four bucks—''

"Well, I can tell you something about him," said the witness loudly. His name was Ron Haney. They were both middle-aged men, Oakley bald and paunchy, Haney taller and thinner. "See, we'd come out nearly together—getting off work at ten, see? We're both short-order cooks at the El Rio Café up the street—it's a twenty-four-hour place, and Bob and I are both on from two to ten. Bob left just ahead of me, and I went to the restroom before I left. I saw Bob just ahead of me up the street, we was both parked in the public lot, see? It'd stopped raining, thank God, but looked like it might start again any minute, and I was walkin' fast, get to my car and get home—I see Bob turn into the lot, and then this bastard came runnin' up from the other direction and jumped him—hit him with something, a big stick of wood it looked like—and Bob went down and I yelled, but I was a good half-block away. I started runnin' up there, the guy was bent over Bob, gettin' his wallet I suppose, and I don't know if he heard me, but just as I got to the lot he took off, same way he'd come. No, I didn't chase him, I wanted to see if he'd killed Bob—he was clean out, Bob I mean, for a couple of minutes, and then I called the cops from the pay booth there—and then Bob come all the way to and started to cuss—''

"Only about four and a half dollars, thank God—but then I tried to get up, and by God, the damndest thing—''

"I saw him pretty good by the lights of the lot, and he was a black guy—pretty big, bigger than me anyway—I couldn't say how old, but he was damn quick on his feet—and I told Bob not to try to get up right away, maybe he'd better see a doctor, and then the squad car come up—''

"I was only a couple of blocks away," said Gibson. "But this is one for the books all right. He went for the wallet, but—''

"Ron helped me up," said Oakley, "and I says where the hell are my shoes—that bastard stole my shoes as well as the money! Perfectly good pair of shoes, I just bought them three months ago, and they cost forty bucks—bein' on my feet so much I have to be careful about corns and calluses, get decent shoes—"

"Well, I'll be damned," said Conway. "That is a funny one all right." Maybe the mugger had needed some new shoes too. He hadn't run off with Oakley's wallet, just grabbed the bills from it, and taken the few seconds of additional time—even with Haney yelling at him—to strip off the shoes. It wouldn't have taken much time; they were slip-on moccasins, and, Oakley said indignantly, real leather with a special arch support.

It was one for the books, but there wasn't much to do about it, with such a general description and no physical evidence.

Conway went back to base and wrote a brief report on it. He had just finished that when Piggott and Schenke came back; they had been put on another heist. "And it's probably another dead end," said Piggott. "All-night pharmacy on Wilshire, only the pharmacist there and he can't give any description, just a young dark fellow, didn't ask for any drugs, just the cash from the register. Didn't touch anything. Nowhere to go."

"Just the paperwork," said Schenke.

For a Saturday night at Robbery-Homicide it was quiet and peaceful.

MENDOZA WAS SUPPOSED to be off on Sundays, but usually he dropped in to see if anything new had gone down. He had just come in about nine-thirty when the word began coming in from Sacramento, the list of all the Model A Ford sedans registered in the state. As expectable, there weren't many of them, and when the list was complete there were nineteen registered in Los Angeles County. That was enough to cover, addresses from Topanga to Irwindale; but they would like to catch up to the hit-and-run driver who had killed little Alice Crane and badly injured her mother, and it was possible that the car had sustained some damage, still bore some evidence the lab could pinpoint. They'd have to chase down all those owners, find out where they and the cars had been at eight-thirty Friday night, and look at the cars.

"Well, it's a change from hunting possible heisters," said Tom Landers philosophically. He went out on that with Higgins and Palliser.

There had been a wire waiting for Hackett when he got in; Dr. James Cannaday would be arriving at L.A. International at midnight, would come to headquarters tomorrow morning. "We'd better ask some questions at the hotel," said Hackett.

"I don't know, Art." Mendoza was looking again at the photographs of the scene the coroner's investigator had taken. "It could be the straightforward thing. So she had a bang on the head, it could have been an accident, and somebody was with her and panicked, tried to set it up to look natural."

"Who?" asked Hackett. "At least I've got the lab going over the car. It's not much use guessing about it until we know more about her, why she was here, who she knew here, what she might have been doing. But we'd better find out what the hotel knows, at that. Not that I expect it'll be much."

They drove out there in the Ferrari. It was raining again slightly. The Sheraton Plaza was one of the classiest hotels in town, and being in close proximity to the airport it got a lot of business. Tourists, mere visitors to the southern California area, would prefer something closer into town; a good many of the people here would be business people, executives flying in and out, with the convenience of being ten minutes' drive from the airport.

Mendoza told the story to the desk clerk, and produced agitation and consternation. But, as was expectable, the clerk couldn't tell them much. It was a big hotel, and it didn't keep tabs on everybody registered. An assistant manager appeared and looked up records. Mrs. Louise Cannaday had had a reservation for Friday and had checked in around noon. "The desk clerk on weekdays isn't here today, that'll be Mr. Keeler, I'll see if I can get him at home." But Mr. Keeler wasn't answering his phone. "This is Mr.

Elgin—'' The clerk was looking interested, a little dapper man in expensive tailoring. ''But if, as you say, this woman died on Friday night, he wouldn't be able to tell you anything—''

''Now I wouldn't say that,'' said Elgin unexpectedly. ''It's an unusual name, Cannaday. I don't know that I'd ever heard it before. And the circumstance was kind of unusual too, and of course it was only yesterday.''

''What was?'' The assistant manager turned on him instantly.

''Well, I never laid eyes on this woman, obviously. Keeler would have checked her in, and know if she'd left her key and gone out—but that would be Friday. But about two o'clock yesterday afternoon I had a call from some woman asking about her.''

''Why?'' asked Hackett.

''Well, it wasn't usual. You know, phone calls go through direct from the rooms. The switchboard's just for long distance or some other call that's going to be charged on the bill, and people calling in. This woman asked if Mrs. Cannaday was in her room, said she'd been calling and got no answer. She said she had to ask the switchboard for the room number—it was six thirty-two—and she'd called four or five times, couldn't get an answer, and Mrs. Cannaday had been supposed to meet her and she wanted us to check, see if she was all right.''

''Unusual,'' admitted the assistant manager. ''So what did you do?''

''Well, I looked to see if the key was there, and it was. So that looked as if she'd gone out. But the woman was kind of persistent, and just in case—I mean, she could have come in and been taken sick or something—''

''Then what would the key have been doing here?''

''Funny things can happen. I didn't know. Just in case, I sent one of the maids up to look and she said it all looked kosher, room in order, open suitcase, nobody there. Which is all I could tell the woman on the phone?''

''Did she give any name?''

Elgin shook his head. "I didn't ask her." He shrugged and repeated, "Funny things happen. Maybe the Cannaday woman just decided not to meet her, who knows? It wasn't any of the hotel's business, so long as she hadn't been taken sick up there. Her key'd been turned in, so as far as we were concerned she was just out somewhere."

"Yes, well, here's a little something else." The assistant manager had been leafing through a card file from a drawer under the counter. "Here's the record we have for her. She had a reservation for Friday and Saturday nights. She checked in at eleven-forty on Friday morning. Then, by what this shows, she asked to keep the room for Sunday and Monday. I couldn't say whether she called or approached the desk clerk personally—you'll have to ask Keeler. It was three o'clock on Friday afternoon. As it happens, this is rather a slack period, and we could oblige her, she was to keep the same room until checkout time on Tuesday. Possibly Mr. Keeler can give you more details."

"We'd like to see her room, please."

"Oh, certainly, I hope there isn't going to be any publicity about this, officers—Of course we're very sorry to hear of her death, but you understand—" The assistant manager was eyeing Hackett's broad sandy bulk and Mendoza's elegant tailoring with glum disfavor.

"Was she murdered?" asked Elgin avidly.

"We haven't any idea yet," said Hackett.

"I'll let you have the key." The assistant manager was resigned.

But on the way to the rank of elevators, Mendoza paused, his gaze drifting across the lobby to the small gift shop, the florist shop, the Western Union counter. "Just a thought, Art. That card in her handbag—"

"By God, yes, and the son said something about a wire—"

They tried the florist shop first. A small floral arrangement had been ordered delivered to Mrs. Cannaday's room on Friday morning; it had been ordered by phone on Thursday afternoon by a Mrs. Adele Mowbray, been charged to a Visa account. There wasn't any address, just the account number. And Mrs. Cannaday had phoned in a telegram from her hotel room late Friday afternoon. Western Union looked it up for them; the pretty dark girl at the counter was efficient. "Oh, yes, sir, the call came through the switchboard, she asked for it to be charged to her bill here." It had been addressed to Dr. James Cannaday in Indianapolis and read simply *Staying over couple days. Arrive ten-forty Tuesday night. Love Mother.*

The hotel room was as anonymous as most hotel rooms. She wouldn't have been in it long, and had left only a few vestiges of her personality visible: a half-full bottle of Cachet cologne, a comb, in the bathroom a jar of cleansing cream, a box of tissues. The one suitcase was open on the rack at the foot of the bed, and its contents were as anonymous: a nylon print dress, a slip, clean underclothes, a cosmetic case, stockings, a carton of Pall Mall cigarettes, a nylon nightdress, a pair of folding bedroom slippers. There wasn't any address book.

"She was traveling light," said Mendoza.

"She had quite a lot of stuff in the handbag," Hackett reminded him. "Airline tickets, charge card, checkbook, cash, everything she wouldn't want to leave in the room."

"And she'd only planned to stay for a couple of days, apparently. What was she doing here?"

"We'll hear some more from the son tomorrow. And the weekday desk clerk, if he knows anything to tell us."

TWO

HIGGINS, PALLISER, and Landers had been out hunting for the Model A Fords most of Sunday. On Sunday a lot of people weren't home, and Higgins reflected that he was lucky to chase down three of them from that list, one in Malibu and two in Hollywood. None of them could have been the car that had struck the Cranes. The owner of the one in Malibu had been working on the engine most of Friday, with at least four witnesses and helpers to back him up; one in Hollywood was owned by the head mechanic at a Ford agency and had been visibly parked in the agency lot until he left work at nine that night, and the other one belonged to a student at U.S.C. who had been in bed with the flu for the last four days, attended by a common-sensible mother, who hadn't left the house on Friday and could swear the car had never left the garage. He was obviously in no state to drive, and she said he was so proud of that old piece of junk he never let anyone else drive it.

At four o'clock Higgins landed back at the office to find Landers and Palliser just back, equally empty-handed; they had found two others that could be crossed off. Grace and Galeano had brought in a possible suspect on the liquor store heist for questioning, but didn't expect much to come of it, and it didn't; twenty minutes after Higgins came in they let him go. Mendoza and Hackett were still out somewhere. When the phone rang on Hackett's desk Higgins picked it up, and it was Scarne up in the lab.

"I've got the kickback from the Feds on some prints. This Joseph Naysmith."

"Oh, him. For once they got on the ball."

"They haven't got him," said Scarne. "Don't know him from Adam."

"So that's that," said Higgins. "The city'll have to bury him." There hadn't been anything on Naysmith to say where he'd been living or working, who he had been associating with.

"The coroner's office sent the slug over, it's a .32 out of a Smith and Wesson."

"Which says nothing unless we get hold of the gun," said Higgins.

"Bricks without straw," said Scarne.

As soon as he put the phone down it buzzed at him again; it was one of the dispatchers relaying a call about a possible homicide. There was nearly an hour and a half left of the day shift, and Higgins got up resignedly to go and look at whatever it was.

The address was on Baldwin in Lincoln Heights, and when he got there the squad was parked at the curb, with Dave Turner sitting in it waiting for him. The house was an old rambling frame place needing a coat of paint, in this old and tired residential area. Turner came up to him on the sidewalk, a tall, thin, black young fellow. "I don't know that this is anything for you, Sergeant, but after I'd heard what she had to say I thought I ought to pass it on. I hadn't been on tour fifteen minutes when I got shot out here, and when I'd listened to her—well, I thought somebody in the front office ought to hear about it. She's a nice woman, this Mrs. Poole, Rita Poole, and she's pretty upset."

They went up the front walk to the wide front porch and Turner pushed the bell. The door opened instantly, and at one glance Higgins could agree that Mrs. Poole looked like a nice woman. She was big and buxom, about sixty, with untidy gray hair and a round motherly face with friendly blue eyes behind round plastic glasses. She was wearing a pink cotton housedress and old felt bedroom slippers. "This is Sergeant Higgins, Mrs. Poole. I'd like you to tell him what you told me."

"Certainly, and I just hope I'm wrong about it all. I've been fretting on it since yesterday and first I thought it wasn't anything to bother the police with, and then I thought if anything was wrong you ought to know, and the upshot was I finally called—'' She was ushering them into a large old-fashioned living room full of shabby furniture, urging them to sit down. "It just don't bear thinking of if it is so—"

"Well, what's it all about, Mrs. Poole?"

She planted herself in a chair opposite Higgins and regarded him with interest. "I must say, anybody'd know you for a policeman just from one look at you, Sergeant." Higgins, tall and broad and bulky as Hackett, didn't need telling that he might as well have *COP* tattooed on his forehead. "It's like this, I've got a pretty good pension from Ed, my late husband, he worked for the railroad, and I own this house clear. But you can always use more money, and I got three good bedrooms upstairs I don't use, so I rent them out. Mr. Wilkins, he's been with me ten years, he's a nice quiet gentleman, retired on Social Security and no trouble, he's out most of the day at the library or sitting in the park. And Miss Glover, she's been here about five years, she works at a beauty shop, and she figures to go and live with her sister up in Visalia when she retires next year. But I just lost my third one, Mrs. Lee, she was a lively sort of young woman, divorced, and she met some fellow at the store where she worked and they got married, so she left. So I put an ad in the paper and a sign up at the front window. And the very next day—that was last Wednesday—this couple showed up. I didn't like the idea of a couple, and a young couple at that—the kind of people I want here is quiet older people, you know the kind—I'd hesitated about taking Mrs. Lee—but the man said it was just temporary, they only wanted the room for a few days, they were on their way up the coast to Ventura, to her sister's, he had a job waiting for him there. And his wife wasn't feeling so good what with just having had the baby, and they wanted to stop over for a rest. Well, I felt sorry for the girl," said Mrs. Poole frankly. "She was just a little thing, maybe about twenty, and she looked sort of pale and run-down like, and the baby wasn't more than a few days old, I thought she must be just out of the hospital with it. A little girl it was, and a puny-looking baby, I know about babies, I had six of my own.

Three of each, and all grown with their own families and all doing fine too.''

"This was last Wednesday," prompted Higgins.

"That's right. I let them come in. He said their name was Leeper. They only had a couple of suitcases and a little overnight bag like. And they'd come in an old car. She told me they'd been over in Arizona. Well, from the first I was kind of worried about that baby. You see, I like babies, and know about babies, and the little thing cried all the time, all fretful and sounding sort of weak. I asked her did she have enough milk, she was nursing it, and she said yes, it was all right, but that baby sounded hungry to me. I offered to help her with it, I said maybe it needed to see a doctor, but she was real sharp to me, just sort of snapped at me that everything was all right. And on Friday he said they'd be leaving the next day. They'd stayed in mostly, she hadn't gone out at all, but he went out that night. I was just out on the front porch to see if it'd started to rain yet, it was about eight o'clock, when he came out. He was carrying the little overnight bag. He walked down the street, didn't take the old car, and I can say when he came back, because I was just going to lock up and I was thinking he'd have to ring the bell to get let in, I was just going up to bed, that was around nine-thirty. Mr. Wilkins and Miss Glover had been home since around six-thirty. And I was just as glad these Leepers was going, because they'd both complained about the baby keeping them awake, Mr. Wilkins and Miss Glover, I mean. Well, he came back just then and went on upstairs. So I locked the door and went up to bed. But you know," and Mrs. Poole looked suddenly frightened, "I never heard that baby cry all night, not a sound, and the poor mite had cried nearly all the time they were here. And when I got up yesterday morning they were already gone, and the old car gone from out in front, and they'd left twenty dollars on the chest of drawers up in the room, which was fair enough with the ten he'd already paid." She took a deep breath. "So naturally I went in to clean up the room, and nearly the first thing I found was this. I'd looked to see if they'd forgotten anything—and there was the little overnight bag." Higgins hadn't noticed it there beside her chair. She pushed it toward him with one foot. "I can't hardly bear to look at it again. I sort of had the horrors about it, I thought, Rita, you're just imagining something awful, people don't do such awful things, but I couldn't help thinking, suppose they did—and finally I thought I'd better tell the police." She shuddered.

Turner bent and ran the zipper open across the top of the bag and Higgins looked at it. It was an ordinary cheap canvas bag, faded blue with a yellow stripe, and it was empty. But inside it was heavily covered with stains, sides and bottom, ominous dark brown-red stains. "Oh, my God," said Higgins. Quite obviously a good deal of blood had been spilled in the bag, fairly recently.

"It was pushed back in the closet," said Mrs. Poole. "Maybe they thought I wouldn't find it. But when I saw inside, I had this horrible idea, suppose he had the baby in the bag when he went out? That he'd killed the baby—oh, it don't bear thinking about, but I never heard that baby cry afterward—"

"Good God almighty," said Higgins. "Well, the lab will tell us if it's human blood."

"But what could he have done with the poor thing?"

If this was so, that was the question. There were a lot of empty lots around, the big refuse dumpsters in a hundred alleys, the sewer drains—Higgins felt a little sick, even after all he had seen on this job. Alert patrolmen to be on the lookout, that was about all they could do. The man couldn't have gone far on foot in an hour and a half. He hadn't given her a first name, and she hadn't noticed the license plate on the car. All she could say, the girl had said they had been in Arizona. She thought the girl was about twenty, small and dark; the man might be a few years older, about medium height, also dark-haired.

On the sidewalk outside, Turner said, "God, you think it could be?"

"You've already seen enough of the job to know you never can tell what people might do," said Higgins heavily. It had begun to sprinkle again. He sent Turner back on tour and took the bags back to Parker Center, up to the lab. God knew if there were any prints left on it, after Mrs. Poole had handled it.

Marx wrinkled his brow at the stains and said, "We'll get to it sometime."

Higgins didn't go back to the office; it was six o'clock and he headed for home. It began to rain harder on the way, and by the time he pulled into the garage behind the comfortable old house in Eagle Rock it was pouring. He came into the service porch, shrugging off the trench coat, and was enveloped in the warm sense of home. There was a good smell of dinner in the oven, and Mary was setting the table in the dining room. He gave her a bear hug, his lovely Mary with her serene gray eyes. "What's that in aid of?" She kissed him back soundly.

"Just for getting home," said Higgins. He had never had much of a home until he had married Mary. And it was a fading memory now, Bert Dwyer dead on the marble floor of the bank with the heister's slugs in him, and his first look at Mary when he and Mendoza had gone to break the news.

"Steve and Laura are getting their homework done. You've got time for a drink if you want one."

"I think I need one," said Higgins. The little Scottie Brucie was bouncing under his feet. Bert's kids were good kids, Steve sixteen now and more like Bert every day, Laura at fourteen nearly as pretty as her mother. And their own Margaret Emily came trotting to be picked up, patting his face and calling him George, which Mary disapproved of, but she wasn't likely to cure her now. He got himself a drink and Mary brought a glass of sherry into the living room with him. He told her about Mrs. Poole because it was still in his mind.

She said sickly, "Oh, George, no. It couldn't be, could it?"

"Anything could be," said Higgins. "Not everybody likes babies. You know what I can't help thinking of. The Graces. Jase's wife can't have children, and they waited so long to adopt them—now they've got that cute little girl and just lately the little boy. They're crazy about them, Jase always showing some new snapshots. Good parents, those kids getting brought up right and having a good happy life. And then other people—'' He sampled his drink gratefully. Sometimes he wished he'd gone in for almost any other job but the thankless job of being a cop.

"WELL, THERE WE ARE," said Hackett, and took off his glasses to polish them. "And it doesn't tell us much, at that."

The autopsy report on Louise Cannaday had been waiting on his desk when he came in on Monday morning; he had scanned it rapidly and now passed it on to Mendoza. The night watch had left them a new heist, that was all. It was Palliser's day off and everybody else would be out on the heists and the Model A's.

Mendoza sat back in Landers' desk chair and glanced over the report. It told them a few things. Louise Cannaday had died of a severe depressed skull fracture, described in technical terms and illustrated with one of Dr. Cox's precise sketches. A blow behind the left ear with some weapon neither sharp nor cutting enough to produce an external wound; there had been no external bleeding. She would have been unconscious from the time she sustained the blow until she died. The estimated time of death was between eleven P.M. on Friday night and one A.M. on Saturday morning, but they could narrow that down because she'd been found in the car at about half-past-twelve on Saturday morning, and she'd been dead then, if recently. Unfortunately the doctor couldn't give them any idea when she might have had the blow with the blunt instrument; she could have lived for an hour or several hours before dying. He thought she had probably lived for at least a couple of hours, by the amount of internal bleeding, but it was impossible to say definitely. There had been no food or alcohol in the stomach; she hadn't had a meal in some hours. Otherwise the body was that of a healthy middle-aged woman of temperate habits, well-nourished, with no chronic disease. There had been an appendectomy, no evidence of any other surgery.

Mendoza blew smoke at the ceiling. "See if anything shows in the car."

"I don't see how she could have got that blow by hitting anything in the car," said Hackett. "And even if she did, somebody moved her, tried to make it look an accident in a stupid kind of way. That's what struck MacDonald. She couldn't have hit the back of her head on the steering wheel, for God's sake, or the dashboard. Well, we'll be seeing the son sometime today, but he won't know anything about it."

"Background," said Mendoza tersely.

The son came in about nine-thirty. He was a tall, good-looking man about thirty, well dressed in a conventional suit and white shirt; he looked a little like his mother, with the same high cheekbones and wide mouth. He looked pale and still shocked but was in control of himself and anxious to give any help he could. "But I still don't understand what could have happened, Mother was a good driver—but an accident can happen to anybody, of course—" He listened to what Hackett had to tell him and gestured helplessly. "So, not an accident, somebody running into her or—but I still can't understand it. Who'd want to murder Mother? Do anything like that to her? It doesn't make any sense. Why, she hardly knew anybody here any more."

"Why was she here, doctor? She lived in Indianapolis?" Hackett offered him a cigarette and he refused absently.

"Yes, of course. She wasn't going to be here long, in Los Angeles that is, just a couple of days. I suppose you want all the details—she'd been staying with Sue, my sister, up in San Francisco. Mrs. Daniel Sperling. Dan's with a big insurance firm, he got transferred to California just after they were married a couple of years ago. And Sue just had the baby last month—a little girl, Gail—and Mother came out to be with her when she came home from the hospital. She'd been there nearly a month. God, that was the worst thing I ever had to do, telling Sue about this. She's all broken up—I don't want her to come, Dan agreed with that, no point, I'll have to make all the arrangements, have Mother sent home—" He ran a hand through his dark hair. "And you see, since she was already here—in California, that is—she wanted to come down here to see Aunt Helen and Uncle John. It's funny, of course they're relatives but I'd never met them—or Sue—Dr. John Lorne and his wife, he's Mother's uncle, he was her father's younger brother. Mother's parents were killed in an accident when she was only eighteen and she lived with Aunt Helen and Uncle John after that, while she was going to college here, U.C.L.A. Then she met Dad—Do you really want all this? I'm sorry, I'm just rambling—"

"Just go on with whatever's relevant, doctor," said Mendoza.

"Well, Mother has a very close friend, Aunt Adele—We call her aunt, she's just my father's cousin—yes, Mother grew up here, Pasadena—until she went to live with her aunt and uncle—and they were in college together, and just after they graduated Aunt Adele got married, and her aunt and uncle and their son came out for the wedding, that's how Mother and Dad met. And they got engaged and about six months later they were married—here—and went back to Indianapolis. Dad was an attorney, he just died last year— that was an awful shock for all of us, he was only fifty-nine—it was a coronary. Of course Mother had always kept in touch with Aunt Helen and Uncle John, she corresponded regularly with Aunt Helen until around four or five months ago, when Aunt Helen had another stroke and couldn't write. They're both pretty old, in the eighties. And Mother came down to L.A. to see them and Aunt Adele, before she came home."

"That'll be Mrs. Adele Mowbray," said Hackett.

"That's right. They were still close friends, kept in regular touch. I can give you the address, it's Pasadena—her husband's with some oil company, they've got three grown children—"

"These Lornes," said Mendoza. "She'd come down on her way home to see them principally."

He nodded. "As long as she was here. She hadn't been back to California for ten or eleven years—She'd come out for Aunt Adele's daughter's wedding then, Linda was her godchild. The Lornes live in West Hollywood. I remembered to bring Mother's address book—my wife said you might want it—I've got keys to her house, of course, we'd been taking care of her mail and so on while she'd been gone. They—Aunt Helen and Uncle John—they'd been getting to where they couldn't take care of themselves, and their daughter and her husband had moved in to look after them. Mother had been corresponding with her since then— her cousin Eleanor—she'd never known her very well, she's a little older and she was already married and away when Mother went to live with them. I know there'd been some discussion about getting them into a convalescent home. Uncle John had been a gynecologist with a big practice, but he retired about twelve years ago, I think. Anyway, that's why Mother was here. She was only staying two days—she was going to see the Lornes on Friday and Aunt Adele on Saturday, and fly home on Sunday. Then I got that wire—" He put a hand to his head. "I don't understand that either." After a moment he added, "All her things still at the hotel, I suppose I'll have to claim them, pay the bill."

They wanted to talk to the desk clerk, and let him ride along. He came out with a little more irrelevant information. The Lorne daughter was Eleanor, married to a man named Schultz; he owned a chain of hardware stores and was reputedly well off. They hadn't any children. Cannaday thought his mother had kept in desultory touch with a few old college friends here, but probably it had been a matter of exchanging Christmas cards, no more.

At the hotel, they found the regular weekday desk clerk on duty, John Keeler, and he greeted them effusively. "Oh, yes, Mr. Armbruster was telling me about it, a very tragic thing," and that was conventional. "I'm sure we all sympathize with the family." Cannaday just nodded. "But of course I thought back to remember what I could about her. I don't know that I could tell you much. I remember Mrs. Cannaday checking in, she had a reservation, it was about noon on Friday." She had, Cannaday had said, flown in from San Francisco on the ten-thirty flight. "She registered, and she said she'd wait in the lobby, and it was just then that this man came up and spoke to her."

"What man?" asked Cannaday. "The Hertz man?"

"Oh, no," said Keeler smoothly. He was a foxy-faced man with reddish hair and a narrow jaw. "She seemed to know him, they seemed to know each other. He came up and spoke to her, and she shook hands with him. I didn't hear her mention any name, no. They moved away from the counter then and stood talking for a few minutes. I was registering a couple in, I didn't really pay much attention, just remembered it when Mr. Armbruster asked me to re-member what I could about her. All I can tell you about him is that he was a very tall man—must have been six-five or six-six."

"Was he a guest here?" asked Hackett.

"Oh, no, I'm sure he wasn't. I'd never seen him before. I think he was middle-aged," said Keeler vaguely. "Well, that's about all I can tell you."

"Does that ring any bells, doctor?" asked Hackett.

Cannaday shrugged. "I can't imagine who it could have been. She didn't know anybody here except her aunt and uncle and Aunt Adele."

"Anyway, then the Hertz man came up and asked for her, and when I looked she was sitting across the lobby so I pointed her out. I was just going to take a break for lunch, Mr. Armbruster spells me between twelve-thirty and one-thirty. And I'd just got back to the desk when she dropped off her key and went out."

"At a guess," said Hackett, "she settled into the room and went to have lunch at the coffee shop here or the res-taurant. Before going to see the Lornes."

Keeler was watching them interestedly. "Did she come back to the hotel?" asked Mendoza. "Do you remem-ber?"

"Oh, yes," said Keeler. "Of course there are always a lot of people coming and going, but Mr. Armbruster asked me to remember what I could, and when he mentioned the room number I did remember. Naturally I don't remember a room number for everybody staying here, but that sort of jogged my memory, because it was just before I went off duty at six. It might have been ten minutes to six, I was just registering a family party and hoping Eisner wasn't going to be late coming in. She came up and asked for her key—six thirty-two—and I gave it to her, I remembered the room number, how I know it was her. Oh, but I forgot to tell you that. She'd called in before. About three-thirty, I think. She had the reservation for Friday and Saturday nights, but she called to ask if she could keep the room for Sunday and Monday. I looked up the reservations ahead and told her she could.''

That said a little something, if not much. The wire had been phoned into Western Union in the lobby here at six-ten. "When did she go out again?" asked Hackett.

"I don't know," said Keeler. "Eisner came on at six when I go off duty. He might know, but people generally just leave the key on the desk if the clerk's busy." They would chase a night man out to ask. That was all Keeler had to tell them, and they rode the elevator up to the sixth floor in silence.

It hadn't been touched; there'd been nothing for a maid to do here. Cannaday looked around drearily at the few vestiges of her personality left behind. "She'd sent all her main luggage directly home. She wouldn't have needed much here, just for a couple of days." He packed the few items in the suitcase, locked it. Adele Mowbray's little welcoming bouquet was wilting in its vase on the bureau. They went back to the lobby and Cannaday asked for the bill, paid it with a check.

"I suppose you'll be seeing the Schultzes," he said wearily. "But if she'd been there, which I expect she had, we know she came back to the hotel. Only where could she have gone later? I called Aunt Adele this morning—she went right up in the air, all to pieces, and I couldn't get much out of her except that Mother had called her about twelve-thirty on Friday and she hadn't heard from her since. She was supposed to be at Aunt Adele's for lunch on Saturday, and when she didn't turn up Aunt Adele had been calling the hotel, but—look, she didn't know anybody here! And why was she staying over?"

"We'd just as soon you didn't leave right away, doctor," said Hackett. "We may have a few more questions for you."

"Sure," said Cannaday morosely. "I'll have to find a mortician, make some arrangements. And I'll have to see Aunt Adele. She was back for Sue's wedding, the last time we saw her." He was staying at the Biltmore downtown; they dropped him off there and went on up to Federico's on North Broadway for lunch. It had stopped raining but a high gusty wind had got up, cold and dank. Nobody else from the office was there, probably out all over the county chasing down the Model A Fords.

"Did you see that funny thing in Saturday night's report?" asked Hackett, glancing at the menu. "The mugger stealing the shoes."

Mendoza grinned. "Maybe he just needed some new shoes, Art."

"The witness said he was a lot bigger than the victim. I wonder if they fit him."

"One of life's little mysteries," said Mendoza. "We'll never know."

They got to the house in West Hollywood at two-thirty. It was a big Spanish-style stucco house with a red tile roof, on a quiet well-maintained street. There were twin rectangles of lawn in front, a small rose garden. The door was opened to them by a stocky balding man in expensive sports clothes. He eyed the badges in dismay. "Police!" he said. "Oh, my God, don't tell me it's something about Louise! We've been trying to contact her all morning. Calling the hotel. Eleanor—" A woman came up behind him in the wide entrance hall. "My dear, it's police—What's it about, gentlemen? Oh, come in—" He gestured them in to a large, handsomely furnished living room.

Mendoza told them what it was about. The woman began to cry, gulping into a handkerchief. "You'll be Mr. and Mrs. Schultz?"

"Yes, of course—my God, I can't take this in—" Schultz's fattish face had gone pale, and he was obviously shocked and astonished. "My God, this is terrible, how could anything like that have happened to Louise? She was perfectly all right when she left here—"

"She was here then?" asked Mendoza. "On Friday afternoon?"

"That's right," said the woman in a quavering voice. She sniffed into the handkerchief. She was a thin blond woman with protuberant pale blue eyes and a rather slack mouth, smartly dressed in a black sheath dress and high heels. "She's dead—killed? But how could she be? We couldn't understand it when we couldn't reach her at the hotel. We've been trying since this morning, she was expecting us to call—How could that have happened to her?"

"I can't believe it—" Schultz was very shaken; he brought out a handkerchief to mop his half-bald head. "Perfectly fine when she left here, that was about four o'clock. As far as we knew she was just going back to the hotel, and going to meet this old friend for lunch the next day—oh, my God!" he said in sudden exasperation. "That damned anniversary party!"

"Oh, dear, you know we had to go, Fred." She was still sniffling.

"Naturally," said Schultz, "in the ordinary way we'd have had her stay to dinner, or taken her out. But there was this party set up, old friends of ours, the Garsteins, it was their thirty-fifth anniversary, it had been set up since last month, a big affair at the Beverly Hills Hilton. We couldn't back out—Louise understood about it, but we were sorry, you see how it was."

"We were going to take her out tonight," said Eleanor Schultz mournfully.

"She came that afternoon to see your parents? What time did she get here?" asked Hackett.

"About two o'clock or a little later. But she couldn't, I mean we couldn't," she said incoherently. "The convalescent home—"

"It was just one of those damned mix-ups," said Schultz vexedly. "Nobody's fault, just the way things happen. That was why she was going to stay over. She called the airline from here and got her reservations changed, and called the hotel. You see, the old people—well, since Eleanor's mother had that last stroke, and her father had been getting so feeble, it'd just got to be too much for Eleanor to look after them. We'd been looking around for a good convalescent home—"

"I hated to do it," she said. "But it was just too hard— all the washing and lifting, we had a nurse coming in but they really needed more care—"

"And this is a pretty nice one, but those places don't always have vacancies. And it came up all of a sudden. Of course we were expecting Louise, she called from San Francisco last Monday to say she'd be down. And it was Tuesday when they called from this home—we'd had an application in—to say there was a new vacancy, they could take both of them right away."

"We were so thankful," she said. "I hated to put them there—but Mother understands, and it's a nice place, they'll get good care. The way Fred says, it was just getting to be too much for me. Mother's eighty-four and partly paralyzed, and Daddy's pretty helpless."

"So we moved them in on Wednesday," said Schultz. "And of course it never crossed our minds but what it would be all right to take Louise over so she could see them, but when I called on Friday morning to ask about them, and mentioned we'd be coming, the nurse said it should have been explained to us, they've got a policy, no visitors for a week. She said they've found it's easier to settle the old people in to a new routine if they don't have distractions, like visitors coming, even family. Well, if that's the way they operate—only nobody had told us that, and of course we'd figured on visiting them that day even if Louise hadn't been coming. But I explained about Louise, how she'd only be here for a couple of days. And the nurse said she was sorry, the only one who could give permission was the administrator, and she'd gone off for the weekend, wouldn't be back until Monday. She was sure it would be all right but we'd have to call on Monday morning and check."

"Oh, I see," said Hackett. "That's why Mrs. Cannaday was staying."

"That's right. Just a mix-up," said Schultz. "Naturally she wanted to see them while she was here. And the conva-

lescent home. We said we'd call her this morning, as soon
as we knew it'd be okay. I checked with this administrator
first thing and she said we could come, so we'd been trying
to call Louise—and now you come and say she's dead. I
can't believe it—''

"She was all right when she left," repeated Mrs. Schultz.
"She was looking forward to seeing this old friend the next
day—''

"Did she mention meeting someone she knew at the hotel?'' asked Hackett.

They stared at him in surprise. "Why, no, she never said
anything like that,'' said Mrs. Schultz.

"Or did she say anything about where else she might be
going?'' asked Mendoza. "After all, she had an unexpected day to fill in—Sunday.''

They shook their heads. "That was another thing, of
course,'' said Eleanor Schultz. "It seemed so dreadfully in-
hospitable. I'd never known Louise very well, but she was
a relative after all, and here for such a short time. But I had
a club meeting on Sunday and Fred had a date for golf, we
didn't know it was going to rain then. But she wouldn't have
known many people here, she hadn't lived in California for
about thirty-five years, since she married and moved back
east.''

"If it hadn't been for that damned party she'd have been
with us,'' said Schultz. "By what you say she was in that
rented car, got a knock on the head some way. Couldn't it
have been an accident? I don't know what kind of driver she
was, but of course there are damn fool drivers all over the
place—''

"It doesn't look that way,'' said Hackett. "You've cleared
up a couple of things anyway, thanks very much. We know
why she was staying on. You couldn't say whether she knew
anyone else here at all besides this Mrs. Mowbray?''

Eleanor Schultz looked ready to cry again. "I didn't really
know her well,'' she said again. "When she lived with
Mother and Daddy, Fred and I were down in San Diego. It
was Mother she corresponded with, until that last stroke in
June. Of course she'd grown up here, there might be old

school friends. I don't know. But when I think—it's just terrible, she was so happy and cheerful, talking about her daughter's baby, and her son's wife's expecting a baby too, he's a doctor, you know, and she said he was doing so well and they were so happy. No, she didn't say a thing about any plans—except meeting this old friend—and she'd see us on Monday."

"If it hadn't been for that party—" said Schultz. "Did you say the son's here? Terrible shock for them. We'd better call him at least, Eleanor, least we can do. Do you know where he's staying?" Hackett told him. "Thanks, we'll contact him. This has really shaken us up—an awful thing. I hope you can find out what happened to her."

Back in the Ferrari, Hackett said, "Ordinary people. It fills in a few gaps."

Mendoza shoved in the cigarette lighter, looking pensively through the windshield at the trees being whipped savagely by the wind. "Gaps," he said. "She had an unexpected day to fill in, Sunday. She'd changed the airline reservation and arranged to keep the hotel room. She went back to the hotel and sent that wire to the son. All expectable. And then what?" He inhaled thoughtfully. "A woman like that—everything we've heard about her—you might expect her to have had a quiet dinner at the hotel, pick up a paperback to pass the evening with, and go to bed early. But she didn't."

"What I'd like to know," said Hackett, "is who was the man at the hotel? The tall fellow she seemed to know, who spoke to her at the desk? An old friend or acquaintance turning up unexpectedly? And maybe saying—the clerk said he wasn't a guest—I'm at the Biltmore, or the Ambassador, or the Century Plaza, so when she found herself with a blank Sunday, maybe she called him—after she sent the wire—and he asked her out to dinner right then?"

"She hadn't had dinner," Mendoza reminded him. "She went out sometime that night, but where did she go? Where would she have gone, damn it? She hadn't had anything to eat, probably since she had lunch at the hotel. Or a drink. A movie? But she'd surely have had dinner first."

"It's more likely," said Hackett, "that she called the Mowbray woman and said she had a free day and why not get together on Sunday. Hell, I forgot that—Cannaday said he'd talked to her, and she said Louise had called her about twelve-thirty Friday to thank her for the flowers probably, and she hadn't heard from her again."

"She was meeting her for lunch," said Mendoza sleepily. "They could have arranged something about Sunday then. Maybe she started out to have dinner and just happened to pick up a likely-looking gent at the hotel."

"Oh, now, Luis. She doesn't seem to have been that kind of woman."

"You never know," said Mendoza cynically.

"And then what happened? They started off somewhere in her car, and got into an argument and he banged her over the head? Why?"

"Queerer things have happened. So all right, not a pickup. The gent at the desk—She knew him from somewhere. He was still hanging around the hotel for some reason, and asked her out to dinner. And then in the car he turned all amorous and made, as the saying goes, the unwelcome advances. And she said, Sir, I'm not that kind of girl, and told him to get out, and he lost his temper."

"Where did he come by the blunt instrument, in the rented car?"

"Don't quibble," said Mendoza. "They'd got to the restaurant by then and he found a handy two-by-four or something in the parking lot. She was a damn good-looking female, Art. Even if she did have grown-up children and a granddaughter."

"Well," said Hackett thoughtfully, "we'd better see the Mowbray woman. She can tell us whether Louise did know anybody else here, old college friends or whoever, she might have contacted. But the time's so damned tight, Luis. She was at the hotel at six. She might have got that knock on the head any time after that. So we know she did go out—she was in the car. Even if the night clerk can say when, it's all up in the air."

Mendoza switched on the ignition. "We can ask." But back at the office he called that address in Pasadena, which Cannaday had passed on, to get only a phlegmatic-sounding maid.

"Oh, Mis' Mowbray isn't home. She got a phone call this morning that threw her into a tizzy, and the mister's out of town on business or he'd of calmed her down. She just said she was going to see some doctor at the Biltmore Hotel, that's all I know."

As Mendoza put the phone down, Hackett said, "Look, Luis, why did she take that long to get back to the hotel? If she left West Hollywood at four o'clock—"

"Rush-hour traffic on the freeway. And she hadn't lived here in thirty-five years. She probably wasn't familiar with the freeways."

"True," agreed Hackett. And then Higgins came in, having been out chasing Model A Fords, and having missed Mendoza this morning told him about the baby and the bloody bag.

"*¡Dios Mío!*" said Mendoza.

"I haven't heard from the lab yet."

"And that's all up in the air too," said Hackett. "We don't really know. Even if it's human blood—"

"I can have a good guess," said Higgins. The other men began to drift in toward the end of shift.

THE NIGHT WATCH didn't get a call until nine-thirty. It was Schenke's night off and Piggott went out to look at it. It was a liquor store on Third, and the proprietor was talking animatedly to the uniformed man, Carlson. "These god-damned punks," he was saying disgustedly. "Of course they've got no damned sense or they wouldn't be crooks in the first place, but I ask you. I ask you. Does anybody can add two and two think I'm going to leave the day's take in the register overnight? And there's a sign on the door says we close at nine. Naturally I'd bagged everything for the bank at a quarter to, and my night clerk Al Tinsley dropped it at the bank on his way home. There was only twenty bucks in the register, bills and coins, to start out making change in the morning. And this damn fool comes barging in here as I'm on my way out, just about to lock the door, waves a gun at me and says he'll take all the money. Well, he was three sheets in the wind.''

"Can you give us a description?" asked Piggott.

"Sure, for what it's worth. I hadn't turned off the outside lights yet, the switch is around back. He was sure old enough to know better, not one of these young hellions—a big guy with shoulders on him like a wrestler, an old windbreaker, tan pants—kind of square face, he needed a shave, I'd say he was about in the fifties.''

"Did you notice a tattoo on his left arm?"

"He had this windbreaker on, I wouldn't see a thing like that."

It wasn't much, but Piggott would be willing to bet—if he'd been a gambling man—that the tattoo had been there, that this was the heister from the market and the other liquor store. "Do you think you could recognize a picture?"

The proprietor looked interested. "In your mug shots? Well, I'd sure as hell be willing to give it a try.''

THREE

ON TUESDAY MORNING the liquor store owner, whose name
was Gerber, came in about nine o'clock and Landers took
him down to R. and I. "I don't know if I can do you any
good," said Gerber, "but I'll have a stab at it. You got quite
a setup here." He looked appreciatively at the pretty trim
blonde behind the counter. "And some damned good-
looking females, I see."

Landers grinned at him. "You'd better not get any ideas
about this one, Mr. Gerber. She happens to be my wife."

"You don't say," said Gerber. "Keep the job all in the
family, hah?"

Pretty blond Phil, whose parents hadn't known she would
turn into a policewoman when they christened her Phillipa
Rosemary, twinkled at him. "And what's more we've got a
baby. But she takes after Tom, not me."

And how lucky they had been, thought Landers, as he
watched her fetch the books of mug shots. After the bad
luck. Things ran in cycles. Phil sticking them with that impossible house in Azusa—a bargain, she'd said—but the
drive in was murder, and then her car giving up the ghost—
but another pair of idiots had shown up to buy the house,
and the apartment in West Hollywood was at least close in.
The only regret they had had was leaving motherly Mrs. Ja-
cobsen across the street, but the guardian angels had been
on the job and right across the hall in the apartment building they had discovered Mrs. Peck, whose grandchildren all
lived back east and who was delighted to babysit Sara El-
len.

He saw Gerber settled down with the mug shots and went
back to the office. He and Palliser had been going over the
reports on those Model A's, and picked up where they had
left off. "You know as well as I do," said Palliser, "none of

it's good enough, Tom.'' They had found four more to look at, all of which could be crossed off for this reason or that, and there were still five to look for. It was surprising there weren't more that could have been involved in the hit-run, but nothing definite to say any of them had been. That the owners looked like respectable citizens didn't mean much; even that kind occasionally got drunk. A chiropractor in Glendale, a salesman in San Marino, a vet in Tarzana, an electrician in Glendora: they all said they'd been home last Friday night, the cars not driven, but they weren't backed up on it except by their wives. In two cases the cars had been parked on the street when not being driven, and the downpour of rain would probably have destroyed any evidence.

"I don't think any of them is likely," said Landers, "but obviously there's nothing to add up to a charge. Well, we've still got five to look for, and at least it's stopped raining.'' But the five remaining Model A's were in Pacoima, Thousand Oaks, Playa Del Rey, and La Cañada, and neither of them made an immediate move to start out on the legwork.

"We'll never get enough for a charge," said Palliser pessimistically. He stroked his handsome straight nose absently. "Even if we think we've spotted him.''

"On the other hand, John," said Landers, "suppose we'd got a definite make on a Mercedes or a Dodge or something, there'd be a thousand more to track down.''

"Don't mention it," said Palliser.

They were still sitting there kicking it around when a call came up from one of the dispatchers, an assault. Just as happy to forget about the hit-run for a while, they both went out to look at it.

The address was Laguna Avenue, an old single frame house, and the squad was waiting for them; the uniformed man was Don Dubois. There were quite a lot of people milling around, apparently neighbors, standing in little groups on the sidewalk, in the front yard. "So what's the story?'' asked Palliser.

Dubois was looking half amused and half serious. "It sounds like a joke, Sergeant, but it isn't really. The ambulance just left before I called in, and the guy looked pretty bad, bleeding like a stuck pig. He was out cold and the paramedics weren't sure he was going to make it. By the time I got here all these people had messed up the scene, but there isn't any big mystery about it. It was his wife. The victim's. His name is Henry Bacon.'' Dubois laughed and then sobered. "By what the neighbors say it isn't the first time she's gone for him." He beckoned to a big fat man with one of the groups in the front yard. "This is Mr. Hubler, he called in."

"You're damned right," said Hubler, coming over. "You more cops? That's very damned right, it was time somebody did something, and when we heard her yelling at him again—this time that damned female really clobbered him! Me and the wife came out when we heard her yelling—and the Irwins from the other side—everybody else came out when the ambulance came, they can all tell you, all the neighbors, how that female is. I called the ambulance too. Henry was bleeding all over the backyard, and I think he busted his leg when she knocked him down the last time, but his head was all cut open too and she'd busted his glasses, his face was all cut—''

A few other people came drifting up to listen and add comments, among them a short plump woman with improbably blond hair—"This is my wife Milly, she can tell you about it too—" plus a thin little man with a bald head, and a couple of other middle-aged women.

"Just disgraceful," said Milly, pursing her small mouth, "the way she treats him! I think the woman's crazy! She ought to be shut up somewhere. Why, just last month she knocked him right across the lawnmower, it was running and he got a nasty cut on the hand, might have lost a couple of fingers, for heaven's sake. She's a terrible woman. None of the neighbors have anything to do with her."

"Henry's a good little guy," said Hubler. "Not the kind to set the world on fire like they say, but a nice enough fellow, kind of meek and not much to say for himself, but a good enough guy. He's lived here nearly thirty years, got left the house by his folks. Like I was telling this other officer, it's not the first time that female's taken after him—sweet Jesus, you'd think he deserved some peace and quiet at his age—he's sixty-five, just retired on Social Security, he worked all his life for Sears Roebuck, drove a delivery truck."

"Well, what happened?" asked Landers. "His wife attacked him?"

"All the time after him," said Milly vigorously, "because he didn't take care of the yard the way she wanted, always finding fault with him over anything, and using language—well, I think she's crazy. And maybe the other one was too."

"The other one?" asked Palliser.

"The first wife," said Hubler. "Erma. This one's Edna. My God, poor Henry, he's sure had bad luck with wives, all I can say. Her, the first one, I guess they was married about twenty years, she died of a heart attack about three or four years back, and then Henry up and married this one not long after, I don't know where he met her, and I'm damned if she doesn't treat him the same way Erma did."

"What happened this morning?" asked Landers.

"Well, we'd heard her yelling at him in the house," Milly took up the tale, "and I was out on the back porch emptying the garbage when he come out the back door with her after him. She was shoutin' out about how he ought to mow the lawn and he was a lazy no-good bastard—excuse me, but that's what she said—never did no work around the place at all—and he does, only you don't need to cut the lawn in winter, but it was always something—if it wasn't that, he'd forgot to take out the trash, he hadn't raked up the leaves, or there was something to fix in the house, always something—anyway, I saw Henry come out but I couldn't hear what he said back to her but it must've made her madder, she's a great big strong powerful woman, you know, and he went into the garage and her after him, and the next thing he come runnin' out and her after him with the hammer, for goodness' sake, and she hit him on the head and he ran down the yard and she ran after him and I called to Al to come and see—"

"And," said Hubler, "I went out the back door just in time to see her hit him a good one on the back of the head and he fell down, but he got up and ran away again over toward the fence, she was calling him every name in the book, and next time she hit him he fell down in that compost hole she'd made him dig, and he yells out like he was really hurt, and I yelled at her to leave him alone, and she just yelled back at me and slammed back into the house. So I went to look at Henry, and, my God, he was clean out and blood all over, and I says to Milly, my God, maybe she's killed him this time, and I called an ambulance and then the cops.''

"It does beat all," said Milly, "how that poor man got two wives acted so mean to him. That first one, one time she hit him on the head with the frying pan and he got concussion, he was in the hospital, only he told the doctor he'd tripped and fell down against the garage door.''

"But this time he sure looked bad," said Hubler. "I don't know but what the woman is nuts, Officers. Maybe next time she would kill him.''

Landers and Palliser rejoined Dubois by the squad. Dubois' black intelligent face wore a wholly amused expression now. "You see what I mean. Either of you feeling brave enough to tackle the amazon?''

"Does she seem to be still on the rampage?" asked Palliser.

"Nary a sound from the house since I got here," said Dubois, "and the neighbors say she's still in there.''

"Well, we'll have to see her eventually, but we'd better check on Bacon first," said Landers. "The female of the species—wasn't Mr. Kipling right. I will say, Phil has a few little habits, she will drape her stockings on the shower rod to dry—but she's never taken after me with a frying pan yet.''

Palliser was laughing. "Not really funny, Tom. Wives—now you mention it I've never been able to break Robin of squeezing the toothpaste tube the wrong way, but that's the worst I can accuse her of.''

The amazon would keep. With all the witnesses, they wouldn't need a statement from her to apply for the arrest warrant, simple charge of assault, probably with intent. They sent Dubois back on tour and drove out to Cedars-

Sinai to find out about Henry Bacon. Eventually they talked to a doctor in Emergency who said, "Well, he's not too good, but he'll probably survive. He lost a good deal of blood and he's got a nasty concussion. He's still unconscious, probably will be for some time. We'll let you know when you can talk to him. What was it, an accident of some kind? The paramedics just dumped him and gave us his name."

Palliser said gravely, "You could say a matrimonial accident, doctor. You'll let us know how he gets on."

Even if Bacon didn't want to charge her, it might be a salutary lesson for the amazon. They went back to the office and Landers typed up a report on it before they started out for lunch. He was just finished with that when Phil called from R. and I. "Gerber didn't make any pictures, sorry."

"I didn't really expect it," said Landers. But he too would have bet that the bumbling heister last night had been the same one on the market job and the other liquor store.

"He picked out three or four, said they weren't him but the general type. They're all in the forties or fifties, fairly big, with big stupid-looking faces, if that's any use."

"We know the general type, yes."

"And I may be a little late home," said Phil. They had managed to find her a middle-aged Chevy in pretty good condition. "I forgot to pick up orange juice and milk yesterday. See you about six-thirty, darling."

MENDOZA AND HACKETT had found Adele Mowbray at home this morning, at an expensive new condominium in upper Pasadena. James Cannaday was with her. She apologized distractedly for any disorder. "We've only just moved in last week. We'd put off selling the big house, but it just wasn't sensible to go on living there, now the family's gone—Greg and Michele way off in New York, I don't expect they'll get back here often, and Linda and Mike just over in Glendale, they won't be coming to stay, and Derek in his last year of college and that good job set up, it wasn't sensible to keep up the big house, and oh dear, I was so looking forward to showing this place to Lou—it just isn't possible she's gone, Jim's been telling me about it and I just can't understand what happened.'' There was evidently money here, expensive new furniture, plush carpeting. She was another nice-looking woman, not looking her age, slender and well groomed with tinted blond hair in a smart cut, discreet makeup, casually well dressed in a navy pant-suit. "Oh, come in and sit down—'' She looked at them with interest, dapper Mendoza in his usual elegant tailoring, big sandy Hackett looming over him. "I just can't conceive—it has to have been an accident of some kind, who'd want to hurt Lou deliberately? Just as Jim says, it doesn't make sense.'' She was given to elaborate gesture, dramatic over-emphasis on every third word, but the deep voice was vibrant with sincerity. "You said you want to ask questions, but I can't tell you anything, I don't know anything about what happened! It seemed a little silly to send flowers to the hotel, but we hadn't seen each other in so long, I was looking forward to seeing her so much—you know, we'd been friends since we were in the first grade together, and that's longer than I like to think, fifty years. She called me from the hotel when she got in, and that's all I know. I never heard from her again—she was coming for lunch on Saturday and when she didn't come I called the hotel—''

"Yes, we know that," said Hackett. "She called you about twelve-thirty on Friday?"

"Yes, it was about then, she'd just checked in. She thanked me for the flowers—she said she was going to see her aunt and uncle that afternoon—I didn't know them at all, of course. We were in and out of each other's houses all the while we were growing up, when she was living here with her parents, but after they were killed—that was an awful thing, they'd been driving back from Lake Arrowhead and there was fog, the police thought Mr. Lorne had missed a curve—Lou went to live with this aunt and uncle, and we were in college then, I don't think I was in the house half a dozen times, we went out on dates together—and just shopping, going around together, we both had our own cars then. She was dating Jerry Lemoyne in college mostly, everybody thought they'd get married. But then when Alden and I got married, my aunt and uncle came out from Indiana and she met John, John Cannaday, my cousin—''

"I told them all that," said Cannaday.

Hackett managed to stem the flow. "What else did she say when she called, Mrs. Mowbray? Did she mention meeting someone she knew at the hotel?''

"No, Jim told me about that and I can't think who it might've been. A very tall man—no, she didn't. That's funny.''

"I don't know who it could've been either," said Cannaday. He was sitting back on the couch gloomily contemplating a couple of used cups on the coffee table.

"Well, she never said anything about it. She thanked me for the flowers—I said that—and she said she was going to have lunch at the hotel and then go to see these Lornes, and she'd be here at noon the next day. Oh, it was just all the usual things," and she gestured widely. "You know, how we'd be glad to see each other, and about Sue's baby and their apartment—we didn't talk long, about ten minutes.''

"Well, what we'd like you to tell us," said Mendoza, "is about any other friends she had here. You'd know of any, I suppose. We know now why she'd arranged to stay on a couple of days." He told them what the Schultzes had said.

"Oh, that was it," said Cannaday. "Of course she would have, she wanted to see them.''

"As she was staying over, was there anyone else here she might have contacted?''

"I can't think who," said Adele Mowbray. "We've been talking about it, did you say Lieutenant? I told you, Jim. I've looked in that address book, and there's nobody—she was only going to be here an extra day, now we know that. We'd have been together most of Saturday.''

"You said something about her address book, doctor," said Hackett.

"Well, Peggy—my wife—said maybe I'd better bring it. I had Aunt Adele's address but I didn't know the Lornes', and I didn't know what information you might want.

Mother hadn't brought it with her because of course she knew those addresses.'' He produced it, a well-worn black leather address book, and handed it over. Hackett got out his notebook and started to go through it, noting down the California addresses.

"I can tell you about any of those, there's nothing in it,'' said Adele Mowbray impatiently. "People like Betty Mc-Cauley and Georgia Hayworth and Stella Booth, they were just old college friends, I'd only kept up with Stella myself and Lou hadn't really kept up with any of them, they just exchanged Christmas cards. Lou wouldn't have called any of them—well, she just might have, that night, for something to do, only we know that after she went back to the hotel she went out again somewhere. That's funny too. Where would she have gone, alone?''

"That's what I've been trying to think,'' said Cannaday. "It is a little funny, I wouldn't have expected her to go out anywhere alone in the evening. Here. I mean, she'd lived here, but a long while back. You could say it was a strange place to her now. Unless she went out to meet someone—but who?''

Hackett was leafing through the address book. Mendoza sat smoking, watching them. "Well, we know now from the night desk clerk that she must have gone out sometime before around seven-fifteen.'' Rich Conway had gone out to ask last night. "He thinks it was around then he found her key on the counter. He didn't know her, of course, but he remembered the room number, the tag on the key. Do either of you know an Ann Kessler?''

"That's another girl from college,'' said Adele. "Just another Christmas card thing. There's no reason Lou would have called her. Really the only people she knew here were me and this aunt and uncle. Oh, I suppose she might have phoned any of them—for something to do—but why should she go out to meet any of them at that hour? And Stella lives in Burbank, miles away. Why should she? I just can't imagine where she might have gone.''

Cannaday said suddenly, "The mileage on the car—the rented car. The tank would have been full when Hertz handed it over. Couldn't you tell how far it had been driven from that?''

"Unfortunately," said Mendoza, "the engine was left running, the tank was empty."

"What about Miss Ernestine Jardine?" asked Hackett. "Granada Hills." Which was a little far away from that Sheraton, and leaving the hotel sometime before seven-fifteen, Louise Cannaday hadn't had all that time to phone many people.

Adele laughed a little hysterically. "Oh, for heaven's sake. She was our English professor in college. Advanced Lit and Shakespeare. Lou was crazy about her, of course she was always better than me at that kind of thing, a real book-worm, and she had the idea she'd like to try to write, Miss Jardine used to encourage her. But I suppose that was another Christmas card thing, Lou had kept up with her that much. For heaven's sake, she'd be about ninety and retired years ago. You don't think Lou went to see her?''

"Why did she go anywhere, is what I can't make out," said Cannaday. "Damn it, she'd had kind of a full day, flying in from San Francisco, seeing those Schultzes, driving in a strange place to her—I'd have thought she'd have had dinner at the hotel and stayed in."

"Yes," said Mendoza, "but looked at another way, she had only a short time here, and that unexpected bonus day coming up. If there was anyone she wanted to see she could have called, possibly to set up a meeting for Sunday—and if whoever it was said 'I can't make it then but how about tonight'—''

"Well, I suppose so," said Cannaday.

"Who's Bruce Mallory?" asked Hackett. "Address in north Hollywood."

"I haven't any idea," said Cannaday. "Oh, wait a minute—''

"That poet," said Adele. "How funny, is he in there? I knew she'd written to him once but I didn't think it was a regular thing."

"A poet," said Mendoza. "Where'd she meet him?"

"She hadn't," said Cannaday. "My God, I'd forgotten the name—she'd just mentioned it casually. It was just a—you know—desultory thing. Mother was a great reader, and she liked poetry. Tried to write some herself, she'd had a few things printed in our church magazine. She subscribed to some poetry magazine, and this fellow had some poems in it, she liked them and wrote to tell him so, that was all. I didn't know she'd heard from him, had his address, she knew I wasn't much interested, she wouldn't have bothered to mention it. But why on earth should she have contacted him, even if he does live here? She didn't know him, they'd never met."

"All I remember about that," said Adele, "and it was months ago, about last March, Lou said she thought his work was very fine, she sent me a copy of one of his poems, it was something about dead leaves and I couldn't make head or tail of it, but I don't go for poetry much. She said she'd had a nice letter from him, but I certainly didn't get the impression they were corresponding regularly, anything like that." Suddenly she gave a little forlorn laugh. "Of course there's Jerry."

"Jerry who?" asked Cannaday.

"Oh, that's just silly," said Adele. "She wouldn't have. I mean, it just came into my head. But I don't really think—"

"Jerry who?" asked Hackett.

She looked at Cannaday apologetically. "I don't really think it could be, Jim. You know Lou and your father had a very happy marriage. It was just a silly thought."

"So who is this Jerry?" asked Cannaday.

"Well, you know, she'd been going steady with him the last two years of college. With Jerry Lemoyne, I mean. Everybody thought they were going to get married. And then Alden and I got engaged and the wedding was set for July, and it was a big wedding, everybody there and Lou one of my bridesmaids, and Aunt Kate and Uncle Ben came from Indiana with my cousin John. And it was one of those love-at-first sight things, they just fell for each other as soon as they laid eyes on each other, and got engaged. I don't think she ever saw Jerry after that, and of course they were married that fall—September—and Lou went back to live in Indianapolis. And when I had an invitation to the wedding I said to Alden, She caught him on the rebound, because of course he was just crazy about Lou. And—''

"What wedding?" asked Cannaday blankly. "Slow down and say what you're getting at.''

"Jerry Lemoyne and Claire Blanding, for heaven's sake. I never liked Claire, she was a terrible snob and oh-so-ladylike you wanted to shake her. She'd done some chasing after Jerry—oh, Lord, it's all such a long time ago—his father was a pretty well-known architect and had scads of money, and Jerry was going in for architecture too. That's what she was after, of course, the money.''

"Well, it's a long time ago and Mother didn't marry him, he married this other girl," said Cannaday.

"Yes, Jim dear, but that's what I was getting to. I ran into Jerry—I'm sorry, Jim, you won't have heard anything about it, but it was quite a joke between Lou and me—it was at our class reunion last June. I hadn't been to one before but I thought it might be fun to see what everybody looks like now, how they'd turned out. And I'd have known Jerry anywhere. Some of them were fat and bald, but he's kept his hair and looked just the same except for being older—he always was good-looking. And he asked if I'd kept up with Lou and he was terribly interested when I told him she was a widow. He kept pestering me for her address and finally I gave it to him. And he wrote her, she told me all about it, it was quite a joke. He wrote and told her he'd been divorced for fifteen years—I wasn't surprised, that Claire was just an impossible person—and they'd never had any children and he was lonely, and he'd always thought the world of her, they'd always got along so well, and if he came back to see her would she let him take her out—''

"This is all news to me," said Cannaday, looking angry.

"Yes, she wouldn't mention it to you, dear," said Adele. "She was awfully amused but of course she was a bit flattered too. She just wrote him back politely, said it was nice to hear from him again and know he still remembered her, but squashing him. It was a joke. And I don't think she ever heard from him again, she never mentioned it.''

"Do you know where he lives?'' asked Mendoza.

"Heavens, I don't—oh, I seem to remember he said something about Long Beach. But for heaven's sake, he wouldn't have known she was here. And she wouldn't—''

Hackett shut the address book. ''Mrs. Mowbray, do you happen to have a good photograph of Mrs. Cannaday?''

"Why, yes, I have, she had one taken about six months ago, why?''

Mendoza lit another cigarette and contemplated it. ''We'd like to know where she went that night. It might turn up some information if we got the press to run a picture.''

Cannaday said distastefully, ''Anyone who has seen this woman, notify the cops? I'm sorry, I can see that. But the idea of spreading her picture around—''

"Don't be silly, Jim. It's a very good idea. We would like to find out where she was, after all.'' She cocked her head at Mendoza. ''And I know the police are supposed to be awfully smart these days, but the more I think about it the more I think it must be something quite simple. Because Lou just wasn't the kind of person to be deliberately—well, killed. Murdered. That's just silly.''

"What do you think happened to her, Mrs. Mowbray?'' asked Mendoza placidly.

"Well, I think she could have decided to go out to dinner someplace else than the hotel. And she'd have had the car doors locked, but maybe when she got there, in a parking lot somewhere, she was attacked by one of the muggers.''

"She wasn't robbed,'' said Hackett.

"No, you said that—so maybe it was just some young crook after the car, maybe he was high on drugs, and he hit her on the head and just drove off with her in it, and then when it ran out of gas he just left it.''

"Anything's possible,'' said Mendoza noncommittally.

"I'll get you the picture.''

It was a very good professional portrait, showing even better than the casual one on the driver's license what an attractive woman Louise Cannaday had been, with the striking white streak in the black hair, the big dark eyes, the smiling mobile mouth. "We'll see you get the address book back, doctor." Cannaday thanked them disinterestedly.

"I should think," said Hackett in the Ferrari, "the lab ought to have been over the car by now."

"Let's have lunch before we go and ask," said Mendoza.

At the usual table at Federico's he brooded over black coffee. "Anything hit you about any of that?" asked Hackett.

Mendoza lit a meditative cigarette. "Something," he agreed. "The old flame. Could there be something in that?"

"Now look," said Hackett, "she seems to have been a nice conventional woman, Luis. Settled down, with a family. One grandchild and another expected. Why you have to keep imagining sex rearing its ugly head—"

"It so often does," said Mendoza with a grin. "Substitute the old flame for the mysterious gent at the hotel, Art. Whoever he was. She was going to have Sunday free. From what Mrs. Mowbray says, this Lemoyne sounded eager. We don't know that he hadn't written her again, that she hadn't written him. She wouldn't mention it to the family, and she might have been enough self-conscious about it that she didn't mention it to Mrs. Mowbray. So he didn't know she was here, who can say that? Say he did, that she told him. She'd expected to have Friday night free. Suppose it was all set up, they were going to meet for dinner."

"Then he'd have come to the hotel to pick her up, wouldn't he? What was she doing in the rental car?"

"Maybe he did." Mendoza interrupted himself to give the order to the waiter. "And when he got there, his car had a flat tire in the parking lot, or battery trouble, so they took hers. And read it just as I said before from then on."

Hackett sighed. "You know we'll never get anywhere on this damned thing. It's all too anonymous. It could even be, crazy as it sounds, something like what the Mowbray woman imagines—the young punk jumping her in a parking lot somewhere, getting scared when he found he'd hurt her seriously."

"Not with the cash still in her handbag," said Mendoza. "Scared or not, the punk would have grabbed that. And one like that would have just run, not tried to set up the fake accident."

"Well, I just don't see us finding out much more about it."

They landed back at Parker Center at one o'clock and rode straight up to the lab. Scarne was just ahead of them, everybody else evidently out to lunch. "That Hertz car," said Hackett. "Have you had a chance to go over it yet?"

"Oh, sure," said Scarne. "I was just about to get out a report on it, not that there's anything to give you. It's clean as a whistle. I understand it had just been rented that day, well, you know the rental agencies, those cars get polished up like nobody's business. There weren't any prints in it at all, and of course that means that somebody had been busy. There should have been some. At least on the wheel, the dashboard. I went over to the morgue and got hers—the Cannaday woman. There were a few of hers on the outside of the driver's door, but inside, nothing. The wheel was polished clean, or whoever drove it last was wearing gloves."

"That figures," said Hackett. "Setting up the fake accident."

"There was a woman's coat on the front seat, I've got it here. Nearly a new cloth coat, fairly expensive. Nothing in the pockets but a woman's handkerchief. A county map also on the front seat, and that's it." Louise Cannaday had been wearing a tailored dark suit and white blouse; possibly, like many women, she had disliked driving in a coat and had taken it off; there was a heater in the car. "Sorry we can't give you anything useful," said Scarne perfunctorily. "Oh, by the way, that overnight bag. Higgins dropped it off yesterday. The stains are human blood all right, I haven't had time to type it."

"Oh, my God, that baby," said Hackett. "And just what the hell do we do about that?"

"Something," said Mendoza rather savagely. "The young couple named Leeper. The old anonymous car. Said to have come from Arizona."

"And heading for Ventura. Only were they? It's going through the motions," said Hackett.

"Yeah, Higgins was telling us about the baby," said Scarne. "Hell of a thing. What some people get up to—but I'll tell you one thing. If it was a baby that bled in that bag, it lost most of its blood supply."

"Thanks, we had deduced that," said Hackett.

They went on down to the office and ran into Landers and Palliser just back from lunch, and heard about the amazon and the meek Henry Bacon. "Don't laugh," said Palliser seriously. "She might have killed the poor fellow, by what the doctor said. He's still unconscious, I checked a while ago. Do we talk to the D.A.'s office or just go for a warrant? It adds up to assault with intent to kill."

"I don't think we'll bother the D.A.," said Mendoza through a grin. "Set up the machinery on the warrant, John. And you'd better take Art or George along to execute it. These females."

"And these damned Model A's," said Landers. "We'll never collect enough for a charge there. Of course there are five still to look at—Nick and Pat went out chasing them. What are you picking up on the Cannaday woman? That's a funny one."

Mendoza sat down at Higgins' desk; when he wasn't involved with paperwork he tended to neglect his own office. Hackett told them briefly what new they'd heard about Louise Cannaday. "Sounds like a handful of nothing to me," said Palliser frankly.

"Oh, trust the boss to come up with an inspiration. He's building a story about the old boyfriend."

"From college thirty-five years ago? That's the longest shot in the book," said Landers skeptically.

Mendoza had the appropriate phone book out. "Never underestimate the power of that old devil, sex," he said briskly. "Here he is in the Long Beach book, Jerome Lemoyne. Twice. At a good residential address, and Lemoyne and Ellis, Architects. You go and set up the warrant on your amazon, John. I think I'd like a little talk with Mr. Lemoyne. And there is that— If he can be the answer on

Louise Cannaday, nobody knew he knew she was here. I don't think we'll let him know we're coming. Come on, Art, let's take a ride down to Long Beach.''

But the trip on the freeway was abortive; in the anteroom of a handsome set of offices in a new building in the heart of the city, a pretty blond receptionist told them that Mr. Lemoyne was out in Tarzana inspecting the site for a new condominium, and not expected back in the office that day.

"Mañana es otro día," said Mendoza philosophically.

ABOUT FOUR O'CLOCK Calhoun and Galeano came back to base and passed on their news gloomily. The other five Model A's could be written off as possibles for the hit-run on the Cranes. Three of them had been out of the county since before last Friday, their owners off on trips to a family reunion, a rock-hunting party, and a wedding. One of the others had been on display in a vintage car show at an agency in Santa Monica for the last week, and the fifth had been sitting in the owner's garage, waiting until he got around to installing a new radiator.

"Well, that's the way the ball bounces," said Landers.

Calhoun slumped into a chair and contemplated his long legs with a scowl. "Damn it to hell, Tom, with the make on the car, and such a car—not so damn many around—we should have got him. That poor damned kid—"

"Cheer up," said Palliser. "These were just the Model A's in L.A. County, Pat. I think there are another thirty or so in the rest of the state." Calhoun snarled at him. "Get some other forces to work on it, find out whether those owners were down here last week." There was time still left on the shift; he found that list the D.M.V. had dredged up and went off to communications to set that up.

Landers had already sent off a request to the Arizona D.M.V. about those Leepers, and what that might turn up God knew. Arizona wasn't going to be happy about it; at least it wasn't as common a name as Smith, but it wasn't outlandishly unusual and Arizona was a big state. Now he sat back in his desk chair and said to Galeano, "And we're not a police state."

"What?" said Galeano. "Thank God, no."

"All the identity cards, and tabs kept on every citizen on official forms in every police station. Of course, if we were, the average citizen wouldn't be able to afford a car. But as it is, there's absolutely nothing on a car registration that says how old the owner is or what he looks like."

Galeano massaged his jaw, which gave evidence of needing a shave at this time of day. "That young couple and the baby. God, what a thing. No, even if Arizona finds anything, there might be a couple of dozen—needle in a haystack, no telling which is which. The baby—this can be the hell of a job for an honest man sometimes, Tom." He brooded at his desk blotter for a minute. "Did I tell you Christine's trying to walk? Marta says it's at least a couple of months early, but she's a smart one." Galeano had come to the domesticities a trifle late and was inclined to be fatuous about his single offspring.

"Oh, Sara's been walking for the last month."

"Yeah, but she's nearly three months older."

Calhoun the bachelor and girl-chaser wasn't interested.

MENDOZA GOT HOME early and found his household strangely peaceful. The twins were out at the corral riding their ponies under the supervision of Ken Kearney, Cedric supervising them, and the Kearneys' large black tom Nicodemus was sitting on a fence post surveying his domain in a lordly manner; Mendoza had waved at the party on his way up the hill. Mairí MacTaggart was ensconced in her kitchen rocker knitting. Two-year-old Luisa, her hair as red as Alison's, was playing with a stuffed cat on the living room floor, and Alison was nursing the new one in her armchair. Mendoza went back to the kitchen to get himself a drink, inevitably pursued by El Señor. The other three cats were mysteriously absent. He sat down in his armchair and contemplated Alison, taking a swallow of rye.

"You're a widow," he said. "A very attractive widow with a nice family and a reasonable amount of money. Before you married your late husband thirty-five years ago, you dated steadily with a nice young fellow at college. You hadn't seen him since. He's just contacted you again, finding out you're a widow. He's divorced and feeling lonely and proposes renewing the acquaintanceship, so to speak.''

"Yes?" said Alison.

"You've been living back east all this time, but for reasons I needn't go into you're on a short visit to Los Angeles. You're not really—I don't think—interested in renewing the romance, but you find yourself here—he lives here—with a free day to kill. You're here alone. Do you phone him and tell him so? Or would you—this widow, who's a very nice conventional woman, nothing fast or flashy—think it was—mmh—a little forward and unlady-like?"

Alison considered, readjusting the blanket around Cecelia. "This widow. You said attractive. How old?"

"Fifty-five. Didn't look it. Very good-looking female, and a smart dresser. She'd just acquired her first grandchild and was expecting another."

"Oh," said Alison, and wrinkled her tip-tilted nose at him. "I think quite possibly she might, Luis. She might not have been remotely interested in renewing the romance, but considering—if she hadn't worn well, if she looked her age, she wouldn't have especially wanted him to see her after all those years, but when she didn't look her age and was still attractive, she might have wanted to see him. Or him to see her. Perfectly innocently."

"That's exactly what I thought," said Mendoza. "You'll be seeing her picture in the *Times*." Hackett had gone to arrange about that before heading home.

"Yes, you didn't really need to ask me," said Alison amusedly. "You know too much about women, rake that you were before I reformed you."

Mendoza grinned at her. "*Sin mujeres y sin vientos, tendríamos menos tormentos*—without women and without wind, less trouble."

AT SIX-THIRTY Mr. Ernest Hoffman had come to the end of his patience. He was a peaceable man, but he liked to abide by an orderly routine, and that meant getting home from work at five-thirty—he had his own upholstery shop in Hollywood—sitting down to dinner at six, and at six-thirty settling down for a session with the evening paper while his wife cleared up the kitchen. Their two children were grown up and married. And the paper delivery boy was getting more and more unreliable. Last night he hadn't come until they were having dinner, and tonight so far he hadn't come at all.

"I'll speak to him when he comes to collect," said Mrs. Hoffman.

"That does me a lot of good now, doesn't it," said Hoffman. "Maybe he came while we were eating." It was dark outside by now, and he switched on the porch light, opened the front door, and stepped out on the porch. Sometimes the stupid boy left the paper halfway down the front walk. Fuming, he started down there, and suddenly spotted something out there on the sidewalk. Thirty seconds later he came rushing back into the house.

"We've got to get the police—an ambulance—it's some poor little girl out there, bleeding all over the sidewalk, I don't know if she's dead—" Waiting for the squad car, the ambulance, he forgot about the evening paper.

FOUR

RICH CONWAY was another one like Calhoun, a good-looking bachelor with an eye for the girls, but he was also a compassionate man and a good cop; and Matt Piggott, besides being an earnest Christian, was the fairly new father of a baby girl. Their brief look at the pitiful slender body on the surgery table shook both of them. A nurse shooed them out, and presently a doctor came to them in the corridor of the Emergency wing.

"It's lucky she was found when she was, if we hadn't got to her for another hour she could have bled to death. Do you know who she is?" They didn't. "I suppose you'll find out. I'd say she's eleven or twelve. She's been beaten up and raped, pretty damned savagely, by a fairly big strong man. She's got a broken arm and collarbone besides all the head injuries and the rest of it. Where was she found?—on the street, well, he could have banged her head on the sidewalk, I don't think there was any weapon. She's concussed, still unconscious. She's just a little thing, she's pretty badly torn up inside. Oh, she'll live, but it remains to be seen if there's any brain damage, she took half a dozen hard knocks on the head."

"We'd like to see her clothes," said Conway. "We'll have to try for an identification."

"Yes, of course," said the doctor. "We weren't looking for that." A nurse handed over the clothes in the cubicle where they had first examined her, and there wasn't anything helpful in them. A blue wool skirt, the waistband ripped half off, a blue polo shirt, knit cotton panties torn to pieces, white T-shirt, knee-length wool socks, scuffed brown leather moccasins, a navy wool cardigan. In the pocket of that was a coin purse containing a dollar and twelve cents in change, nothing else.

"They're fairly nice clothes," said Piggott. "She isn't a street kid, Rich." They reached the same conclusion at the same time: the girl might have already been reported missing. But in case there was a shortcut they went up to where she'd been found, an address on a residential block on Elden Avenue, and had a look around the sidewalk and yard there. The householder who had found her came out to ask questions but he couldn't tell them anything.

"I don't think I've ever seen the child before, but all the blood—my God, I thought she was dead, we were afraid to touch her, try to help, but the ambulance got here fast—" There wasn't any purse to be found, or schoolbooks or papers, but there was a steady wind blowing which might have dispersed anything like that. Emergency would notify them if the girl came to and identified herself, but from what the doctor said that wasn't likely to happen soon. They went back to headquarters and down to Traffic to ask if there had been a call on a missing child. It was seven-thirty. The watch commander said, "Why's Robbery-Homicide asking questions? You got E.S.P. up there? There was a report about half an hour ago—probably just another nervous parent, the kids roam all over and forget to come home when they should. There's a squad there now. Twelve-year-old late home."

"What's the address?" asked Piggott.

He looked it up in the log. "Westmoreland Avenue."

"That's got to be it, Matt," said Conway. "That's the cross street up from Elden."

It was one side of an old stucco duplex, and the uniformed man, Powell, was still there, talking to Mr. and Mrs. Dale. They looked ordinary solid citizens, in the thirties, Dale short and stocky, his wife thin and dark, and they were trying to keep their heads and be sensible. She turned to the plainclothesmen with a kind of wild relief.

"He's just been saying it isn't very late and sometimes kids lose track of time, but you don't understand about Sandra, that's what I been trying to tell him. She's a good sensible child, and after Mrs. Moore told us when she left—

we didn't call the police until then, Chuck had looked all up the block—"

Another woman, tall and plump, came in, apparently from the kitchen, with a glass of water and a bottle of aspirin. "You just take a couple of these and try to calm down—" but she looked nearly as agitated as the Dales. "Oh, more police?"

"Mrs. Dale, how long has your daughter been missing?" asked Conway. That attack had been recent, very likely within half an hour of the time she'd been found.

"That's just it," she said frantically. "Since about five-thirty, and she was late then, she knows she's supposed to be home before dark, and it gets dark early now, she should have been home by five, we have dinner at six, when Chuck gets home, and when she wasn't here by five-thirty I called Mrs. Moore. Sandra had gone home with Carol after school, they like to do their homework together. But she knows she's supposed to be home before dark. I was annoyed, I said to Chuck, you'll have to go round there and walk her home, and then when I called nobody answered—"

"We'd just gone out," said the other woman. "I'm Mrs. Moore, Officers. I'd had quite a day what with all that laundry, I got behind when the washer went out last week, and my husband said, why not just go out to that fried-chicken place on Vermont, so we never got back till after six-thirty, and when Mrs. Dale called and I told her Sandra had left at five-thirty—she and Carol were in Carol's room doing their homework or something, and I'd reminded Sandra about the time when it was starting to get dark, I know the Dales like her in before then, and she said she'd leave in a minute. It wasn't until a good twenty minutes later I realized she was still there, and she'd forgot the time too—she went off in a hurry. I did think of asking Harry to walk her home, it was dark then—oh, dear Lord, if anything's happened to her I'll never forgive myself—but he'd just come in, he was tired and hungry, and it's just a little way, a block over on Elden and a block on this street, and she said she'd run, she'd be all right, and Harry was already out at the car—''

"I think we may have found your daughter," said Piggott gently. "We don't know, but we'd like you to come to the hospital and see if it is. She's been hurt, I'm afraid, yes."

"Oh, my God," said Dale. "An accident? Yes, all right. Now, Dorrie, don't give way, we've got to keep our heads and do what we have to do. Where is she?" He looked a little wildly at the detectives. "What happened to her?"

"Let's be sure it is your daughter first, sir," said Conway. "We'll take you to the hospital." She had begun to cry but controlled herself with an effort.

"You let me know," said Mrs. Moore on the tiny front porch. "Let me know if it is Sandra. Dear Lord, I'll never forgive myself is she's hurt bad, I should have had Harry walk home with her, but it's such a little way and no main street to cross, and she's twelve after all, not a little kid—but I should have—Carol's all upset about it—you let me know." She was starting off down the street as they got into Conway's car at the curb.

The Dales rode out to the hospital in silence. By now the hospital had the girl in another cubicle in Emergency, with an I.V. going and a nurse in attendance. She was still unconscious, her head heavily bandaged, looking very small and flat in the cot. The Dales took one look and she said faintly, "Yes, it's Sandra. Oh, baby, what's happened to you? Oh, Chuck—''

"Now take it easy, they're looking after her. What did happen?"

"We better find a doctor," said Piggott.

It was the same doctor they had talked to first, and he told the parents what had happened, the savage attack, the forcible rape. Mrs. Dale did break down then, sobbing in great gulps, huddled on the bench in the corridor, and Dale began to swear. "I'll kill him, I'll kill the bastard—doing that to my little girl—you'd better catch him, some goddamned son of a bitch hurt my girl like that—''

"We'll certainly try, Mr. Dale. We'll hope Sandra can tell us something about him." And the doctor touched Conway's arm and beckoned them aside.

"They haven't quite taken it in yet, about the possible brain damage," he said evenly. He was a tall lanky man with gray hair and glasses. "It's possible the girl won't be able to tell you anything, even if there's no permanent impairment. It might be quite a while before she remembers anything, if she ever does. That would be merciful in a way, but of course you ought to catch up to one like this, find out who he is. We'll hope for the best, but it's early to say. We won't try to get any X-rays yet, she's holding her own and we'll see how she looks tomorrow."

He discouraged the parents from staying; there wasn't anything they could do. And there wasn't anything more to do tonight except take the parents home and assure them they'd be hunting for the rapist.

"Those houses down there," said Conway, "on Elden and Westmoreland. Not very far back from the street. But if anybody along there had heard anything, maybe the girl screaming—if he chased her, say—they'd have gone out to look. Or would they? The wind's been making a racket—"

"And there was Kitty Genovese," said Piggott. "Screaming her head off—that murder back in New York—and nobody who heard her wanted to get involved. I don't know, Rich. If anybody did, they're not going to admit it now. I think he may just have followed her, not chased her, maybe in a car. Spotted her alone on the street just by chance, and jumped her right there where she was found. That's where it happened, by the blood."

"Let's just hope to God," said Conway, "the poor kid will come to okay and be able to tell us something about him."

THAT WAS WAITING for the day watch on Wednesday morning. Both Calhoun and Higgins were off. Mendoza passed the night report around and they talked about Sandra Dale briefly. Hackett called Emergency and talked to one of the nurses. The girl was still unconscious but considered stable, and the parents were there. He reported that and added, "So we ask Records for any likely suspects." That was the obvious way to go on one like this, and most of the heisters. He got R. and I. and asked them to put the computers on the job. The computers made life easier these days.

The night watch had also left them a new body and a new heist. Grace went out to have a look at the body. The first piece of business that turned up was the heist victim, to make a statement, and Hackett talked to him. He was the manager of a chain drugstore on Virgil, a small thin man with a nervous Adam's apple and a high voice.

"I'd never been held up before, I don't mind telling you I was scared, you hear about all these crazy young punks on drugs, never know what they'll do. Like I told the officers last night, he came in just before closing, business had been slow, I hadn't had a customer in the last hour. Oh, I can give you a kind of idea what he looked like, he was in his early twenties, around there, kind of tall and thin, clean shaved, he had dark hair—yes, he was a white man—He came up to the counter and said, 'This is a stickup, give me all the money'—No, he didn't ask for any drugs, just the money."

"Could you say anything about the gun?"

"Oh, I didn't see his gun, he had it in his coat pocket, he pointed it at me through that, and I wasn't about to take any chances, you hear of such things, all the violence. I just handed over the money, all the bills from the register. It wasn't all that much, it'd been slow, like I say, and we're insured. About sixty dollars."

Hackett suddenly remembered something in another night report a few days ago about one like that. No gun visible, and the same general description. "Do you think you could recognize a picture?"

"Oh, goodness no, I don't think so, he was only there a couple of minutes. That's really all I can tell you. I don't know when I've been so shaken up. I had to take a glass of brandy when I got home to settle my nerves, and I don't usually drink spirits at all, but I don't mind admitting I was scared. I'd never been held up before—"

He had just signed the statement rather shakily and gone out when the arrest warrant came in on Edna Bacon. "The boss thought you ought to ride shotgun on this," said Palliser with a grin. "You like to come and meet the amazon?"

Mendoza was on the phone in his own office. Hackett said amiably, "I don't mind."

"I wonder how Bacon's doing," said Landers. "I called in first thing, we'll need a statement from him sooner or later, and he hasn't come to yet. She really did clobber him."

They took Hackett's garishly painted Monte Carlo out to Laguna Avenue. "I trust she's still here," said Palliser. "I asked, and she hasn't even called to ask how Henry's doing."

"Well, wives," said Hackett. "Like other people, they come all sorts."

She was still there, at the old frame house. She opened the front door to them and gave them an aggressive stare even before they showed her the badges. She was at least five-ten and probably weighed upward of two hundred pounds, a big hefty woman with scanty pale-red hair in a knob on the back of her head, and considering her figure she was inappropriately wearing baggy blue jeans and a pale pink T-shirt.

"Police," she said. "What the hell do the police want?"

"We have a warrant for your arrest, if you're Mrs. Edna Bacon," said Landers.

"Yeah, that's me. What the hell you mean, arrest? Me? What the hell for?"

"Assault with intent to kill," said Palliser. "You nearly did kill your husband yesterday, you know. He's still unconscious."

She uttered a braying contemptuous laugh. "Henry? Did that good-for-nothing little squirt say that? Carting him off to the hospital, it was foolishness, he was all right, just knocked out—if he told the cops that he's just shamming, and if he had the nerve to lay a charge on me, I'll see he gets paid for it good. That damned little bastard!"

"It's not what he said, it's what the doctor said," Landers told her enjoyably. "We'll have to take you in, Mrs. Bacon. Right now."

She glared at them incredulously. "To jail? You're goin' to try to put me in jail? Just because I knocked that no-good little squirt down in the backyard? That's crazy! He's my husband, I guess I got a right to treat him like he deserves."

"Short of murder," said Hackett. "You'll have to come along with us, Mrs. Bacon." He was about to show her the warrant, tell her about her various rights, when she started to shout.

"I'll be damned if I do—you can all go to hell—"

"Now let's not have any trouble here," Palliser started to say, when she aimed a fist like a ham at him and connected solidly with his jaw like a man, and taken by surprise he staggered back, tripped over the doormat and sprawled on his back down the front steps, swearing. Then she turned on Landers.

"Wasn't Luis right," said Hackett. "Now, Mrs. Bacon—" It wasn't exactly according to Hoyle, they weren't supposed to manhandle prisoners, especially female ones, but they had to take her in and even if their female detective had been along—Wanda was still busy on that juvenile thing—she wouldn't have been much use with this one. Hackett got a hammerlock on her but she broke loose and got in another telling blow at Landers before they got a pair of cuffs on her and bundled her into the car. On the way downtown Palliser went on swearing.

"Goddamn it, it feels as if I've fractured my spine—I hit that step right on the tailbone, damn it—"

Landers was nursing what would probably turn out to be a fine black eye. "My God, I'll never hear the end of it from Phil. A female. But what a female." At the Sybil Brand Institute, the women's jail, they handed her over to a matron and Hackett passed on a warning before taking off the cuffs. The matron looked fairly tough herself. She said tranquilly, "Oh, don't worry, Sergeant, they usually settle down once they're booked in." She led Edna Bacon off to a cell and they saw her go thankfully.

"I wonder where in God's name Henry found that one," said Landers.

There was legwork to do, but none of them felt like starting out on that. They went back to the office and found Grace typing a report. The new body, he said, looked like a typical derelict, spotted by a patrolman on the sidewalk along Hoover at three this morning. "They haven't got to an autopsy yet, of course, but he had on the usual collection of worn-out clothes, forty cents in change, no I.D., and he smelled to high heaven of cheap wine. Just another bum dying the hard way, alcoholism or whatever. He looked to be around seventy. I sent the prints to R. and I. in case we've got them, there may be a family to pay for a funeral. What's the matter with your eye, Tom?"

"You may well ask," said Landers bitterly. "I'll never hear the end of it, damn it."

WHEN ALISON had found her historic old Spanish *estancia* in the hills above Burbank, Mendoza had called the local architects' association for a recommendation, somebody competent to evaluate the building, and the current president, Ralph Guilfoyle, had been fascinated by the historical interest of the place. He was still a casual acquaintance, and Mendoza thought he could bear to know whatever might be to know about Lemoyne and Ellis, Architects. Guilfoyle, unsurprisingly, was rather proud of personally knowing a real live lieutenant of police, and would open up on anything he knew, but of course there were a lot of architects in the country.

Just on the chance, Mendoza got hold of him at his office and put the question. "Never mind why I'm asking. Is the firm solid? Good reputation? I'm interested in Lemoyne. Do you know anything about him?"

"Happy to be of any help," said Guilfoyle obligingly. "As it happens I can tell you something. I don't know Lemoyne personally, but I do know Gilbert Ellis. It's a sound firm, they're good people, but they got into a little trouble last year through nobody's fault. They'd got a contract to build a big new shopping mall in San Gabriel, and the

ground was broken before it developed that the title to the
land wasn't clear. The developers were a big realty company, Gold Carpet, and while the property was still in es-
crow the cloud on the title showed up—I don't know the ins
and outs of it—and there was a lawsuit, against the realty
company and Lemoyne and Ellis. It went against them and
they both dropped some money on it.''

"Oh, really," said Mendoza. "You don't know anything
about Lemoyne personally?"

"Not much," said Guilfoyle. "I've met him, of course,
at association dinners and so forth. All I can tell you is, I ran
into Gil Ellis somewhere recently, and among other things
he said he was a little worried about Lemoyne, that business had sort of demoralized him, they'd lost a good deal of
money and Lemoyne had been having some kind of trouble
with his ex-wife, she was asking for more alimony, and Lemoyne had been worried and doing some drinking." Guilfoyle laughed. "Ellis is a pretty strict churchgoer, he doesn't
approve of drinking. I don't know how much there is in
that."

"Thanks so much," said Mendoza. "Did the lawsuit have
any effect on the firm's reputation?"

"Well, some. Inevitably. People can be muddleheaded,
Mendoza. It was the realty company that goofed, not to
make sure of the title before making the contract, but the
suit was against the architects too and they lost the case. Oh,
it's a very sound firm. I'm sorry I can't tell you anything
more, I don't really know much."

"Thanks very much," said Mendoza again, and put down
the phone and thought about that. Hackett was out somewhere. Just going through the motions, they'd said. Contact everybody in Louise Cannaday's address book who
lived here—Did she call you, if so what did she say, did you
see her that night? But they were mostly women, and by
what Adele Mowbray said very casual contacts. He finally
stabbed out his cigarette and got up. The *Times* hadn't run
the photograph in the morning edition; hopefully it would
be in a later one.

At the tall new office building in Long Beach, the sleek receptionist finally condescended to admit him and showed him into a handsomely furnished inner office. He produced the badge and presented himself to Jerome Lemoyne, sitting at a big walnut desk facing a huge picture window overlooking the city.

"You're police?" said Lemoyne. "What's it about, what can I do for you?"

Mendoza surveyed him with leisurely interest. Lemoyne would be somewhere around the middle fifties; he was a handsome, virile-looking fellow, a six-footer with good broad shoulders, and he'd kept his figure. He had a lean face with regular features and a head of thick fair hair going gray. "Oh, sit down—What's it about?"

Mendoza told him, briefly and economically. "We'd like to know if you knew Mrs. Cannaday was going to be here, Mr. Lemoyne. Did she contact you by any chance? Did you contact her? Did you see her that night, last Friday night?"

Lemoyne just sat in his tall leather desk chair, staring at the blotter, and then he said in a dull voice, "Louise. You're telling me she's dead—I'm sorry, give me a minute. That's a shocker. She was killed somehow, an accident? God, we were the same age—it's too soon, too young." He fumbled for a cigarette in the leather box on the desk, lit it, and inhaled strongly. "My God," he said quietly, "I wish I'd seen her. I wish—" and he laughed, and said bitterly, "Wishful thinking. Who said it, you can't go home again. It's never been any good thinking about what might have been."

"Mrs. Adele Mowbray told us you had been in contact with her," said Mendoza.

"And I suppose she told you the hell of a lot more than that. She's a talker. Yes, if you can call a couple of letters being in contact. Life's a funny proposition, isn't it?" He laughed briefly, sounding genuinely amused. "Isn't there a saying—Life is what happens to you while you're making other plans. Which is too true. Lou and I—" He picked up a ballpoint pen and poked aimlessly at the blotter "—I'd thought it was a settled thing between us, all that time back. We'd never said anything, but we dated regularly, we got along so well, enjoyed the same things, had the same interests—she knew I'd be going into my father's firm after I graduated, be set with a good job—you know, that very last date I was going to say to her, Let's make it official, honey, I'll get you a ring tomorrow, let's get married this summer. And then she was all full of the wedding, Adele's wedding, and talking about these people from Indiana—'' Suddenly he got up and stood looking out the window, his back to Mendoza. He was silent for a long moment, and then said, ''You know, it's absolutely irrational, it's thirty-five years ago, but I still hate that fellow. That Cannaday. What right had he to show up and take my girl away? Oh, you do the decent thing, the conventional thing, goodbye and good luck. And I wasn't a fool, anybody could see that Lou was crazy about him, really in love more than she'd ever been with me, and he felt the same way. There wasn't anything I could do about it. And it's the hell of a long time ago. I'm not going to pretend I've brooded over it ever since. Life goes on and other things come along. But—I'd have liked to see Lou again.''

''Mrs. Mowbray said you had written to her, suggesting you'd like to see her.''

''Yes,'' said Lemoyne. ''It was a silly idea, when I heard she was a widow, that we might pick up again. You really can't do that sort of thing, can you? She'd been living back there all that time, had new friends and other interests. She wrote me—'' He turned, and his mouth twisted a little to bitterness—''a nice proper letter. Nice to hear from me, but she wasn't interested. She didn't put it that crudely, but that's what it amounted to. Well, I understood that. There was too much water under the bridge.''

''You didn't hear from her again,'' asked Mendoza, ''or write to her?''

Lemoyne went back to the window. ''I didn't say that. She dropped me a note, from San Francisco.'' So she kept his address, thought Mendoza, and then amended the thought. The phone books for anywhere in the state would be available in any city library. ''Last week. It was just a note, she said she was going to be here, not very long, she'd be at the Sheraton Plaza and free that Friday night, if I liked we could have a friendly drink together, she'd be pleased to see me again.''

''And did you take her up on it?'' asked Mendoza.

He came to sit at the desk again. ''I wanted to. I'd have liked to see Lou again. I tried to call her at the hotel about one o'clock that day but she was out. So I called again about six-thirty but she still wasn't in.'' She had sent that wire at six-ten but they didn't know when she had gone out; it could have been as early as six-thirty. Whenever. ''I tried again about seven, but no luck. And I called on Saturday—but you say she was killed that night. Friday night. God, I'm sorry.''

''So what did you do that night?'' asked Mendoza conversationally. ''Go out to dinner? See some friends?''

Lemoyne looked up and stared at him. ''What the hell do you mean? I had dinner at home—I watched some TV and went to bed—why the hell should you want to know?''

''We don't know just how she came to be killed, you see,'' said Mendoza gently. ''She'd gone out, as yet we don't know where, and it doesn't seem likely she'd have gone out alone. Somewhere, somehow, she sustained a blow on the head that killed her.''

''And you think I could have had something to do with it?'' asked Lemoyne roughly. ''No, Lieutenant. Not guilty. I don't suppose I could prove it, but I never saw her. I wish I had. The little she said in that first letter—I'm glad she had a good life with that fellow, the children, a happy time. More than I had, but that wasn't Lou's fault. I just wished I'd been able to see her again.''

And all that sounded nice and straightforward, reflected Mendoza, but there was nothing to back it up. He admitted he'd known she was here; he could have contacted her at the hotel, could have taken her out somewhere. He was a virile, full-blooded man. He probably hadn't suffered any lack of varied female company since his divorce, or before, as far as that went. And it might not have been any sudden attack of *amour*; there was the suggestion that he had harbored some bitterness against her all those years, for walking out on him. Whatever the circumstances had been, that had probably been an unpremeditated attack. And Lemoyne was an intelligent man.

Mendoza ruminated on it, watching him. A sudden flare-up of that bitterness?—and she hadn't looked like a meek woman. The sudden quarrel—in a parking lot somewhere? Not at the hotel, too public and too many people coming and going. The sudden violence erupting—but, the blunt instrument? He could have knocked her down against the trunk of the car, that would do. Or even on the paving of a parking lot, a sidewalk. But, setting up the fake accident, how could he have known she wouldn't come to and tell about it? How had he known she was seriously enough hurt that she'd die of it some unspecified time later? He was of an age to have served in the Korean war at least; he could know something about depressed skull fractures. He could have called an ambulance, told the frank tale, she tripped and fell, hoping she'd back him up. For old times' sake? On the other hand, there was what Guilfoyle had said. There had been that trouble with the business, cutting into their reputation; and purportedly he'd been having trouble with his ex-wife. He might have been leery of having any more scandal, any publicity. Unexpectedly stuck with what he might well be aware was a dying body, he might have panicked. Even if it was Lou, the old flame—the girlfriend who had walked out on him, however much he'd thought of her. And water under the bridge—thirty-five years, and he hadn't seen her since. He could have set up the fake accident, not really thinking, in a blind panic.

But it was a trifle early for that, wasn't it? The car rammed into a light pole on Fourteenth off Sepulveda—yes, making it look as if she'd been on her way back to the hotel, which was at Sepulveda and Century. And turned into the side street for some reason? That was a residential street; had that car been sitting there more than a couple of hours before it was found?

And the rented car? In the course of casual observation, could she have said, they gave me a red two-door Ford, last year's model, so he knew what to look for in the hotel parking lot? They would have been in his car. Or, for God's sake, in the hotel room? thought Mendoza, and immediately damned himself for a fool. Whatever had happened or hadn't happened, nobody had carried Louise Cannaday's unconscious body down from the sixth floor of that big and busy hotel to locate the rented car and set up the fake accident. No, they would have been out somewhere. And how had he gotten back and forth? From the scene of the fake accident back to the hotel parking lot? Walked all that way, taken a cab?

And speaking of intelligence, Art had been halfway wrong. The fake accident hadn't been altogether stupid. If she'd had that bang on the head in front rather than from behind and if X had only thought to put her prints on the steering wheel, it might have passed as an accident. With less meticulous police work. Possibly X didn't realize that the L.A.P.D. had some strict regulations about accident investigation.

At the outset of the Cannaday thing Mendoza hadn't been particularly interested, but anything a little offbeat always stirred his curiosity. There seldom was anything offbeat on this job, the monotonous repeated crudities and violence. On the face of it this was such a very simple thing, but there was no shape to it; it was all so ephemeral. She came back to the hotel, and then she went out, and then she was dying or dead in the rented car. Somebody had taken a little trouble setting that up, polishing prints off the wheel, and that hadn't been the casual mugger. Her belongings hadn't been touched. Even if it had been an unpremeditated attack some vestige of a personal motive there had to have been. And the only people she had known here hadn't had any remote motive to quarrel with her over anything. Except Lemoyne?

Mendoza felt annoyed at circumstances in general. And Lemoyne was saying again, "God, I wish I could have seen Lou again. But I don't understand what could have happened to her—this accident—" and he was asking questions about that, which was quite natural if he didn't know anything about it, and Mendoza felt more annoyed.

He extricated himself with some difficulty and at random stopped at a rather expensive restaurant for lunch. Restaurants, he thought. Louise suggesting a friendly drink, presumably at the hotel. Why would Lemoyne have taken her somewhere else, probably suggesting dinner? There was quite a good restaurant in the hotel. The waiter poured Mendoza's coffee and he lit a new cigarette to go with it. Something fleeting passed across the back of his mind and he grasped for it without success. Restaurants—well, there were quite a few good restaurants around that area, and elsewhere. Maybe Lemoyne had a favorite place, and she wasn't familiar with the city now, she would have left it up to him. Yes?

He didn't know quite how he felt about Lemoyne. But he was the only one here who had much personal feeling about Louise Cannaday, and it was personal feelings which erupted into quarrels and potential violence. Adele Mowbray had loved Louise as an old friend. The Schultzes had been neutral, she was just a relative not well known. Those old college friends out of her remote past, they'd be neutral too. The old college professor, about ninety and retired years ago—*"¡Maldición!"* said Mendoza to himself impatiently. Woolgathering.

He began to think Hackett might be right, that they'd never find out exactly what had happened to Louise Cannaday. There just wasn't any handle to it. And he felt annoyed all over again about that. He didn't like things left up in the air.

PALLISER AND LANDERS had just got back from lunch when a plaintive teletype came in from the D.M.V. in Arizona. If L.A. could supply them with more information, they'd be happy to cooperate. "The damned fools," said Palliser, who was still feeling that bruise on his tailbone, "they ought to know if there was more information to be had we'd send it along. Damn it, they've got computers too." He went down to Communication to pass that thought along.

Meanwhile the computers down in R. and I. had been busy, and a list of names and pedigrees was coming into the

Robbery-Homicide office: the known local rapists out of their records. It was a big country, and most people had access to cars. Whoever had jumped Sandra Dale as she was hurrying home last night might have come from anywhere, but they would look first at the known addresses and question the men who were living in that general area. Galeano and Grace were going over the partial list now, sorting those out.

Palliser called the hospital. Sandra Dale was still unconscious and so was Henry Bacon. He swore again, feeling his back. "That goddamned female," he said to Landers at the next desk, "I hope I don't end up seeing a chiropractor." Landers' eye was developing nicely and by tomorrow would be all colors of the rainbow. Mendoza came in and took Hackett into his own office for a conference. They settled down over the list of rapists, weeding out the most likely-sounding ones to look for on a first cast, and the office was quiet for the next hour. Then one of the dispatchers sent up a call to a hit-run, and Palliser did some more swearing and got up.

The only address was on Wilshire, the Good Samaritan Hospital. So it had happened at the right place, thought Palliser, only he didn't think they had an emergency ward. He found a squad parked at the corner, no other evidence of an accident, and asked the squad-car man about it.

"You can't prove anything by me," said the Traffic man, "I didn't get here until it was all over. The clerk at the drugstore on the corner up there saw it and called in, called the paramedics. The ambulance was just getting ready to leave when I got here, and all I've got for you is the victim's name, Peter Cusack, before they whisked him off. I don't think he's hurt serious, he was cussing a blue-streak."

He would, of course, have ended up at Cedars-Sinai, so Palliser had to drive out there. He had to wait awhile, but was finally let in to one of the cubicles, where Peter Cusack was stretched out on a cot with assorted bandages here and there. He was still cussing. He was a rather handsome man in the late twenties with a crest of tawny hair, and he looked at Palliser's badge and cussed some more.

"So now the cops come to ask questions, did I see the car, what happened. They fetched me in here with the siren going before I laid eyes on a cop—well, just the one out of the squad, and they didn't let me talk to him, and goddamn it, now he'll be checking all the parking meters. And of all the goddamn times to be laid up! We've started to take inventory early, and the boss's out with a virus, and the only secretary with any sense is getting married next week, and now for God's sake I've got a broken thigh and a broken right arm—and I'll tell you something else, goddamnit—" He looked at Palliser balefully. "There was only five minutes left on that meter, and the cop on the beat's going to slap a ticket on my car and there'll be a fine, and whose fault is that? That goddamn drunk driver, that's who! Sweet Christ, you'd think a man could go to visit his wife at the hospital without getting run into by a goddamn drunk! Now wouldn't you?"

"Yes, sir," said Palliser. "You'd been at the hospital? The Good Samaritan?"

"Where else?" said Cusack. "Ruth just had the baby day before yesterday, just what we wanted, a girl—the boy's two years old—and they're both fine, and she asked me to bring her that other bedjacket from home, so I took it to work this morning and I stretched my lunch hour to go and see her. I found a parking slot around on Witmer, and when I came out I knew the hour was about up, I was hurrying to get back. I'd just turned the corner and was jaywalking across the street to the car when this goddamned drunk mowed me down—"

"Did you see the car closely enough to give us a make?" asked Palliser.

"Oh, my sweet Jesus," said Cusack, "did I see it? How could I help but see it, I'm about in the middle of the street when I heard it, there's not much traffic on a side street like that. I looked before crossing and there wasn't anything either direction, and then out of the blue this thing came around the corner going like a bat out of hell and the driver probably drunk as a skunk, it was weaving all over, and I couldn't tell which way to jump and besides, I'm not a mountain goat! I didn't have a split-second to think before the damn thing sideswiped me and knocked me flat and went roaring off toward Wilshire—No, for God's sweet sake, I didn't get a look at the driver, what more do you want? Goddamn driver drunk in the middle of the afternoon—he could have been Rip Van Winkle for all I know," said Cusack bitterly. "Driving an old piece of tin like that—"

"What was it?"

"It was, believe it or not, one of those goddamned old Model A Fords, a sedan, and it must have been doing sixty. And Ruth due to come home on Saturday and her mother back east and they say I'll be laid up for six weeks with this goddamn leg, and who in hell is going back there to get my car and drive it home? No, for God's sake, I didn't notice the license plate. I had something else to think about right then. And don't I know, if you catch up to that bastard he'll get probation and a fine and that'll be the end of it."

"Something a little stiffer," said Palliser, thinking of Alice Crane. That had to be the same car, of course. Well, there were all the other Model A's in the rest of the state, but they could take a second look at those four just possibles here.

Being there, he went to ask about Sandra Dale. As he was talking to the nurse at the station, a doctor came down the hall in something of a hurry and spoke to a couple sitting on the bench. "That's Dr. Ferguson, he's been checking on her," said the nurse. "Those are the parents."

Palliser went up to him and he turned irritably. "Oh, police. Of course you'll want to know, she's been restless and may be regaining consciousness shortly." Grudgingly he let Palliser follow him and the parents into the cubicle down the hall.

Sandra was moving painfully on the narrow bed, moaning. She looked very small under the thin white sheet. Her mother bent over her. "Darling, can you wake up? It's me, it's Mom, Sandra—"

Her eyes opened suddenly, bright blue eyes looking a little dazed. They stayed on her mother's face. She licked her lips and tried to speak, after a difficult moment got out a dry whisper. "I was hurrying—get home for dinner—sorry I was late, Mom—"

"Oh, my darling, my baby, it's all right—but can you tell us who hurt you?"

"Don't know—man, big man—grabbed me from behind—" she closed her eyes again with a long sigh.

The doctor was holding her wrist. "That's very satisfactory," he said. "She'll do better. Mrs. Dale, I'd like you to stay, the nurse will bring you a meal and make you comfortable—if she should wake up again it'll reassure her to find you here."

"Oh, yes, anything—anything we can do—thank God she'll be all right," and the mother put her head down on the side of the bed and wept.

Palliser didn't think it was satisfactory at all. If the girl could have given them some sort of lead—but evidently she couldn't. Of course, she might remember more later, but she might not, too.

PALLISER GOT STUCK in a traffic jam on the Hollywood freeway, and was half an hour late home. He went in the back door to the old-fashioned service porch and was met by the big black shepherd Trina, who offered him a polite paw. Bending to take it, he felt a sharp twinge in his back and groaned.

"Where have you been?" asked Roberta. "I was starting to get worried. And what are you groaning about?"

He told her about Edna Bacon. Davy came running to be picked up and he begged off. "You're too heavy in the condition I'm in right now." The other offspring would be tucked in bed at this hour.

Roberta was giggling. "I'm sorry, darling, but a big strong handsome officer like you, and a mere female—"

"You wouldn't say mere if you'd seen her. Seriously, Robin, the damn thing's giving me hell, I came right down on that top step, I'll bet there's a bruise as black as Tom's eye—"

"I'll have a look. You get undressed and after dinner I'll
find the heating pads for you, you can lie on that and see if
it's any help. The things you do run into," said Roberta.
"And I'll have a stiff drink before dinner."

FIVE

THE DAY WATCH was coming in on Thursday morning, and Rory Farrell had just settled at the switchboard when he plugged a call through to Higgins; it was Jeff MacDonald at the coroner's office. "You again," said Higgins. "What now?"

"You've got a little more business over here," said MacDonald. "The hospital sent the body over at some ungodly hour and he's been stabbed—your jurisdiction by the location of the paramedic station. I suppose you'll want to find out what happened."

"Hell and damnation," said Higgins. Something else showing up to work just when they had all the rapists to locate and question. There were at least three very hot suspects. The girl's clothes had been sent up the lab but it would be some time before there was any report on that. Everybody else would be out chasing the rapists, but this job was like what was said about women's work, always something else showing up to be done.

"All we've got is his name," said MacDonald. "And the notation from the hospital, brought into Emergency at three A.M., expired three thirty-five. His name is Luke Doolittle. I suppose the hospital will know something more."

"Thanks for nothing," said Higgins.

Landers and Calhoun, Palliser and Galeano, were already on the way out. They were still looking for a couple of heisters. At least the night watch hadn't left anything new. There had been a mugging at a parking lot on First, but there wasn't any more to be done about that. Grace was brooding again over the list of Model A Fords, and said they might take another look at those four who were just possibles. It was Hackett's day off. It was supposed to start raining again; evidently they were going to have a wet winter.

Higgins drove out to the hospital to find out if they knew any more about the man who had been stabbed. In the Emergency wing the only nurse at the station was yawning her head off. "We had a busy night," she apologized. "I'll be glad when this shift is over. Oh, that one—It was Dr. Delgado had him, he was brought in just as the shift changed at three A.M. I'll get him for you."

Delgado was a dark youngish fellow needing a shave, and his eyes looked bleary. "God, what a night," he said. "Drunks and accidents—you'd think people would stay home and sleep nights when they can. What do the police want? Oh, that one. He was brought in just as I came on. Knife wound, the hell of a lot of internal bleeding, and we got him on the table right away, started to pump plasma into him, but it was no go. The aorta had been punctured and he was in shock. We lost him in the middle of the surgery. Even if we'd got him sooner I don't think we could have saved him."

"Was there anybody with him?" asked Higgins. "Do you have any record of next of kin?"

Delgado yawned. "Yes, I think there was a girl with him. I wasn't paying attention, the paramedics brought him in in a hurry and we were just concerned with trying to save the man's life. I didn't hear what happened to him. I suppose one of the nurses got some information on him."

The nurse at the station was still yawning too. "I've got it somewhere, of course we asked for his name and address. The girl said he had medical insurance on his job." Presently she found the record. Luke Doolittle, an address on Thirty-Fifth Street. The girl's name was Beatrice Doolittle.

By the time Higgins came out it had begun to rain slightly. He found the place on Thirty-Fifth Street, a small single house on an old block of similar houses, but nobody answered the door. Annoyed, he tried the house next door, and a big black woman opened the door to him.

"Oh, we knew there was trouble some kind when the ambulance come in the middle of the night," she said, looking concerned. "We thought maybe Mrs. Doolittle was took sick, she hasn't looked so good lately. I put on a bathrobe and went over to see could we help—they lived next door since the girls were little—but Bea was just getting into the ambulance and she says to me, Oh, Mrs. Olson, it's Daddy, but I can't talk to you now, and off it went.''

"There doesn't seem to be anybody home," said Higgins.

"No, I know, I went over awhile ago. I suppose they'll be over at Ethel's—that's Bea's sister, Ethel Gill, she just lives over on Thirty-Seventh, she just got married last year to a nice young fellow works for the city. I can give you the number.''

Higgins found that address, an old six-family apartment. Gill was listed on the top floor. The door was opened by a nice-looking young black woman, who looked at the badge and said over her shoulder, "It's the police, Bea. We were expecting you, we knew you'd come asking questions. You'd have to. It's all just too awful to think about, I guess neither of us has got over the shock yet, nothing like this ever happened in our family. Come in, sir. Joe, my husband, he said you'd be coming, he wanted to stay home from work, but I said there wasn't any sense to that, he didn't know anything to tell you and I guess Bea's sensible enough to tell the truth and shame the devil like they say. Even with Daddy—oh, it's just awful—'' Her face crumpled suddenly and she got out a handkerchief, blew her nose. "Sit down, sir. This is my sister, Bea.''

The other girl was younger, not quite as pretty; both were medium black. She had been crying, a couple of limp tissues clutched in one hand. She looked up at big broad heavy-shouldered Higgins, who might as well have COP tattooed on his forehead, with a listless expression. "Miss Doolittle, you know I have to ask you some questions about what happened last night. Is that right, Mr. Luke Doolittle was your father?''

She nodded. "I'll have to tell you. I can hardly believe it happened yet, like Ethel says nothing like that ever happened in our family, and I just don't understand about Mama. I know she thought the world of Aunt Norma—but things happen and you've got to figure God's got some reason for it, like the Reverend Thornton says." She gave a dry sob.

"That was Mama's younger sister, Aunt Norma," said Ethel. She had sat down in a chair across from the couch where Bea crouched forlornly. "We've been worried about Mama, Officer. We never knew her to do like that, but she was all broke up when Aunt Norma was killed, it was an accident on the freeway, back in July."

"Never," said Bea, coughing into the tissues. "Why, all our lives Mama was such a good woman, she never missed church on Sunday and she was right down on liquor and cards and swearing and a lot of other things, like the Bible says. But ever since that happened, Aunt Norma I mean, it's just been terrible, we were worried about out of our minds. She'd got to drinking, she'd go out and get drunk and come home in a terrible state. And Daddy tried to get her to go to the doctor but she wouldn't. He went and talked to Dr. Gregson about it—he's our family doctor—and Dr. Gregson said something about change of life and depression, and he gave Daddy a prescription for some tranquilizers, but Mama wouldn't take them."

"Well, what happened last night?" asked Higgins.

She sat up straighter and looked at him miserably. "She wasn't home when I got there, I work at a title guarantee company uptown. I'm a file clerk. Why, up to a couple of months ago I never remember coming home and Mama not there, getting dinner ready—you know, Ethel, she always had dinner ready when Daddy got home. But lately she wasn't there mostly. I got dinner and Daddy came home the usual time—he works at Durfee's Heating and Plumbing, he's worked for them twenty-five years—oh, Ethel, we'll have to tell Mr. Durfee—" Higgins gave her time, repeated the question. "Yes, sir, I've got to tell you, I know. Daddy was worried, we both were, when she didn't come home. He'd tried to hide money from her so she couldn't go out and get drunk, but she'd guess where and get it. Finally we went to bed, there wasn't anything else to do. And it was way in the middle of the night I heard her come in, at the front door. Daddy hadn't locked it because she wasn't home. And I heard her knocking into things in the front room, and then she turned on the stereo. She turned it up real loud, it was the Mills Brothers singing a lot of old hymns, Bringing in the Sheaves, and Brighten the Corner Where You Are, all those old ones. And that's what woke up Daddy, he came out of the bedroom and I came out too.''

"She was drunk?'' asked Higgins.

"Yes, sir, I've got to say she was just awfully drunk. She was sitting on the couch by the stereo. And Daddy knew it wasn't any use trying to argue with her when she was like that, he just said, Frances, turn the volume down, it's the middle of the night. She didn't say anything so he went and turned it down, and he said to me, we might as well go back to bed, and he went back in their bedroom and I was just going back to my room when she turned the volume way up again, and Daddy came back. And he just said in kind of a quiet voice—Daddy never uses swear words—he said, Frances, I've got to get my sleep, turn that off and come to bed. He turned it off and Mama got up and went out to the kitchen and when she came back she had the bread knife. And Daddy was back in the bedroom then and I tried to take the knife away from her but I couldn't, and she just went up and stabbed him, right in the stomach. He was sitting on the bed then. And I didn't think he was hurt bad at first, there wasn't much blood. I just said, Mama, how could you do that, and I got her to lie down on the bed and a minute later she, well, she just passed out and started to snore. And then Daddy sort of collapsed on the floor and he said, girl, I reckon I'm hurt some, and then he passed out too and I was awfully scared but I tried to keep my head, I phoned for an ambulance—''

"As far as you know your mother's still at home?''

"Yes, sir, I didn't go back. I went to the hospital with Daddy, and I called Ethel and told her what had happened, and she and Joe came right over—and then they told us Daddy was dead—'' She began to cry again. "It didn't seem possible, all of a sudden like that, and Mama doing it, but she wasn't in her right mind. She was just awful drunk—''

Automatically Higgins thought about legalities. The woman had deliberately gone to get the knife. If she'd already had it in her hand, this might have been called voluntary manslaughter. As it was, it could amount to a charge of murder two, but a smart public defender might get that reduced on account of the drunkenness, with medical testimony concerning her mental state. He looked at the two girls and reflected that it was all a damned shame. Apparently it was a decent respectable family, and just because this damn fool woman had gone off the rails—and of course this would add up to more paperwork. They'd need statements from the daughters, the woman herself when she was sobered up, and meanwhile she'd have to be stashed away pending the arrest warrant. He told them about the statements and they said they could come in the afternoon. He went back to the office and found Mendoza about to leave, out to chase rapists with Grace. Mendoza swore about the Doolittles, and went back to his office and told Farrell to get him the D.A.'s office. Higgins sat beside the desk, looking out at a cold gray sky and the view over the Hollywood hills, while Mendoza kicked the thing around with a deputy D.A. They settled on a murder two charge. Mendoza set up the machinery on the warrant, and then he and Higgins went down to Thirty-Fifth Street to pick her up.

Frances Doolittle was just out on bed and obviously suffering from a painful hangover; she was a medium-black woman with a sagging figure, draped in an old bathrobe over her underclothes. She wasn't in any state to take in much of what Higgins said—it was possible she didn't remember much about what had happened, and she didn't offer any resistance. Mendoza surveyed the bedroom, with the bread knife still on the floor, the few spots of blood, and said, "We'll need the lab out to get some photographs. Print the knife, and get hers to match."

Higgins called in on that, and they waited until Horder came out. "You can lock up here when you're finished—" He had found the front door key on the dresser in the bedroom—"and drop off the key at our office." The daughters would be coming in, they could hand over the key then.

They ferried Mrs. Doolittle down to the Sybil Brand Institute.

"I do get tired of the stupidities, George," said Mendoza as they got back into Higgins' Pontiac. Then he began to laugh.

"Something strike you funny?"

"In a way," said Mendoza. "All those detective novels, *amigo*." When he had time Mendoza was a voracious reader, with a somewhat catholic taste. "Especially the older ones. All those elaborate plots and alibis worked out to timetables. Hardly realistic, as any cop could have told them. That's not how real people behave. This a very typical homicide, the average kind we see day in day out, isn't it? Somebody gets drunk, somebody gets mad for a minute, there's a little argument, and hey presto, somebody's dead. No mystery, no plots, no subtlety."

"Just human nature," said Higgins. And somebody would have to stay in this afternoon to take down the Doolittle girls' statements.

THEY WOULD VERY MUCH like to get the rapist who had jumped Sandra Dale, and this kind of thing was just dogged legwork and then dogged questioning. There were three hot suspects on that list from records. William Agar had a pedigree of two counts of assault, two counts of forcible rape, and one of those had been on a girl of fourteen. He was just out of Folsom on that, still on parole. He was described as twenty-eight, Caucasian, six-one, a hundred and seventy, blond and blue, and he was living with his mother on Monette Street, which was very much in the general area. Antonio Flores had a short pedigree but a significant one: forcible rape and beating of a twelve-year-old girl. He was off parole but his last known address, as of six months ago, was Harvard Boulevard, also close in the general area; and he was described as twenty-six, Caucasian, six feet, a hundred and sixty. Bernard Kinney had been charged with two forcible rapes, one as a minor, and had last been heard of on Breed Street in Boyle Heights; one of those girls had been fourteen, the other sixteen. He was black, six-three, a hundred and ninety, and would be twenty-five now.

Palliser and Galeano went to look for Agar, and didn't have any trouble locating him. His parole officer had gotten him a job at a fast food place on Sunset Boulevard, and he was there manning a broom on the kitchen floor. He was annoyed at cops showing up and taking him in for questioning. He said the boss wouldn't like it. "And do I lose the job, the P.A. officer won't like it, what the hell do cops want with me. I've been clean, you've got nothing on me." He was surly-looking, with skin pockmarked by old acne, and unkempt clothes.

They sat him down in one of the tiny interrogation rooms and started the monotonous round of questioning. Where were you on Tuesday night? Have you got a car? Were you anywhere near Elden Avenue? This kind wasn't usually very bright, and the flicker of an eye, a sudden wary look, a gesture, might betray guilty knowledge, tell them where to go on pounding at a suspect.

"I wasn't anywhere, I was just home. Watching TV."

"Not out beating and raping a girl? On Elden Avenue?"

"No, for Gossakes. I never done anything like that."

"You did before," said Galeano coldly. "Twice."

"I got railroaded by the cops. I never did no such thing."

"Can anybody say where you were that night? From five o'clock on? Your mother?"

"Oh, Jesus, she was out somewhere when I come home. I get off at four, I just went home. She was goin' out with some other old lady, friend of hers." The father wasn't on the scene, she had divorced him years ago. "She come home about nine o'clock. Whatever you're askin' about, did it happen after that?"

"No," said Palliser. "What about a car?"

"Oh, hell, I got an old heap, the P.A. guy'd tell you that."

They went on at him but it wasn't very satisfactory. He might be X, he might not be. By what little they'd got, the girl hadn't had a chance to put up a fight, and the fact that he wasn't marked up in any way—they'd got him to roll up his shirt sleeves—was neither here nor there. Besides, it had been a chilly night and he would have been wearing a jacket or sweater. They might commandeer all his clothes for the lab to examine, but at this stage they hadn't any real reason and there was no guarantee that if he was X, he hadn't been just bright enough to get rid of what he'd been wearing.

"What were you watching on TV?" asked Galeano. "When?"

"Oh, Jesus, when I come home. Or sometime after. I don't remember, some old movie."

"What was it about?"

"Jesus, I dunno exactly. It was some kind of western, some guy havin' a fight with some other guy about a girl—"

And that synopsis would embrace a lot of westerns. And what with all the channels these days there would probably have been one like that showing somewhere. It was up in the air. He was uneasy, he was belligerent, but that wasn't evidence. They took a break, left him there and went out to the narrow corridor.

"What do you think, Nick?" said Palliser.

Galeano rubbed his jaw. "Hell, I don't know. He's done two stretches, he won't be eager to go back to the joint. You'd think he'd at least wait till he's off P.A. to pull anything, but with the sex fiends there aren't many rules. Most of the time, a thing like this is just the moment's impulse. They don't think ahead. See something, want it, bingo. He might have been just driving around, on the prowl or not, spotted her and followed her."

After a while they went back to him. It was tedious, it was elemental, and to anyone who didn't know much about police work it might have looked stupid, but it often paid off, the primitive way of going at it. So they went back to it. Where were you on Tuesday night at six o'clock? Were you anywhere near Elden Avenue? Were you in your car? Can anybody say you really were where you say you were?

He blustered at them feebly, surly and aggrieved. "You damn cops got nothing on me, I'm clean. Whatever kid got raped I didn't have nothing to do with it—"

"Oh, you know it was a kid?" said Palliser. "That's interesting. You think it was a kid who got raped, what put that in your head?"

"Wasn't it? You said so, damn it—"

"No, nobody said so," said Galeano. And even that wasn't just so much use, he'd done one stretch for the rape of a minor and might assume they were tackling him on a similar case. Finally after a session of two hours they let him go; they could always bring him in again.

THE ARIZONA D.M.V., without comment, had sent over a list of twenty-seven cars registered to people named Leeper, and Landers showed it to Palliser in some dismay. He and Calhoun hadn't found Antonio Flores, been chased from pillar to post; Flores, off parole, had held several different jobs, lived with several different relatives, but they now had a pretty firm address for him in Hawthorne, as recent as a month ago. "What the hell do we do with all this?" asked Landers. "Twenty-seven! That woman said they told her they were heading for Ventura, but we don't really know that. And we can deduce that poor damn baby's dead, but we don't really know that either. Send all these plate numbers up to Ventura and say, Have a look for all of them? I can hear what they'd say."

"Well, it seems to be all we can do," said Palliser.

"My God," said Landers. His eye had taken on several hues and he was feeling it gingerly. Reluctantly he went down to Communications to contact Ventura, and Palliser could imagine too what Ventura would say about it. The only description they had on the Leepers was that they were a couple in the early twenties, and conceivably, among the twenty-seven registrations, there could be more than one young couple, but hopefully, not all travelling in California. He and Galeano went up to Federico's for lunch and talked about Agar some more, came to no conclusion.

MENDOZA HAD CARTED Higgins off to lunch, and talked about Louise and his speculations about Lemoyne at length. Higgins listened, and over a second cup of coffee said,

"You've always had an imagination, Luis. Even if any of that's so, we'd never prove it. There's just no handle to the damn thing. We know from the autopsy report there wasn't any external bleeding, there'd be nothing to show anywhere. So he says he was at home that night, what's to say he wasn't? So he knew she was here, even says he tried to get in touch with her. We couldn't prove he did."

"Damn it," said Mendoza, "he says he tried to call her at six-thirty. If he knows anything about it, George, that's either damned smart or damned stupid. We don't know exactly when she left the hotel, just sometime before seven-fifteen. At six-thirty she could have been in the bathroom and not heard the phone or she could have answered it. Agreed to go out to dinner with him."

"All right," said Higgins, "it's up in the air. I don't see any reason they should have had any kind of fight—two old friends, damn the dead romance, that was half a lifetime back and in my experience these things get buried and forgotten. It would have been the sentimental thing, remember when, remember so and so, nothing else. Why should they get into an argument?" He drained his coffee cup and got out a cigarette. "If we're imagining things, I can do some too."

"Such as?" said Mendoza.

"You mentioned some of what the Mowbray woman said. What she thought might have happened. Of course, says she, she'd have had the car doors locked. Oh, yes? Any sensible woman driving alone at night does lock the car doors, sure, but we don't know that she did. The car was a strange one to her, she'd just been driving it that day. Maybe she thought the driver's door was locked, the passenger door, and they weren't. Say she was going to take herself out to dinner somewhere, a restaurant somewhere around, and somebody jumped her at a light. It happens. The mugger trying the door on a chance, climbing in beside her."

"It happens," agreed Mendoza, "but I'll remind you that she wasn't robbed. And somebody set up the accident."

"How do we know that?" said Higgins, and Mendoza looked at him with raised brows. "Look, Luis, we're only guessing. Fourteenth off Sepulveda—she hadn't had dinner, so she was heading up Sepulveda? The mugger said, turn down the side street, lady, and she did. But you said, and from the little we know about her I'd agree, she was the kind of woman to keep her head and stay cool, and so she deliberately rammed the car into that pole and opened her mouth and yelled for help, hoping to attract some attention. Well, she didn't, but it scared him. That's a residential block, people would be home. He could have expected that somebody might show up any second, what's the matter, lady. And he banged her over the head to stop her yelling any more—''

"What with?" asked Mendoza.

"How the hell should I know? The muggers don't go in for guns, but four out of five of them are equipped with something, a piece of two-by-four, a wrench, anything handy. He banged her on the head, he was nervous about her yelling, and he got out. Cutting his losses.''

"That's fairly nice imagining, George, but I'd like it better if he'd taken her handbag with him. And why was the steering wheel wiped clean?''

"She'd been driving in gloves," said Higgins. "It was a cold night.''

Mendoza was silent, looking at his empty coffee cup. "There was a pair of gloves in her handbag," he said mildly, "but a lot of people don't like to drive in gloves, however cold it is. And I don't think you're going to tell me that she rammed the car into the pole, screamed for help, and then carefully removed her gloves before he banged her on the head.''

Higgins regarded his cigarette ruefully. "No, that doesn't fit," he admitted. "There'd be no reason in that. All I say is, I agree with Mrs. Mowbray that whatever happened it must have been something simple, nothing so elaborate and far-fetched as this Lemoyne suddenly getting mad at her all over again because she'd walked out on him thirty-five years ago. It's just what you were saying about Doolittle. The elaborate plots and alibis. Human people, real people, don't operate that way. I know some people harbor grudges, but

damn it, they also settle down and forget their first youth-
ful romantic urges.''

Mendoza stabbed out his cigarette. ''But you can't always generalize about people,'' he said thoughtfully. ''You
know, I like some of that very much, George. The idea of
her deliberately hitting that pole when a passenger suddenly turned into a dangerous nuisance—yes. Substitute
Lemoyne for the mugger. But why were they in her car?
Or—or,'' he said suddenly, ''he was driving. Yes, I can see
that. He turned into the side street and parked, they'd got
into the argument and he didn't want to be distracted. He'd
been driving in gloves. And he lost his temper—''

''Having the convenient blunt instrument in his hip
pocket?''

''He wouldn't have needed one,'' said Mendoza. ''He
could have taken her by the shoulders and shaken her hard,
bringing the back of her head down on the passenger door.
That would produce exactly the kind of blow she'd had.
And realizing what he'd done, he got out. All he had to say
was that he hadn't succeeded in contacting her, which is
what he did say.''

''I don't know the man,'' said Higgins dryly, ''but you
make him out a damned cold-blooded character, Luis. She
wasn't dead. If he knew enough about depressed skull fractures to know she might die, he also knew that if she got
prompt help she might have been saved. You don't tell me
he wanted to let himself in for a murder charge when he
didn't have to.''

''Oh, for the love of God, I'm not sure what I mean,''
said Mendoza. ''Talking off the top of my mind, and then
the pretty deduction comes to pieces when you think about
it twice.'' He stood up abruptly. ''That warrant ought to be
coming through sometime this afternoon.'' And rummag-
ing for change for the tip, he added, ''Just a wild thought—
I suppose those Schultzes really did attend that anniversary
party?''

''Oh, now, really, Luis,'' said Higgins. ''We can find out
if you think it's relevant.''

"And all the college friends—I'd better talk to them. But when they say no, I didn't know she was here, she didn't call me, who's to say otherwise? And the old college professor—no, damn it, I refuse even to think about Miss Ernestine Jardine. About ninety and retired years ago. The hell of it is, the time is so tight. If she'd left the hotel by six-thirty she hadn't had time to call anybody at all, and when she talked to Adele Mowbray at twelve-thirty and then went out for lunch, she hadn't had time then either. Lunch," said Mendoza distractedly. "What's in my mind about lunch?"

"At the coffee shop there," said Higgins helpfully, "and she struck up an acquaintance with somebody there who suggested having dinner together."

"Don't gibber, George," said Mendoza. "There was something, but it's gone."

They went back to the office, and the warrant wasn't in yet. Calhoun and Grace were questioning a suspect. Besides the three fairly hot ones, there were a lot of known rapists to look for. Everybody else was out, and Farrell was reading a paperback at the switchboard. Mendoza sat down at his desk and got out that address book.

"It's nothing but a damned waste of time to talk to these people, but it'd better be done. Why in hell should she have called any of them? Just people she exchanged Christmas cards with. When she had such a short time here? Shorter than she knew at that. *¡Por Dios!* I'd forgotten the poet. There won't be anything in that either, of course." He looked up at a hearty loud sneeze from the door.

"Well, see who's here," said Higgins. "We haven't laid eyes on your happy face in quite a while. They been keeping you busy?"

Captain Saul Goldberg came in, putting a handkerchief away, and sat down in the chair beside Mendoza's desk. "Hello, Saul," said Mendoza. "Anything we can do for you, or are you just visiting?"

Goldberg gave them an amiable grin. "I'm looking for a body."

"Well, we haven't too many on hand at the moment," said Mendoza. "Any particular body, or will any old corpse do?"

Goldberg brought out his notebook. "He's Caucasian, forty-one, five foot eight, a hundred and forty, brown and blue, a very snappy dresser, very particular about grooming and so on. His name's Jean-Pierre Vaquier."

"I don't think we can oblige you," said Mendoza. "Never heard of him. Is he one of your dealers or just a user?" Goldberg was the nominal chief of Narco division.

"Oh, we don't want him especially," said Goldberg. "That is, of course, we do, but it's Interpol is curious about him."

Mendoza sat up. "You don't say. Who is he?"

Goldberg sneezed again and said, "Damn allergies. Well, he's somebody very damn important in the European syndicate, Luis. The section arranging all the deals for bringing the stuff in from wherever and getting it distributed to the sellers. He's only been nabbed once, by the French police twelve years back, and it wasn't much of a charge, and of course with all the syndicate money behind him a smart lawyer got it reduced and he only served about nine months. But he's one of the big boys, and Interpol's had an eye on him along with all the rest of them. I first heard of him about three weeks ago, Interpol asked us to keep an eye out. Us and New York. He was said to be heading here. New York just missed him on his way through, he was using a forged passport in the name of Jacob Gold, and they didn't get that from Interpol until he was through customs and had vanished. But Interpol had the word he was heading for L.A. I didn't ask, but I deduce they've got an informer planted middling high on the totem pole."

"And what was he supposed to be up to here?" asked Mendoza interestedly. "We've got enough of that breed native to these parts."

Goldberg laughed. "How too, too true. Something he ought to have known better about. The word Interpol got, he was heading here for a very hush-hush meeting with another big shot from Hawaii to arrange for a series of shipments, H and coke mainly, from a new source somewhere in the Orient. And they were figuring to bypass the syndicate boys here, set it up without cutting them in.''

"Oh, my," said Higgins. "Now that was just asking for trouble. Somebody always knows."

"You're damn right," said Goldberg. "God knows that bunch of ghouls, and the ones here, are taking a fortune out of that dirty trade, they can afford the cuts and pay-offs, but somebody also always gets greedy. Anyway, New York gave us the word that Vaquier had passed by and was probably heading here, and we've been looking and listening with no result. Feelers out to all our informants, but a deal like that would be—um, pretty damned exclusive.''

"Hardly arranged in the back room of a cheap bar," agreed Mendoza. "More likely a million-dollar condo in Beverly Hills. Your street people wouldn't be much use. You're talking about a body. Do we leap to the conclusion that the syndicate boys here found out they were being bypassed and took steps?''

"That's just what," said Goldberg pleasedly. "We had further word from Interpol last weekend, that somebody had spilled the beans and there was a contract out on Vaquier. If he knew about it and made tracks for home, of course, they might have caught up to him anywhere—''

"Where's home?" asked Higgins.

"Oh, Paris. What sounds like, and Interpol says is, a very fancy address. He's got a summer place on the Côte d'Azur too. Evidently the word got out to his friends and cohorts almost as soon as Interpol heard. A couple of his close business associates have taken off on sudden mysterious vacations and his wife has shut herself up in the summer place with a bodyguard. And then just this morning we got an update from Interpol, they've had the definite word that Vaquier has been permanently removed from the scene, and it's supposed to have happened right here. As of a few days ago. The smaller bigshots over here, I could have a guess, are licking their chops and wondering who might step into his shoes, and everybody on both sides of the Atlantic is saying the silly goddamn fool ought to have had better sense than to try a play like that. But naturally Interpol would like to know definitely if they can stop worrying about him. So I come asking you if you know anything about a body that might be him. Of course he might have been taken off in some other division, I'll be asking."

Mendoza sat back and blew smoke at the ceiling. "Let's see that description," he said suddenly. He studied it for a minute and then said, "Now I do wonder." He went to the door and looked into the communal detective office down the hall. "Calhoun around, Jase?"

Calhoun lounged in a moment later. "What's up? We just let that bastard go, he's one we can cross off on Sandra. He had an alibi, believe it or not, he was at his cousin's wedding on Tuesday night."

"Have a look at this." Mendoza handed over the description. "It just slid into my mind while you were talking, Saul—the summer place on the Côte d'Azur, Vaquier a snappy dresser and particular about his gentlemanly appearance. That corpse with the nicely manicured hands, Pat—did it conform to this?"

"Naysmith," said Calhoun. "Well, in a general way, yes. Height and weight and age. Who's this Vaquier? There wasn't much I.D. on Naysmith, but some—driver's license, Social Security card."

"Oh, they'd probably have planted something like that," said Goldberg, "to satisfy the authorities here, just enough. What did he look like?"

"Drifter down on his luck," said Calhoun succinctly. "Nobody knew anything about him. Found shot—it was an S&W .32—on the street."

Goldberg blew his nose. "That would do. The little I.D., and no leads, no reason to work it any further and nowhere to go anyway. It wouldn't matter if he got buried by the city here as Smith, Jones, or Robinson, so long as the word was out in circles where it matters, he got his comeuppance, so everybody else will heed the warning."

"Yes," said Mendoza amusedly. "I don't say it's so, it was just a thought. And Interpol will have his prints from the French police."

"The Feds didn't know him," said Calhoun. "But if he's not a native, who was he?"

"Well, it's just possible he was this big fish Interpol's agitating about. I trust the lab will still have his prints. Go and ask, Saul, dispatch them overseas and find out for certain."

"Service with a smile," said Goldberg. "Thanks very much, boys. I didn't expect to pick the brass ring the first time of asking." He went off happily.

PALLISER GOT BACK to the office about four o'clock, after an abortive hunt for Bernard Kinney, who had also moved around after getting off parole. An ex-girlfriend had just told Palliser the last time she'd seen him he'd been living with some pal at a pad in Hollywood and working at a car wash, but when she'd found out he'd done time she didn't want no more to do with him, she was an honest girl, and that had been about four months ago. Palliser had sent up a request to the D.M.V. in Sacramento for any car registered to Kinney, and slumped into his desk chair tiredly; he was still feeling that bruise, though the heating pad had helped.

Landers and Galeano had just come in when the phone rang on Palliser's desk. He answered it, put it down, and looked over at Landers. "Henry has come back to us. Would you like to go and talk to him?"

"Not particularly, but I suppose we'd better," said Landers.

"We seem to be haunting Cedars-Sinai these days. We can take your car, I've had enough driving for the day."

"You think I haven't? These damned punks, as soon as they're off P.A. they go wandering around, can't stay put anywhere."

On the narrow hospital bed in the Emergency wing Henry Bacon peered myopically up at them, at the badges, blinking weak blue eyes. Palliser remembered that the amazon had broken his glasses. He was a short, thin little man with a round face now marred with several cuts and bruises. He said in a thin voice, "You're police officers? I don't know what you'd want with me, gentlemen—I've just had an unfortunate accident.'' And he essayed a weak smile at Landers. ''I see you've—er—been in the wars too.'' Landers' eye had started to fade a little now.

Palliser told him they wanted a statement, and he listened in growing consternation. ''You've put her in jail?'' he asked. ''But my goodness, she'll be furious. Just furious.''

''So she was,'' said Landers feelingly. ''But you know, she could have killed you, Mr. Bacon. And we understand it wasn't the first time she'd attacked you.''

''What—what kind of sentence might she get?'' he asked.

''Something like a one-to-two, and she'll likely serve about nine months,'' said Palliser.

''Oh. And then she'll be out,'' he said miserably, ''and want to come back.''

''Well, you don't have to let her,'' said Landers. ''You've certainly got grounds for a divorce, sir. And you can get an injunction to stop her bothering you in any way.''

''Oh, that really would make her furious.'' He blinked up at them unhappily. ''You know, I've been thinking about it, since I woke up here. It's possible I've just been unlucky in the experiences I've had—my first wife had a very hot temper too, I don't know whether you heard that. But really, it does seem quite a price to pay for having a woman around to do the cooking and the cleaning. I don't like housework at all, I'm no hand to cook for myself. But I've just about reached the conclusion that it would really be easier to do all that myself, nuisance though it is, if it would mean a little peace for a change. I really think it would. What you say about a divorce, well, I was brought up to be a religious man and normally I don't approve of divorce, but I've come to see that in some circumstances it may be the only answer.'' He shivered and felt the cuts on his face. ''Of course, I wouldn't like to have to move. Our old family home—but I don't suppose that thing, what you said, an injunction, would stop her coming there. Not if she wanted to. Women,'' said Bacon plaintively, ''seem to be very difficult to get along with, for some reason.''

They were speechless until Palliser said weakly, "Well, you'd better get a lawyer, Mr. Bacon. We'll take a statement from you when you feel up to it, just the facts of what happened."

In the corridor, they looked at each other and burst out laughing. "You know what I can't help wondering," said Landers, "what was his mother like?"

BILL MOSS TOOK OVER the squad at midnight, at the change of shift. He didn't mind night watch at all; it could even be peaceful, cruising the largely empty streets in the dead of night. After about two A.M. there wasn't much action around; on weekends it could be busier, of course. Tonight he didn't get a single call for over two hours, and he was beginning to feel slightly bored. The threatened rain had cleared away and the night was still and cold.

At two-thirty he got sent to an address on Logan Street over by Echo Park. It was an apartment building, and there were two men waiting for him, one of them sitting on the top step. The other one said, "I'm Burt Conklin, I called in. This is my pal Ollie Shoemaker. You feel better now, Ollie?"

"I'm okay." They were both middle-aged men in nondescript clothes. "Look, I know there isn't a damned thing you can do about it, but Burt said we ought to report it. See, Burt had a little poker party here tonight, he's not married now and can do like he pleases, and I just live two doors down, the duplex down there, my wife's in Fresno visitin' her sister so I come over to sit in. There were three other guys, we're all pretty old friends. We finished the session maybe half an hour ago, the other guys left and I finished my beer and left too."

"Nobody was drunk," said Conklin hastily, "we only had a couple of bottles apiece."

"Well, for God's sake, I'm only two doors from home, no way at all, but I hadn't more than come down the steps here when this guy falls on me—like he come out of nowhere—hell, no, I didn't get a look at him, the street lights are all off—he hit me on the head with something and knocked me down, I guess I was out for half a minute. I can't tell you nothing more about him. And when I could stand up I went back to Burt's, my head was bleeding some. Goddamnit, I'd got hot tonight, I'd won over thirty bucks, and he got that and the twelve I started with.''

"You can't give me any description, sir?''

"Hell, no. But the crazy thing about it—'' Shoemaker thrust out one leg. "He stole my shoes too! Can you tie that? Stole my shoes, just an old pair, but left me in my stocking feet—what kind of crazy mugger is that?''

SIX

UNPRECEDENTEDLY, Mendoza dawdled around after breakfast, somewhat annoying his adult household. The baby was fretful. Alison shooed the twins off to get ready for school. Luisa was being obstreperous, running back and forth towing an imaginary kite. Mairí appeared at the living-room door, dangling car keys, ready to drive the twins to school, but they were charmed to have their father there to see them off and lingered.

"Only ten more days! We counted!" Johnny was proclaiming loudly. "Then we're grown up!" The twins had a seventh birthday coming up at the end of the month, and it was an important milestone in their lives: after that they would be allowed to have grown-up dinner with their parents at night instead of nursery dinner with Mairí.

"Luisa's got to wait a long time before she's grown up," said Terry importantly. "And Sissy has to wait a lot longer—"

"Cecelia," said Alison automatically. "Put your coat on, Terry."

"And then when we're all grown up," pursued Johnny, "we'll have to get a bigger table, won't we?"

"Certainly not," said Alison. "The table's quite big enough for everybody. Get your coat on, Mairí's waiting."

"Sissy's being an awful crybaby this morning, isn't she?" Terry looked up at her parents, her brown eyes soulful. "I could stay home and help you with her, Mama, if you sent a note to Sister Grace."

"I don't need any help, thank you," said Alison. "Off you go now."

"Sissy won't be grown up for years and years," said Johnny, capering around Luisa.

"Cecelia," said Alison.

"You know, my girl, I wouldn't fuss about it," said Mairí benevolently. "It's a queer thing, but some people go through life picking up nicknames and others never do. There's not much a body can do about it."

Alison juggled the wailing baby in her arms. "But such a silly one—and what's got into her? She never cries—well, hardly ever—"

Mairí bustled the twins toward the front door. "Come along, you two, you'll be late for school. You just sing the *Earl of Moray* to her and she'll settle down. You remember how it goes—'Ye hielands and ye lawlands, oh, where ha'e ye been? They ha'e slain the Earl of Moray and laid him on the green—'"

"But, Mairí," said Alison, aghast, "what a bloodthirsty thing to sing to a baby!"

"Och, she's taken to liking that one fine, just the last few days, I've been meaning to tell you. She did not like *Loch Lomond* and times she likes to hear *Charlie Is My Darlin'* but the *Earl of Moray* nearly always sends her right off to sleep." She bustled out behind the twins, and outside Cedric began to bark.

Luisa barged into the couch with the invisible kite and began to wail loudly. "For heaven's sake," said Alison, "get out from under foot, Luis. Aren't you going to work today at all? I've got a hundred things to do, and these children—"

"The damned place will be full of rape suspects," said Mendoza moodily.

"And you want to brood on your widow. From what you told me you'll never get anywhere on that, you'd better give it up. Stop wandering around and go to the office."

Belatedly Mendoza went out to the garage for the Ferrari. It looked as if it might rain any time, and it had begun to sprinkle by the time he got downtown. He found the office empty except for Hackett at his desk talking to a fat bald man.

"Where have you been?" asked Hackett. He took Mendoza aside, over to Higgins' desk, and handed over the night report. "Nothing in it but a heist, and it sounds like our big fellow with the tattoo again. A liquor store on Wilshire. That's the owner, his name is Minetti. Oh, and that mugger hit again, the one stealing shoes."

"Very funny," said Mendoza. He drifted back to hear what Minetti was saying. Hackett was taking notes for a statement.

"You said you saw the tattoo on his arm?"

"Yeah, he had one, I saw it when his sleeve pulled back when he pointed at that case of Scotch, it's just over his wrist. Did the other detectives tell you he took two cases of Scotch as well as the cash? It's a fact. After I handed him the bills out of the register he says, I'll have some of your stock too, buster, and he makes me lug two cases out of the back room and put them in his car."

"Oh, he did?" said Hackett. "So you saw his car. Do you know what it was?"

"Listen," said Minetti exasperatedly, "how would I see that? He must have figured on taking the liquor too, he had the car backed up to the back door, that's the way he came in, and the trunk lid was up. Any kind of insignia would be on the trunk lid, and I didn't see it. All I can tell you—it was a gray car or maybe light blue, those lights in the parking lot are fluorescent and they change the color of things."

"And as far as you remember he didn't touch the counter or anything else? He wasn't wearing gloves?"

"No," said Minetti. He scratched his bald head. "I know that's what I said, but I got to thinking about it later and I was wrong. I thought back about it, of course I know what you'd be after, any fingerprints, and I remembered he did touch something. The glass on the back door. He followed me there when I carried out those two cases of Scotch, one at a time, and I remember the second time I looked around at him, to see if he was getting ready to leave then, and he was standing there—he had the gun in his right hand, a big gun it was, and he had his other hand on the door holding it open. That's when he did leave, he said, okay, buster, you acted real nice and easy, you go back in there now, so I did, and he slammed down the trunk lid and took off. You asked if he was drunk—he wasn't, but he'd had a few, I could smell it on him.''

"This back door," said Hackett, "have there been many people in and out of it since?''

"Nobody at all," said Minetti. "That was about a quarter of nine last night, and like I say we close at nine, I'd just been starting to bag the money for the bank when he came in. I haven't opened up yet today, the fellows last night said come to make a statement, so I did.''

"Good," said Hackett, and got on the phone to the lab. Marx said he'd chase out to see if he could pick up anything. Minetti agreed to meet him there and let him in. He signed the statement when Hackett had typed it up, and went out.

"If this is the same bird," said Hackett, "and it sounds like it—according to Gerber the other day he didn't pick up much loot on that job—it figures he'd hit again this soon.''

"Very likely," said Mendoza, uninterested. He wandered down the hall to his own office, and when Hackett looked in twenty minutes later he was dealing himself poker hands from the deck out of the top drawer. Probably, Hackett thought from experience, practicing the crooked deals off the bottom of the deck. The domesticities had ruined Mendoza's poker game, but after all he had started out as a Vice cop and still superstitiously claimed he thought better with the cards in his hands.

Palliser and Galeano brought in a suspect to question. "We got a make on Bernard Kinney's car from the D.M.V." said Palliser in passing. "I've got an A.P.B. out on it.''

"Fine," said Hackett absently. They took the suspect down to an interrogation room. Marx called in half an hour later and said he'd picked up a dandy print, a whole palm and four fingers, from that back door, and it had to belong to the heister—Minetti said it was the right place.

"I'll get them classified and sent down to R. and I. You should hear sometime this afternoon if we've got them on file.''

"Step in the right direction," said Hackett. "I suppose it's too early to ask if you've found anything useful on the Dale girl's clothes?"

"I don't know that we'll get much for you there," said Marx doubtfully. "The panties were evidently ripped off before she was raped, there aren't any semen stains or pubic hairs. And the damned hospital never took any swabs. I know it was an emergency, but if they'd got a semen specimen we could have typed it at least. There's miscellaneous dirt and dry leaves stuck to the outer clothes, a good deal of blood on the skirt, but that's hers presumably. Type O."

"Well, thanks," said Hackett. The lab could do miracles these days, but only if they had material to work with.

At eleven o'clock Farrell relayed a call from a dispatcher, a new homicide, and Hackett routed Mendoza out to go and look at it. Two of the interrogation rooms were occupied, presumably by rape suspects, and nobody else was in. The call was to an address on Sutherland Street just the other side of Echo Park. It was an old and shabby apartment building, probably containing about thirty units, and the uniformed man, Frawley, was talking to a citizen on the front steps. He came over to the Ferrari as it pulled up to the curb.

"The apartment manager found the body," he told them. "He's been dead some time, it looks like, the doctors can pinpoint it, I suppose. I just took a look, preserved the scene for you, I don't know what the manager might have done in there before he called in. His name's Griggs, Alfred Griggs, been the manager here for a long time, he says, and knows all the tenants."

"All right," said Hackett. "We'll take it from here. Hang around."

They went over to the other man. He was a gaunt tall man with a thin halo of red hair around a bald head. "This is the hell of a thing," he greeted them lugubriously. "Who'd of thought old Leo'd end up like that, murdered, for God's sake. It just don't seem right, he was a nice old guy."

"We'll have a look, and then we'll have some questions for you, Mr. Griggs," said Mendoza.

"Sure. I'll take you up there." It was a four-story building and there wasn't an elevator. They climbed three flights
of stairs and went down a long dusty hall, and Griggs indi-
cated a half-open door on the right. "That's it."

Hackett shoved the door further open with one foot and
they looked in. "No, don't go in, please." It was a typical
apartment living room for a place like this, about twelve by
fifteen, with a few pieces of old upholstered furniture, a
small TV set on a metal cart in one corner, a thin flowered
rug on the floor, a glimpse into a small kitchen in one
direction, a bedroom in the other. And there had obviously
been a violent struggle of some sort here. One big armchair
was lying on its side, the coffee table had been overturned
and spilled its contents on the floor—a single used glass, full
ashtray, half-empty pack of cigarettes. A straight chair near
the kitchen door had been knocked over. The body was lying
on its side near the coffee table, the body of a big heavy man
with thin gray hair, wearing old tan work pants and a tan
shirt. His glasses had fallen off and lay a few feet away. The
heat was on in the apartment and there was a sweet, faintly
sickening odor of beginning decomposition in the air. He
had been dead awhile.

"Hell of a thing," said Griggs. "Old Leo."

"Have you touched anything in here?" asked Hackett.

"Not me. I just saw it and called the cops. I can't get over
it, old Leo murdered. And I don't want to tell you your
business, but I might have a guess who did it."

"Well, let's take first things first," said Hackett. "What
was his name, what do you know about him?"

"Leo Putzel," said Griggs promptly. "He'd lived here
about twenty years. First him and his wife, she died last
year. They've got a married daughter somewhere up north.
He worked for the gas company most of his life, retired four
years back on Social Security, he was seventy. Nice old guy,
quiet, rent always on time. I guess he'd been lonely since his
wife died. The way I came to find him—I haven't been up
here for about a week, my place is on the ground floor—but
Mrs. Perez down the hall here had asked me to look at a
leaky faucet, so I came up this morning. And I noticed his

door was part open. I thought it was funny because he was particular about locking up. I don't suppose anybody else here would have noticed. He didn't neighbor with the other tenants. So I just looked in, and there he was. Looks as if he'd had a fight with somebody, maybe got hit on the head." There was blood, long dried, on the head and the rug. "Old Leo." He shook his head. "Damn shame."

"When did you see him last?" asked Hackett.

"I thought back on that, and I can tell you exactly. It was last Tuesday morning. He was going out to the market, he said—I'd just come out to the mailboxes to see if the mailman had come yet. He was just the same as usual, but of course he wouldn't have known he was going to get murdered. He stopped and we talked for a couple of minutes. It was about eleven o'clock."

"You said something about having a guess, somebody with a reason to have an argument with him?"

Griggs said apologetically, "Now I wouldn't want to get anybody in trouble, and I don't know anything about it. But like I say he'd been lonely since his wife died, didn't have much of anybody to talk to, and he talked to me sometimes. I know he'd been damned annoyed at this guy who owed him some money. As a matter of fact it was his brother-in-law, his wife's brother. He'd told me some about it. From what he said this guy was pretty unreliable, kind of a no-goodnick, and kind of a lush on and off. But Leo's wife, well, you know women, he was her kid brother and she felt sorry for him. They'd helped him out before when he got behind with his rent or lost another job. And it was just a couple of weeks ago Leo was blowing off steam to me, he said the guy still owed him fifty bucks and kept making excuses why he couldn't pay it back and he was fed up with it, he was going to have a showdown with him, and if he got the fifty back he'd let the guy know it was the last he'd get."

"Do you know his name?" asked Hackett.

"Yeah, Chester something, I guess it'd be in Leo's address book. Anyway, when I saw him last Tuesday I asked him about that and he said the guy was coming to see him that night and he better have the fifty and no more excuses.

I just thought, it looks as if maybe he got killed a little while ago, maybe it was Tuesday night. I know he'd said this guy, he was the kind that got nasty when he was drunk.''

The body might very well have been a body since Tuesday night. "Thanks," said Hackett. "We may have some more questions for you later. Right now you can go back to your own apartment." He went reluctantly, and Hackett followed him down, told Frawley to put in a call for the lab.

In half an hour Scarne showed up in a mobile lab van with Horder. In the apartment they looked around for an address book and found one by the telephone in the kitchen. Scarne printed it before handing it over. Hackett looked through it and said, "Here he is. Chester Rieger, address on Dillon, not too far off. We might as well go and have lunch, the boys won't be finished here for a couple of hours, and the coroner's office won't get to an autopsy until tomorrow or next day. It looks simple enough, the old codger had a fight with somebody, whether it was this Rieger or not, there was some kind of violent struggle, and I don't suppose a quiet old fellow of seventy had many enemies. Just more of the human nature."

Mendoza agreed morosely. They left the lab man to get the necessary photographs and dust the place for prints and call up the morgue wagon. Chester Rieger would keep; they had been late getting on this one anyway. They had a leisurely lunch and got back to the office at two o'clock, just in time for Hackett to take a call from R. and I. The prints Marx had sent down didn't appear in L.A.'s records; they had been wired back to the F.B.I., so there would be a kickback on that sometime. Mendoza headed back for his office and the deck of cards.

"Goofing off," said Hackett. "If you've got a yen to go and see that poet, don't ask me to go with you. We might as well write the Cannaday thing off, it'll never come to anything." But he knew how Mendoza felt, he didn't like things left up in the air either.

A direct call came in then from headquarters in Ventura, which had been surprised and annoyed about twenty-seven plate numbers. Hackett spent awhile on the phone with a

Lieutenant Gonzales, explaining the circumstances, and Gonzales was slightly mollified. "Well, I can see it's the hell of a thing to work, but my God, when we haven't a clue which of these plate numbers belongs to these people you might want—"

"I know, I know," said Hackett, "and no really useful description."

"The hell of a thing, that baby," said Gonzales. "Well, all we can do is put all of them out and see what we come up with. I'll get back to you if anything comes of it."

Hackett put the phone down and yawned. He thought suddenly that somebody ought to call Leo Putzel's next of kin to break the news that he was dead. A married daughter somewhere up north, Griggs had said. She ought to show up in the address book. He went down the hall to the coffee machine, and as he passed the switchboard Farrell looked up from his paperback.

"You all seem to be earning your keep these days. Jase and Nick hauled in another ugly-looking bruiser, and John and Tom are talking to another one. Pat's out with George looking for that Flores, he seems to be an elusive customer."

"They mostly are."

"And another body turned up."

"Oh, hell," said Hackett. "Who's on it?"

"Everybody else was out on the rapists. Wanda had just come in and she went out on it."

They would be hearing about that in due course. Hackett brought a paper cup of coffee to his desk, and clearing up as he went along, had another look at Leo Putzel's address book. He decided the likeliest bet for the married daughter had to be a Florence Bergen, at an address in Fairfield. There was a phone number; he dialed it and after a delay got Florence Bergen. She had a sharp decisive voice, sounded like a sensible woman. She did a little crying, controlled herself, and thanked him for letting her know. "But to think of him dying like that—it doesn't seem possible—you mean somebody broke in and killed him?"

"We don't know much about it yet, Mrs. Bergen. We'll notify you when the body can be released."

She sobbed again a couple of times. "Yes, I'd better come—I'd better call my husband right away, we'll have to decide what to do. I know he'd want to be with Mother, she's buried out at Rose Hills—"

"There's no real hurry, Mrs. Bergen. You understand there'll have to be an autopsy."

"We'll come. Of course we'll have to come."

"We don't like to bother you at a time like this, but can you tell me anything about a Mr. Chester Rieger?"

"Uncle Chester." Her voice sharpened. "Had he been around? You don't mean—you don't mean you think *Uncle Chester*—that he had something to do with what happened to Dad? Oh, my God, that would be the most terrible thing I can think of—of course Dad had trouble with him before, Mother always saying give him another chance—I know he's got to drinking worse than he used to and Aunt Lil's had trouble with him—he got arrested for hitting a man when he was drunk—but you don't mean *Uncle Chester* might have—"

"We don't know what happened yet, Mrs. Bergen."

"We'll come," she said rather numbly. "There'll be all the arrangements, and the apartment—we can probably come tomorrow or next day."

"We'll be in touch with you," said Hackett. He went back to typing the preliminary report on Leo Putzel. They would have to get a formal statement from Griggs. See what the lab had turned up there. And sometime locate Chester Rieger and question him.

JESUS CALDERONE had been a happy man when he came to work that morning. He was a man who was happy by nature, who found his pleasure in simple things, asked not much of life but the simple good things, the love of his wife and children, a glass of wine now and then, the comfort of home even though it was an old house and the roof sometimes leaked. There were good neighbors, and by the grace of the good God he had a job which paid enough to buy food and clothes and a few luxuries for Maria and the children, four good children, healthy and smart, children to be proud of. Carlos wanted to be a doctor and perhaps that would not be so easy, the money it would cost, but if it was intended a way would be found. At the moment, Jesus was feeling especially happy about the eldest daughter, Elena. On Sunday she was to make her first communion before Father O'Sullivan, and she was talking about giving herself to the church, to be a sister of grace. Jesus was a trifle skeptical about that, he was a sensible man. She was only twelve and children had these idealistic notions. One needed a strong call from God to devote oneself like that. Himself, he did not care, all very well if it should turn out so, but he would be just as happy to see Elena married to some good man and producing healthy smart grandchildren for him. All that was in the future.

When he got to work he was sorry to find he would be driving alone. His regular partner Juan Aragon had called in sick with the flu, but he wasn't surprised. Juan had been feeling bad for two days. It would make the workday harder, but one took what came.

Jesus drove a refuse truck for the city, and when he had a helper with him, at every stop Juan got out and emptied the cans; now Jesus would have to do that and also drive the truck. But it couldn't be helped. He set out on the usual route cheerfully enough, though it was cold and might rain again, but of course, working alone delayed him.

It was much later than usual when he got to a certain alley along Mohawk Street. The streets here were all filled with apartment buildings, old and run-down. The tall refuse cans were put out in rows behind their rear doors in the alleys between streets. He turned into this one, maneuvering the big truck expertly, and got out to empty the first row of cans into the maw of the truck. He drove on fifty feet further and got out again, with the truck's grinding machinery chewing up the refuse it already held.

He thought at first the thing lying on the blacktop paving in the dirty alley beside the refuse cans was one of the figures from a dress shop window, worn out and thrown away there, and then he saw that it was too small for that, and he looked again, unbelievingly, and without conscious thought he crossed himself. It was a *niña*, a little girl, a little girl like Elena, only she had blond hair, and she was broken and bloody and dead, there was blood.

"*Madre mía,*" he said in a whisper. The poor little one. But of course the police must be informed, but he said a small prayer for the little soul before he went to find the nearest telephone.

WANDA LARSEN was going through one of those times when she wondered why she had picked this job. It was an interesting job, a lot more so than working in an office somewhere, though God knew there was a lot of paperwork, or selling people things. And she'd worked like a beaver to make detective rank. She liked all the men she was working with, and most of the time she could leave the job behind when she went home, leave the tragedies, the blood, the crudities to take care of themselves. But sometimes it got to her. The juvenile case had left her feeling sick and sorry and wondering if there was any possible hope for humanity in this sick and sorry century.

The two juveniles had opened up boastfully, with no vestige of remorse or consciousness that they had done anything wrong, and implicated quite a few of their pals; they had had an eminently successful burglary ring going, and were quite unreticent about assorted other ventures, mayhem, and a nice little protection racket. But what Wanda couldn't forget were the parents. One set of obviously low intelligence, apathetic and unconcerned. The woman had a record of petty theft and sporadic prostitution, the man had a record of burglary. That boy wasn't going to get any support from them, any constructive help, and what could you expect? But the other set—all sorts of kids rubbed shoulders in high school now—fairly affluent, regarding themselves as sophisticated moderns, and raging at the cops picking on their superior offspring. Kids got into a little mischief, and the damned cops came down to give them a bad time just because they were big bullies. That woman yesterday, a fat raddled woman with coarse bleached hair and a too-tight red pantsuit, leaving the Juvenile office with her fat half-drunk husband—"And I'll tell you something else, you damned nosy Parkers just out to make trouble for everybody, you putting Roy in your damned Juvenile hall, but we don't want any of those goddamned preachers like the one tried to talk to me yesterday, tryin' to teach him about God and all that crap—there isn't no God anywhere, anybody with sense knows that!"

Wanda had come in late today, and been caught up with the current cases on hand by Rory Farrell. She felt a little sick again about the rape. Everybody seemed to be out on that. There was a new homicide, Mendoza and Hackett on it. Galeano and Grace brought in another suspect. She didn't want much lunch; she went out for a milkshake at the nearest drugstore.

It was three o'clock when Farrell relayed a call from a squad, a body. Nobody else was in, and she got up wearily to go and cover it. Visiting the restroom, she thought she wasn't looking her best, rather washed out and tired, and she needed a shampoo and set. It was still drizzling when she went out to her car in the lot and started out to find the address on Mohawk Street. It was a tired old street of ancient apartment buildings. The squad was sitting in front, with the uniformed man and a woman in it. The Traffic man was Dubois.

He got out and said, "You'd better come into the squad, Miss Larsen, it's coming down harder. There isn't much to tell you. The man on the refuse truck spotted the body, it's around in back. We're waiting for the mother to show up now. It's just a kid. This is Mrs. Weiss, she's the apartment manager."

She was a big dark woman with a distinct moustache and round dark eyes, looking shocked and resentful, as if these things shouldn't happen to upset everybody. She hugged a shapeless blue cardigan around her and said, "It's not right, not even a blanket or nothing around her, and all the rain— It's the little Keller girl, Dorothy Keller. It just turned me sick to see her, that Mex fellow rang the bell and asked to use the phone, when he said what it was I went and looked—''

"It looks as if she fell out the window," said Dubois. "They live on the fourth floor. Mrs. Weiss knew where the mother works."

"That's right, I don't know about him, he works at a furniture store but I don't know where. She works at a café on the boulevard, I called her and said to come home, something had happened. She'd have to take the bus—''

"I'd better have a look," said Wanda. Dubois took her around to the alley. She looked at the small slender body lying broken and bloody on the blacktop and said, "It doesn't seem right, the rain, but the lab will have to get pictures." The child looked to be twelve or thirteen, a thin blond girl in a shabby cotton dress.

"The manager says that's one of their bedroom windows up there," said Dubois, pointing. "You can see it's open, and the screen pushed out." The body was lying partly on top of a window screen.

"Well, you'd better call up the lab for photographs," said Wanda.

They had just got back to the squad when the mother arrived, hurrying up the block from the bus stop at the corner. They took her into the apartment lobby and forestalling Wanda or Dubois, Mrs. Weiss broke the news to her dramatically. "Must have fell out the window up there, I don't know how the screen came to be loose, but it's a long way up and like I say she's dead, Mrs. Keller. The policeman said right off, she's dead—''

The woman just stared at them, not seeming to take it in at first. Then she said, "I want to see her."

"Better not, ma'am," said Dubois. "They'll be taking her away pretty soon, you can see her later—''

"I want to see her," said Mrs. Keller flatly, and they let her go to look. She didn't start to cry, only got out a handkerchief and held it to her mouth.

"We'd better go up to your apartment," said Wanda gently. "We'd like to try to find out how it happened."

Mrs. Keller said in a dull voice, "I guess I know how it happened." She looked about forty, might be younger; she had a scrawny figure, mouse-colored hair in no style, uncurled, and wore no makeup, her face round and plain with dull eyes like gray marbles and old fashioned gold-rimmed glasses. In silence she climbed the stairs ahead of them, Mrs. Weiss leaving them at the foot with visible gratitude. Mrs. Keller unlocked the door and they followed her in to a shabby living room. The furniture obviously belonged to the place, nothing personal about it. She said, "Dorothy's room is over here. There's only two bedrooms, we let her have one, Jimmy has to sleep on a cot in the hall."

It was a very small room, square, and barely furnished with a single bed, a small chest of drawers, a single straight chair, and a rag rug. The screen was missing from the window and the window was wide open. Mrs. Keller went straight to the chest of drawers.

"She was in such a state this morning I kept her home from school, I said you just rest and try to forget about it. I had to go to work, I've used up most of my sick leave and I don't dare lose the job. I guess it was the wrong thing to do. I should have stayed home with her." She looked at the thing she'd picked up, and then she sat down on the bed and began to cry, not noisily, in a series of great dry sobs. Wanda took the little sheet of paper from her listless hand.

It had been torn from a cheap lined tablet, and there were wavering lines of pencil writing across its top. *Dear Mom, I guess ther's no hope for me ennywere becas like he said I alreddy made the chois and give my soul to the Devvil and beside ther isnt unythin to go on live for and if I got to go to Hell I mite as well and not stay here any more.* It was unsigned.

Wanda looked at Dubois and said, "You might as well go back on tour." He shrugged and went out. Wanda sat down beside Mrs. Keller on the bed. This wasn't any time to question the woman, but of course she'd have to be talked to. Wanda just sat there awhile feeling helpless, and then she heard sounds below and went to look out the window. A mobile lab van had pulled up in the alley, and a couple of lab men were taking photographs. They would know the futility of looking for prints, any other physical evidence, and that wasn't going to be necessary anyway. Already the body was soaking dark with rain. As soon as they'd got the pictures they'd call the morgue wagon.

Mrs. Keller said behind her, "I'll never speak to him again."

Wanda turned.

"I'm sorry to bother you," she said softly, "at a time like this. But if you could tell me something about it, why your daughter wanted to kill herself—" She had the badge out ready to show, to introduce herself, explain why she was here, but the woman didn't look at it. She looked at Wanda incuriously; it didn't matter to her who Wanda was or why she was here, she was just another human being to talk to.

She said, "This is what it comes to in the end. I'll never speak to him again. My husband. Bernie. He put all that in her head, he's doing it to Jimmy too, and maybe he's right about it and I'm a wicked woman for thinking he's wrong, but I can't help it. I don't feel I am. I just can't believe that God would send a little girl down to hell forever and forever for stealing two dollars. I just can't believe in that kind of God."

Wanda sat down beside her again. "Would you like to tell me about it, Mrs. Keller?"

"You see," she said painfully, "they don't call him God, at that church. They call him Jehovah. It's the Pentecostal Brotherhood Church of the True Grace, that's what it's called. And they're the only ones know how to abide by true Christianity, what Bernie says. I was sent to Sunday School and I always reckoned I was a good Christian, but what Bernie says, you're not really confirmed in faith unless you go to the right church and that's the only right church. He's always been strict with the children but it was for their own good. He's a good, honest, hardworking man. I've stood up to him about such things as Dorothy wearing colored hair ribbons and having birthday parties, he said it was vanity and foolishness, but children don't get so many pleasures, they deserve some. He wasn't quite so strict with Jimmy, but he stood out against the basketball team, said that was foolishness too and he only let him play if he kept up his school marks. But this was just such a silly little thing, it didn't really matter. You know how girls are. Little girls just starting to grow up some. Dorothy's twelve, she's only twelve. She wanted to have her ears pierced. A lot of the other girls at school had their ears pierced. It's just a fashion. The funny thing is, you know, I've seen pictures of some of the people in the Bible—Ruth and Naomi and Bathsheba and Solomon's wives and all—and they had on earrings, you could tell their ears were pierced. And when he put his foot down about it, I told him that, and he acted some surprised but he had to admit it was so. He said she could do it if she saved up the money herself. And there's a place up on Silver Lake Boulevard, a jewelry shop, advertised they'd pierce your ears for five dollars and give you a pair of real gold hoops besides. Dorothy was just crazy to have it done. You know how girls are.''

She stopped there, and after a minute Wanda said, ''Yes. Did she have it done?''

''She had three dollars saved up for it. She gets a dollar a month allowance. Jimmy doesn't get an allowance any more since he's got a paper route, he's supposed to use that to buy his lunch at school and pencils and all like that.'' Mrs. Keller suddenly hugged herself fiercely as if she was cold, so cold she'd never be warm again. ''If she'd only told me, I'd've found the two dollars somehow! As tight as things are— Bernie gives so much money to the church, I've tried to tell him the family ought to come first, and everything so high now—I was ashamed Dorothy hadn't any nicer clothes for school, and Jimmy needing shoes—but all he ever says is, we're putting it where moth and rust do not corrupt, and we owe it to the Lord, only he says to Jehovah. And she never told me. She had three dollars saved up and then yesterday there was a sign on the window at that place, the price was going up to seven-fifty next week, and she wanted to get it done for the old price. And I know it was wrong of her, but children do wrong things sometimes. She knows where Jimmy keeps his money, in a box in the hall closet, and she went and took two dollars out of it while he was doing his homework last night. Only he was going down the hall to the bathroom and saw her, and asked what she thought she was up to with his money. And of course Bernie heard.'' She got out the handkerchief again but just sat holding it. ''And Bernie told her she was a child of the Devil, she'd done other wicked things like wearing the hair ribbons and being greedy for candy and not wanting to go to church but he thought she could be redeemed with enough prayer and sacrifice but this showed she was too wicked for that. She'd already made her choice and she'd chosen the Devil's side instead of Jehovah's, and it didn't matter what else she did now, she'd go to hell and burn in fire and brimstone forever and ever. And Jimmy kept trying to say he didn't care about the money, if Dorothy'd asked he'd've let her have it—Jimmy's a good boy—but Bernie said that made him nearly as bad, aiding a thief, and if Jimmy wasn't careful he'd burn in hell forever too. And there wasn't any hope of redeeming such a wicked child as Dorothy and he washed his hands of her, if she chose to serve the Devil he'd just have to pray all the harder to be forgiven he's raised such a child.'' Mrs. Keller was staring at the opposite wall, rocking her thin body back and forth. ''She was crying and carrying on, she was downright upset, and I didn't say anything to him because it's no use, but I tried to talk to her, like I'd tried before. I told her, I said people have different ideas about God but I don't believe God's like that, waiting to catch us out every minute and send us to Hell when we do the first thing wrong. I wouldn't want to believe in a God like that. I tried to tell the children many a time about Jesus, how he's kind and merciful and loves everybody, and God was his father so how could God be any different? But Bernie was always filling their heads, and that preacher at church too, with this Jehovah, and all I can make out, Jehovah's just watching every second to catch anybody doing wrong and he likes to send people to Hell to burn. And I just don't believe—I don't care but I don't believe it, that any God—if he wanted to take the trouble to create us in the first place—is going to send a little girl down to hell to burn forever just because she stole two dollars." She looked at Wanda, but still not seeing her. "Do you believe that?"

"No, Mrs. Keller," said Wanda, "I can't believe that either."

"But she believed what her father said, and it's right children should pay attention to their father, but this is what it came to. It was just, she wanted to have her ears pierced. And she believed what Bernie said about hell. She was only twelve, she hadn't hardly had time to live yet, and now she's dead."

"Mrs. Keller," said Wanda, "have you any relatives living here, any particular friend?"

She shook her head. "The family's all gone. Jimmy'll come home pretty soon, I'll have to tell him. And there'll have to be a funeral, I don't know how we'll pay for that. But I'll never forgive Bernie. It's his fault Dorothy did that. He'd never believe it but I know it is."

"Would you like me to take you to the hospital? You shouldn't be alone. They'd give you something to put you to sleep, get some rest—"

"No," said Mrs. Keller definitely. "I'll be all right. I'll have to tell Bernie what happened and then when I can think what to do, Jimmy and I'll go somewhere. I'll never forgive him. Telling such lies to my little girl. I don't know how we could live, I wouldn't like to ask for welfare, but I won't stay with him." She still didn't ask who Wanda was, why she was there. Wanda left her sitting on the bed. A report to type on it, and the follow-up: sometime get a statement from her, see that she was notified about claiming the body. Offer her some practical help, refer her to the Social Services?

She sat behind the wheel of her car, feeling helpless and rather savage about the world in general, and she thought about the parents of that juvenile. Was it better to have no faith in any kind of God, or an arrogant faith in some vengeful cruel God happier in punishing His creation than rewarding them? It was raining harder. She switched on the ignition and the windshield wipers and started back to the office.

By the time she got there it was after five. She could make
a start on the report at least. The only one in the office was
George Higgins, and she asked, "Everybody else left
early?"

"Are you kidding, with all these damn rapists on hand?
We may be doing some overtime. John just got word that
that A.P.B. turned up Kinney out in Van Nuys, he went out
to pick him up. He might be hot for the Dale girl and we can
hold him overnight without a charge. You look beat. What
was the new homicide?"

The hell with the report. Wanda sat down, accepted a
cigarette, and told him. "The woman's no responsibility of
ours, but she doesn't seem to have a soul to help her. And
that poor child—"

"Yes," said Higgins, looking rather grim. "I can't say
I'm much on churchgoing. But it always stuck in my head,
what somebody said, I can't remember who it was, that
Christianity hasn't been tried and found wanting, it hasn't
been tried. I don't know all the answers, who does? And it's
time to go home."

As they came past the switchboard he said to Farrell,
"What's happened to the boss, he take off early?"

Farrell was getting ready to shut the switchboard: any
calls after the end of this shift would be relayed directly up
from Communications. "Oh, he and Art took off just before you got back an hour ago. I had a call from some citizen claiming to know something about that Cannaday
woman."

"Oh?" said Higgins. "I wonder what that amounts to.
Well, I suppose we'll be hearing."

THE CALL HAD COME IN at four-thirty, and Hackett took it.
"Listen," said an excited male voice, "it said in the paper
to call this number if anybody knew anything about this
woman. I call, and they say it's Robbery-Homicide, for
God's sake—Was she murdered?"

"May I have your name, sir?"

"Sure, I'm Eddy Delfino. I never saw that picture in the
paper until today, just now. This picture of the dame named

Louise Cannaday." The *Times* had run it in the late edition on Wednesday evening, and up to now it had produced no information. "Yesterday was my day off, and I didn't see a paper, and I didn't see one today until I come on the job. I don't keep up with the news all that much, just the headlines, and I wouldn't have seen about it today except that when I came in Romeo was still off."

"Romeo?" said Hackett.

"Oh, excuse me, that won't mean anything to the cops. Romeo, he's the one on the cleanup crew does the bar, the rest of them take care of the restaurant. They come in after we're closed. And he's got the flu. Of course there's a lot to do in the restaurant, but anyway, things have sort of piled up in here in two days, and when Marty and I came on at four he says for God's sake let's get rid of some of this junk—people leave things around, you know. And there's some newspapers on the bench in the corner, I go to pick them up and this picture's staring me right in the face. This Louise Cannaday. It said to call in—"

"Where are you?" asked Hackett. "Can we talk to you now?"

"Sure. Maxime's, it's Beverly Boulevard in Beverly Hills. I'm one of the bartenders here. Yeah, I asked the boss and he says all right, we got to help the cops, I'll tell you whatever I can."

Mendoza and Hackett got out there in a hurry. That was a very classy, fashionable—and expensive—restaurant, housed in a handsome Spanish-style building with its own parking lot. The bar was at one side of the elegantly furnished entrance lobby; it was long and L-shaped with intimate small round tables embellished with fancy candles in pewter holders, a banquette along one side. At this hour it only had two customers, a couple holding hands at a rear table.

"You the cops?" One of the bartenders looked up at them expectantly as they came up. "I'm Delfino." He was a handsome young fellow with a hairline moustache the twin of Mendoza's. He had the *Times* spread out on the bar. The other bartender, an older man, was listening interestedly.

"Like I say, this is the woman I saw. I saw the picture, I says to myself, I've seen that dame, and then I remembered. I thought about it good, and I remember all right, but it isn't very much."

"Where did you see her?" asked Mendoza.

"Right here," said Delfino. "What it says under the picture, Friday night, and the date—that's a week ago tonight, and that's when it was. She came in here with a guy and they sat right at that table." He pointed. "You can see it's right near the bar and right under one of the spots. I waited on them. The girls take orders for drinks from people in the restaurant, but Marty and I wait on them in here. I noticed the dame because she was sort of unusual looking, that white streak in her hair. Not exactly young, but a nice-looking dame, dressed nice—something dark."

"What time was it?" asked Hackett.

"It'd be around eight o'clock, give or take a few minutes. They came in and sat down, and I couldn't tell you what he had, it was something ordinary, a martini or whiskey sour, but she just ordered ginger ale."

"Yes," said Mendoza. No food or alcohol in the stomach. "What did he look like?"

"Now there I can't help you much," said Delfino. "I didn't notice him much. All I can tell you is, he was pretty tall and he had on a bright red velvet vest, it looked a little funny. Unusual, you know? They didn't stay long. They seemed to be talking pretty serious, he only had one drink and she didn't finish the ginger ale. Then he left the money on the table, a pretty good tip too, and out they went."

And Mendoza slapped one hand down on the bar and said, "*¡Diez millónes de demonios!* The man at the hotel!"

SEVEN

"CONDENACION," said Mendoza, "I don't know where my mind's been. The man at the hotel!" The rain was slowing traffic and they were both going to be an hour late home.

"It could have been," said Hackett. "It's a funny little thing all right, but it doesn't take us any farther in finding him."

"You don't think so? That, no. But, *por dios*, the age must be getting to me, Art. The desk clerk told us he came up and spoke to her, they shook hands and so forth. That sounds as if she wasn't expecting to see him. She expected the Hertz man to meet her, didn't mention anyone else."

"So?" said Hackett.

"So, who the hell was he and what was he doing here? To meet her unexpectedly? I knew there was something in my mind about lunch," said Mendoza. "The clerk said he wasn't a guest at the hotel. Why was he there, whoever he was? It was around lunch time. He could have been meeting somebody there for lunch."

"Oh, yes, I see," said Hackett.

"And that's a nice restaurant, but a little out of the way for the casual lunch date unless there was some reason to meet there. It's at least possible that the other one was staying at the hotel."

"You're leaping to several conclusions at once," said Hackett, "but I suppose it's possible."

"And, damn it," said Mendoza, "what time does the place open? Probably for brunch, and all the staff there at noon will be off until tomorrow. And it's been a week, would anybody remember anything? Damn it, this should have rung a bell with me days ago."

Privately Hackett wasn't so enthusiastic about the brain-wave, but Mendoza was fuming about delay. He let Hackett off at the parking lot and Hackett had a long slow drive home, apologized to Angel for not calling. "Something came up at the last minute and Luis and I had to chase out on it."

"Well, I knew if you'd had an accident I'd hear about it sooner or later," said Angel. "I kept dinner warm for you."

He sat down with a drink and the evening paper first, and Sheila came clambering over him, wanting to show him how she could almost read. He put the paper down to listen to her and fell sound asleep in his chair. When Angel woke him up she said, "You're not getting enough rest lately, Art, they're keeping you too busy."

"Oh, we haven't been that busy," said Hackett, yawning. "I'm all right."

BERNARD KINNEY looked to Palliser and Landers like another good bet for Sandra Dale. Palliser had picked him up from the Valley station last night and stashed him in jail pending questioning, and this morning they brought him down to headquarters and started in on him. He was a big, very black fellow without much brain, and he answered them in sullen growls.

"I don't remember where I was Tuesday, around, yeah, I guess I was in my car, I guess maybe I was with a pal just drivin' around."

"Looking for girls?" asked Palliser.

"Not special."

"What pal?" asked Landers.

"Oh, Ray Fisher. We got to be pals up in the joint." They prodded some more. "I didn't have no place to sleep, I lost that job, and he let me move in his pad."

"Where were you about five-thirty that day?"

"Man, who knows, I don't keep track of time. I guess I wasn't with Ray then, he gets off work at six, he works at a gas station. You said some street, I dunno if I was there, I was just around."

It was so often the way with ones like this, they were irresponsible, they drifted as the wind, but it was possible he was being deliberately evasive and they kept on at him.

When they took a break an hour later, Palliser paused beside Wanda Larsen's desk where she was typing a report. "We haven't really talked to the Dale girl yet," he said. "She ought to be up to answering some questions now, and you'd better be the one to ask them."

"I expect so," said Wanda. "Is she still in the hospital?"

"You can check."

"I'll get on it after lunch."

"It doesn't look as if there'll be any physical evidence. The lab came up with nothing from her clothes. Unless the girl can give us some definite lead—"

"I'll see her," said Wanda.

MENDOZA WAS FIDGETING around his office, looking at the clock every two minutes, and Hackett didn't think he'd be much use in questioning a suspect. He took Calhoun with him to look for Chester Rieger. They found him at home at a shoddy apartment on Dillon Street, watching a football game on TV, and he looked alarmed at the badges, at the two big men in his doorway. He was big enough himself, a pasty-faced man in the fifties with shaggy brown hair and a loose mouth.

"What do cops want?"

"Just a few questions for you," said Hackett. "May we come in?"

"Oh, sure, I guess." Unwillingly he backed in, and they followed him and sat down. The living room was dusty and untidy, with clothes strewn over the furniture, used glasses standing around.

"You're acquainted with Mr. Leo Putzel," said Hackett.

"What do you mean, acquainted? He's my brother-in-law, what about it?"

"Then you'll be sorry to hear he's dead," said Calhoun cheerfully. "Did you go to see him on Tuesday night?"

"Leo dead, gee, that's a shame, did he have a stroke or something? Of course he was pretty old. I'm sorry to hear that."

"What about it?" asked Hackett. "We understand you were going to see him on Tuesday night."

Rieger looked uncertainly from one to the other of them.
Finally he said, "Yeah, that's right, I did. Come to think I
did see him last Tuesday."

"He wanted to see you," said Calhoun, "about some
money you owed him. Fifty bucks. He was pretty annoyed
because you hadn't paid it back. Did you pay it back?"

"I—how'd you know that?" asked Rieger. "No, as a
matter-of-fact I was still short, I'm kinda between jobs, and
my wife's got a part-time job but things are kind of tight. I
explained that to him and he said it was okay."

"Oh, he did," said Hackett. "The word we got was that
he was damned annoyed and meant to have a showdown
with you. You didn't have an argument with him about it?"

"No, I never. I told him how it was and he said okay. I
wasn't there long."

"Not long enough to have a fight with him?" asked Calhoun.

"No, certainly not, I wouldn't have a fight with Leo."

"What time was it?" asked Hackett.

"Oh, I guess I got there about eight, left about eight-
thirty."

"And he was friendly and glad to see you," said Hackett, "and said it was okay about the money, so you parted
good friends?"

"Sure," said Rieger. "What made you think I had a fight
with him?"

"Well, somebody had a fight with him," said Calhoun,
"and evidently knocked him over the head and killed him.
You're sure it wasn't you?"

"What the hell do you mean?" asked Rieger in alarm.
"Somebody killed him? No, for God's sake, it wasn't me, I
wouldn't have a fight with Leo, he was an old man, a lot
older'n me, I wouldn't have touched him whatever he said,
whatever names he called me—"

"Oh, he called you names," said Hackett. "That figures, by what we heard. Called you a damned deadbeat and
a welsher, and you'd better pay back the money, and you'd
never get another dime from him, something like that."

Rieger was very alarmed now. "How'd you know that? All right, all right, he said that, he was good and mad at me—he called me some names, but I never touched him, I wouldn't do that, I never laid a hand on him. He was sittin' there drinkin' whiskey, he never offered me a drink but I didn't think nothing of that, and I told him I was sorry, I didn't have the fifty bucks yet—"

"Had you had a drink or so before you got there?" asked Hackett.

He licked his lips. "Maybe I had a couple. I wasn't drunk, nobody could say I was drunk or nowhere near it. And I never laid a hand on him. He damned me up and down and called me some names and then he said to get out and not to show up again till I had the money. So I got out. Listen, if somebody killed him it was somebody else, after that. He was okay when I left, just sittin' in his chair drinkin' a glass of whiskey. He looked fine. I wouldn't put a hand on him, an old man like that. I don't know why anybody'd think I'd do a thing like that."

"Well," said Hackett, "do you know anybody else who might have had it in for him? Any reason to argue with him? You're the only one we've turned up."

"Listen," said Rieger, confused and scared, "I don't know anybody like that, no, but it wasn't me, I never touched him, he was fine when I left, only I says to Lil when I come home, I don't guess we'd get any more out of him, he was mad. But I didn't do anything to him."

"Did he do anything to you?" asked Calhoun. "Maybe he took a swing at you so you got mad and took a swing back at him?"

"No, no," said Rieger. "He never and I never. He was okay when I left him."

Hackett gave him a benevolent smile. "You'll have to testify at the inquest, you were probably one of the last people to see him alive."

"Oh, Jesus," said Rieger. "But I swear to God, you gotta believe me, I never touched him. If he got killed it musta been somebody else. Maybe a burglar breaking in or something. It wasn't me. He was Bella's husband, she was my

sister, I wouldn't do that to Bella's husband, he was a relative. You got to believe me.''

"We'll probably want to talk to you again," said Hackett. "Have you ever been fingerprinted, Mr. Rieger?"

"Oh, Jesus," he whimpered. "Oh, my God, you goin' to
railroad me for a murder? Murder? They took them at the
jail when I got arrested once, they said assault but it was just
a little argument—I'll admit I had one over the eight but so
had the other fellow—I wouldn't do a thing like that—you
gotta believe me—" They left him to stew, and in the car
Calhoun said, "It looks open and shut. If the lab picks up
his prints there anywhere relevant, next time he'll cave in and
admit it."

"He's the type," agreed Hackett. "Let's see what kind of
record he's got."

It wasn't much of a record, on file at R. and I. He had
been charged with simple assault eight months ago, for at-
tacking a fellow in a bar during an argument. It was the first
count on him and he'd served sixty days, been put on probation. The way this thing shaped up, he was the prime suspect for Putzel, the only suspect. By Putzel's address book
he hadn't known many people, and Rieger was probably the
only one with any reason to quarrel with him. He had been
there that night, which was in all probability when Putzel
had died. Wait for the autopsy report, the lab report.

MENDOZA HAD SHOT OUT to the Sheraton Plaza at ten
o'clock and had to wait until the restaurant opened at
eleven. His guess had been wrong: they didn't go in for the
fancy brunch on weekdays. The restaurant staff came on
this shift at eleven; another crew would take over for the
dinner trade; they were open until ten for that. It was a
tastefully decorated big room with tall windows, brilliantly
lit with outdoor light and many ornate light fixtures, the
waitresses in prim black and white uniforms. Mendoza had
reckoned on there being a maître d' in a place like this, and
there was. His name, despite his impeccable European
manner, a suave sophisticated expression, and slightly for-
eign gestures, was Homer Peabody. At this hour the place

was empty; the waitresses had congregated at a table near the kitchen door.

Peabody looked at Mendoza's badge and listened to questions intelligently. "Well, just as you surmise, sir, anybody in a position like mine has to have an eye for people. For the regular customers. It makes all the difference to a place if you can say, good evening, Mr. Smith, nice to have you with us again, you can see that. If it flatters people, well, it's just good manners and good policy. It's part of the job."

"And I suppose," said Mendoza, "you have some regular patrons at the restaurant as well as at the hotel?"

"Both, that's right," said Peabody. "They don't necessarily overlap, as it were. But it's my job to know the ones like that. Of course we get a lot of people who aren't regulars, just stay at the hotel once in a way, and some of the regulars at the restaurant aren't guests at the hotel."

"Well, I'll take a gamble on your memory," said Mendoza, "and ask if you remember a very tall man having lunch here a week ago yesterday." He didn't mention the fancy red velvet vest; the desk clerk would probably have noticed that. "That's about all I can tell you about him, his height, but the desk clerk doesn't think he was a guest here. It's possible he was having lunch with someone who was staying here, but I haven't any idea who that might have been." And putting it like that, he realized just how thin and unpromising this little inspiration had been.

Peabody ruminated. "A very tall man," he said. "Taller than usual, I take it you mean. That rings a sort of bell—oh, of course. I do remember. I couldn't have said offhand exactly what day it was, but maybe you could tell from the register. He was with Mr. Lounsbury."

"And who," asked Mendoza, "is Mr. Lounsbury?"

"Oh, he's one of the fairly regular guests in the hotel, sir. When I say that I mean he'll be staying here perhaps overnight or a couple of days two or three times a year. He's a very pleasant gentleman, very friendly. Only has one arm, I believe he lost the other in an accident, he mentioned something about it once. He always talks to me and the girl who waits on him. I serve the wine, of course, and he usually has a bottle of wine with lunch and dinner. I believe he's a lawyer, has a lot of business interests that bring him down here every so often. He lives up north somewhere.''

Mendoza didn't believe this was paying off. ''What about the tall man?''

''Well, if it's the one you're asking about, there was a man like that had lunch with Mr. Lounsbury, as I say I couldn't fix the day but it was toward the end of last week, and it could have been Friday.''

Mendoza thanked him fervently and went up to the lobby. The desk clerk delayed him to get the assistant manager's permission but finally turned the register over to him. And there was Abel Lounsbury, registered for one night only, a week ago Thursday night. He had given his home address as San Luis Obispo.

Armbruster, the assistant manager, said, ''Oh, yes, Mr. Lounsbury's with us a couple of times a year, sometimes oftener. No, I don't know much about him, he's a businessman of some kind.''

Más vale tanto que nunca, said Mendoza to himself, better late than never. He drove back to the office and consulted information, got a phone number in San Luis Obispo and dialed. Here his luck ran out. Mr. Lounsbury was not at home, a polite male voice informed him. Mendoza asked for and got Mr. Lounsbury's office number. There, after some argument with a secretary, he finally talked to one Harbuck, who was Lounsbury's partner and deferential to high-ranking police.

''What's old Abel been doing to have the cops after him? I'm afraid I can't say when he'll be back, possibly tomorrow or Monday, I should think Tuesday for certain. He's up in Tehama County looking at some investment property for a client. Would I know who he had lunch with a week ago yesterday? Lord, no, how would I? I'm sorry I can't help you any more.''

Baffled, Mendoza put the phone down. Eventually, he told himself. Surprisingly, the little inspiration had paid off this far.

SANDRA DALE was still in the hospital but was going home tomorrow. She was alone in the small room, propped up in the single bed, and brightened slightly at the sight of Wanda. She was still looking pale and fragile but much better.

"You said you're a detective. Are there many girl detectives?"

"Quite a few these days." Wanda sat down in the straight chair beside the bed. "You know we'd like to find the man who hurt you, Sandra. I'd like to ask you some questions. What you remember about it."

She nodded. "Mom said you would. But I don't really know much to tell you, Miss Larsen. You know, one of the doctors here, Dr. Ferguson, he's awfully nice, he says it was lucky I didn't really have time to be scared. And I didn't. I was thinking about getting home, I was late, and hoping Mom wouldn't be too mad at me. I was hurrying. And it was cold, there was an awful cold wind and I just had my sweater. I was nearly at the corner of our street, Westmoreland, and I never heard anything behind me, he just grabbed me all of a sudden from behind, and that scared me all right because I never knew anybody was there."

"Did he say anything to you?" asked Wanda.

"No, he never said anything, he just knocked me down on the sidewalk and I hit my head an awful bang. He had hold of me by the shoulders, and I tried to get loose—Mom always says if anybody tries to get hold of you in the street, if you're scared of anybody, you should go to the nearest house and ask for help—but I didn't have a chance to do that, he was awful strong and I couldn't get away from him. He held me by the shoulders and he banged my head down on the sidewalk again and that's about all I remember, except that he was tearing my skirt off and he'd, well, he'd got hold of my panties, and then I guess I passed out. It was dark, I'd just passed a street light when it happened, and I never saw him, to tell you what he looked like."

And in one way that was a good thing, thought Wanda, for the girl's own sake, but it didn't make things easier for the cops trying to find him. "Did you get any impression about his size, was he big, tall, fat?"

Sandra shook her head. "He was awfully strong. I think he was pretty big. Oh, and he stole my necklace. My locket." Her eyes filled with easy tears. "It was my best thing, Miss Larsen, my garnet locket. It's real gold, with a real garnet set in it, and that's my birthstone. I just loved it, and besides it's a sort of family heirloom, if you know what I mean. It belonged to my grandma, Daddy's mother, she'd had it since she was a little girl. She died two months ago. Daddy went back east for the funeral, it was Illinois. And just a couple of weeks ago Aunt Rose sent it to me, she said Grandma'd like me to have it, and I was so proud of it, I wore it every day and showed it to everybody at school. And when I woke up here in the hospital it was gone. Daddy went up there, where it happened, and looked all around, but he couldn't find it, so I guess the man stole it." She wiped her eyes with a tissue. "Mom says not to worry about it, just thank God I'm alive. Because the kind of man who likes to hurt girls, do what he did to me, sometimes they do kill them, don't they?"

"They do indeed," said Wanda soberly. "You're lucky to be alive, Sandra." The gold locket, that didn't say much, or did it? The rapists, the molesters, all of those with a sex quirk, sometimes did the offbeat things. It was possible he had taken it as a kind of souvenir. Something to look for anyway.

But that was all Sandra had to tell. Unless they got lucky and the questioning broke down one of the suspects, which had happened before, maybe they would never find out definitely which big man with the dark impulses inside him had pounced on Sandra. And that would be regrettable, for if they didn't catch up to him, sooner or later he would pounce on some other girl—if he was one of the suspects, he had done it before—and she might end up dead. Sandra nearly had.

MENDOZA HAD GOT BACK from lunch and was perched on a corner of Hackett's desk, talking about Chester Rieger with Hackett and Higgins, about two o'clock, when Goldberg ambled in. "Well, Luis, I thought you'd like to know your brainwave paid off. You hit the bull's eye with that phony Naysmith. Interpol confirmed the prints just now, and they're very happy to know they can write off Vaquier and forget about him. Now all they've got to worry about is who's going to get his old job.''

"Good," said Mendoza absently.

"To each his own," said Goldberg. "Now I go back to worrying about the dirty trade on my own beat. You know, sometimes I wish I could believe in the Christian hell. It doesn't make sense, of course, how could a nonphysical soul be punished physically, but it would be kind of comforting to think that these cold-blooded ghouls deliberately creating addicts and sending them to hell on earth would get some of it back hereafter.''

Mendoza laughed. "I can't subscribe to dogma either, Saul, but I think they get paid out. Somehow. It is, as I've said before, an orderly universe. Somebody managing things. Not at random.''

"I hope you're right," said Goldberg, and drifted out. He passed a man in the doorway, who came in and without greeting sat down in the chair beside Higgins' desk.

"Well, we haven't laid eyes on you in quite a while," said Higgins. "That bank job is September. To what do we owe the honor?''

The newcomer was a Fed and of course the FBI men all looked alike; whatever their individual features they were urbane, dressed quietly to the nines in conventional business suits, looking like professional types, which they were. This one, a tall blond fellow named Fothergill, regarded the detectives with bland curiosity.

"Tell me," he said, "you've been busy with all the bodies and heisters? Not a minute to think about anything else? You just haven't had a chance to take a quick look at the N.C.I.C. bulletins?''

"Come to the point," said Higgins. "Have we missed something?''

"Oh, brother," said Fothergill. "I mean, what's the point of N.C.I.C. nattering away day in day out, keeping the local police informed about the latest mayhem and wanted names, if you don't pay any attention to it?'' He took a Manila envelope from his breast pocket. ''You sent some prints back to headquarters. A heister you're after.''

''Oh, yes,'' said Hackett. Those prints from the back door of Minetti's liquor store. ''He's pulled several jobs here lately. Do you know him?''

''Do we know him?'' said Fothergill. ''Hoo-boy. Headquarters shot the word out to us pronto. He's been on the ten-most-wanted list for a year. His name is Howard Gibbons and he's got a pedigree from here to there. Here's the list.'' He handed over a Xerox copy bearing a photograph at the top. ''Name it, he's pulled it. Heists, assault, attempted kidnapping, murder. He's fifty-four and he's spent twenty-six years in one joint or another. He first drew a lifer in New York twenty-six years ago, served ten, and six months after he got out drew a fifteen-to-twenty for shooting a deputy sheriff in New Jersey. He went over the wall with another one like him, fellow named Tombs doing a lifer for shooting another lawman, and they took to heisting post offices. They got into a shoot-out in Kansas and ended up accounting for a state highway captain and two of his deputies.''

''Oh, sweet Christ,'' said Higgins. ''Look, Fothergill, we just picked up his prints. So far as we knew up to now he was just another heister.''

''We'll forgive you,'' said Fothergill. ''Way the ball bounces. But now you know.''

''Have you got a line on him at all?'' asked Mendoza. ''We've got damn all.''

''Nary a lead,'' said Fothergill. ''Regrettably. He's been lose for sixteen months, since he got away from Leavenworth. The last time we heard of him was about eight months ago, he pulled a heist at a supermarket in Denver, shot a clerk dead and left his prints on the register. This is the first time he's surfaced this far west. He's got an old mother up in Maine, but she swears she hasn't heard from him and we believe her. His wife divorced him about ten years ago. The warden of the federal pen says he took that pretty hard, did some grudge talking about it.'' He shrugged. "That seldom comes to anything, but who knows?"

"Where's the wife now?" asked Higgins.

"Chicago. She says she hasn't heard from him either, and we can't see any way he'd know where she is. Naturally we've been looking for him. All over. And the only other thing I can tell you, and it's no use to you—in the course of looking we've talked to some of his former pals, and a couple of them admitted to having seen him since he's been on the run, and they tell us he's been hitting the bottle pretty damn heavy."

Hackett polished his glasses thoughtfully. "The latest job, where we picked up his prints, he took a couple of cases of Scotch as well as the cash."

"It figures," said Fothergill sadly. "He's coming to the end of the line—I hope—and he's got nothing. No family, no money, nobody to care a damn what happens to him. Which is what he's earned. But if he's pulled a few heists here—"

"Three or four, by what we can deduce," said Higgins.

"Then maybe he's not just passing through. He may have holed up here somewhere, at least temporarily. He's probably got a car but there's no way to track it down, it won't be registered to him in the right name. But you'd just better keep it in mind, boys. He's not the average heister waving a gun around to look important. Armed and dangerous is the word." Fothergill gave them a crooked grin. "He's a dead shot and a gun expert. He may be using a .38 or something to pull the heists, but in the past he's favored a submachine gun."

"In other words approach with caution," said Hackett. "We'll bear it in mind. Thanks so much for the word."

"It's a little surprising," said Fothergill seriously, "that he hasn't taken a shot at one of the victims. From what we know about him, he can be hair-trigger, and if he's lapping up the liquor he might be even more so."

"We'll put out the word," said Hackett. "All we can do. We haven't got a damn thing on him, that's the hell of it.

Maybe a gray car, maybe light blue, no make. What's the tattoo on his wrist?''

Fothergill laughed shortly. "Navy insignia. He did a turn when he was eighteen or twenty. So did a lot of fellows, and a lot carry a tattoo." He got up. "Good luck on locating him. At least you know who he is."

"And the hell of a lot of use that is," said Higgins as Fothergill went out. "Put out the mug shot to all the squads, and a mean bruiser he looks—" He held up the Xeroxed sheet to study it. "We haven't got a Deadeye Dick in every squad car. And between heists he may be holed up in some hotel room hardly poking his nose out." It was just something else to think about.

Landers and Galeano came in then and sat down at their respective desks. "We've had another go at Agar," said Landers. His eye was faded back to normal now. "It's in the air, but I don't think much of him for it. He's not scared enough."

"Neither do I," said Galeano. "It isn't exactly that he isn't scared, he isn't worried. He's smart enough to know we've got no real evidence, and that doesn't say anything as to whether he's guilty, but I think if he was the one on the Dale girl he'd be more worried with us picking him up right away. It's just a feeling. We let him go again."

"I'm rather liking Kinney for it," said Landers, "from what John says. But of course there's no evidence there either."

"And," said Wanda, drifting in and making for her desk, "I'm afraid there isn't likely to be. The girl just doesn't know anything. Thinks he was big, he was awfully strong, but she never got a look at him, it was dark. All she gave us is the gold locket—Grandmother's gold locket with a real garnet." She told them about that.

"Damn it," said Landers, "what does that say? Nothing. He could have grabbed it, he could have kept it—as a souvenir, you say—or tossed it away later. The sex fiends do funny things. But equally it could just have been yanked off her neck and got buried in the dirt and dried leaves on the street."

"She says her father went and looked for it."

"It could have got picked up by somebody else," Galeano pointed out. Wanda admitted that. They sat in silence for a minute, and then the phone rang on Hackett's desk.

He picked it up, said his name, and the next minute slammed it down and got up. "Maybe we're making some progress. Somebody's just found the baby."

MR. JOSEPH GAFFNEY was quite frankly horrified. He was a very tough man, an ex-Marine; he had been all through Vietnam and a lot of other grueling experiences, he had held various jobs from bouncer at a waterfront bar in San Pedro to a roustabout with a circus, but nothing had really prepared him for this. He had seen a lot of dead bodies, but not one like this. These days he had his own business, he was doing fine, and when he went down to the place on Venice Boulevard with his foreman Ernie Gomez it was just another job to look over, all in the day's work. His business was tearing down old buildings, and there was a lot of that in L.A. these days. Time had caught up with the city, especially the old inner city, the oldest part, and the developers were tearing down the old places, refurbishing whole blocks, with the blessing of the city fathers. This one, an office building on Venice, had been scheduled for demolition for six months. It had been empty longer than that, its ground floor windows boarded up. But as they walked up to it Gaffney said, "Damn kids always find a way to get in." Several of the boards had been pried off the windows at one side. "Kids! What the hell they want in an empty building? But they will do it."

Gomez said, "Place to go and smoke pot, or make out with the girls." All they were concerned about was the overall condition of the building, what it was going to take to knock it down. Gaffney unlocked the front door and they went in to what had been the lobby. There was miscellaneous junk lying around, a few boxes and barrels, and it was dark in there. Gaffney tripped over something and swore.

He looked at what was lying there and said, "Kids! Leaving dolls around yet!"

And Gomez said in a peculiar voice, "That's no doll, Joe."

And Gaffney looked again, and bent to feel the thing, and jumped back as if he had been shot. He said, "Oh, Jesus Christ, Ernie!" For a minute he wanted to be sick.

"It's a baby," said Gomez, "and it's dead. We'd better call the cops, Joe."

Gaffney was afraid to look at it again, he might be sick. They got out of there fast. There was a pay phone booth at the corner.

THEY COULDN'T DO anything at the scene until the lab had gotten some pictures. Marx and Horder came out in a van. There wouldn't be much hope of prints at the scene, but the lab men dusted a few nearby objects. The very small body had begun to decompose even in the cold weather. Mendoza and Hackett followed the morgue wagon back to the coroner's office and went in to find a doctor.

One of the coroner's younger bright boys took a look, the body transferred to an examination table, and said, "I suppose you'll want a full autopsy, but it's short and not so sweet. Somebody cut the baby's throat. There must have been some blood spilled somewhere."

"We know about that," said Hackett.

"Nobody could guess exactly when," said the doctor. "A week or more."

"Probably," said Mendoza, "a week ago yesterday. We can guess that too."

"Oh," said the doctor. The body had been wrapped in a dirty cloth of some kind, striped blue and white.

"If you can supply us with a plastic sack we'll take that along for the lab," said Hackett.

"You see this and that on this job," said the doctor, grimacing, "but this is the first time I've seen anything like this. Damn it, she couldn't have been more than a few days old, by the size." The one reluctant look they had taken, the baby had a lot of dark hair.

"Any guess about the weapon?"

The doctor shrugged. "Anything would have done, even a pocketknife. It wouldn't take much, a baby this young. We can probably have a guess when we take a closer look. Somebody'll probably get to an autopsy sometime tomorrow or next day. We'll be sending you a report."

He found a plastic bag, and back at headquarters Hackett took it up to the lab. "Even in L.A.," said Higgins in the office, "we're not apt to get two babies with cut throats inside a week. Goddamn it, I wish we had a better lead on those Leepers."

There wasn't anything to be done about that. They kicked it around a little, and the rape, and Leo Putzel, and Gibbons. There was no way to go hunting Gibbons either.

Palliser and Landers went back to talking to Kinney again, got nowhere, still thought he was a hot suspect, but finally let him go. They couldn't hold him without a charge, and there wasn't enough evidence for that. They had a firm address for him in Van Nuys at least, but of course there was no guarantee that he wouldn't take off again somewhere. This could be a discouraging job. Eventually most of them went home a little early.

ON SUNDAY MORNING Mendoza got in earlier than usual, trying to locate Lounsbury. Lounsbury wasn't home yet.

"You'll get him eventually," said Hackett.

"Damn it," said Mendoza, "if he's got anything useful to tell us, I'd like to know what it is."

"Eventually," repeated Hackett soothingly. They'd wait to tackle Chester Rieger again until they'd seen the autopsy report on Leo Putzel. Everybody else was back at the rapists except Higgins, who had gone to see Minetti again and try to pry something else helpful from him on Gibbons.

About ten o'clock Scarne appeared and said, "You don't even look at evidence before you hand it over to us?"

"What?" said Hackett. "What have you got?"

"Of course it is damned dirty," said Scarne, "aside from the blood. I understand the baby's body was wrapped in it. But of course we're used to handling all the muck and blood and dirt. But I would've thought you might have looked."

"At what?" asked Hackett.

Scarne unfolded the object he was carrying on Hackett's desk. "The blood's dry, I won't mess up your blotter. The blood's type O, by the way." The thing was, unfolded and spread out, a bib-type apron made of blue and white striped cotton. It was extremely dirty aside from the bloodstains. Scarne flattened it out and said, "Identification of a sort. If you'd just looked." Across the top of it in dark-blue embroidery was the legend *Dateland Café*.

"Identification be damned," said Mendoza, "what the hell does that tell us?"

"Dateland," said Hackett pensively. "There's something trying to ring a bell in my head about that—Dateland—" and then he said suddenly, *"Dateland!"* and began to scrabble in the letterbox on the desk. "Where the hell's that list, all those damned registrations—" He found it, scanned it in one lightning glance, and said, "By God, here it is, here it is, Luis! I knew that said something, and damn it, it's a town in Arizona and here by God is the right registration—Francis Leeper—a twelve-year-old Chevy registered to an address in Dateland, Arizona, last March. The right one of those twenty-seven plate numbers, by God, it's got to be!" He seized the phone. On Sundays the switchboard was manned by Rita Putnam. "Rita, get me a Lieutenant Gonzales in Ventura, and make it snappy!"

SUNDAY WAS Wanda's day off. She'd had a shampoo and set last night and felt more herself, with the week ended and the rain cleared away. She had a new novel from the library she was anxious to read, but she couldn't seem to settle to it. All yesterday that woman Mrs. Keller had been in her mind. And it wasn't any of the police's business; maybe it was just human business, but on Sunday afternoon she went down to Mohawk Street, to that old apartment building, and climbed up to the fourth floor.

The man who opened the door would be Bernie Keller, a tall and curiously top-heavy man, shaped like a top with heavy shoulders tapering to narrow legs and feet. She asked for Mrs. Keller. "I'm sorry, she's isn't here," he said in a light high voice.

"When will she be back?"

"I fear she will not be back," he said, and his tone was dignified, self-consciously aggrieved. "She has abandoned me and taken my son with her. Are you an acquaintance of hers?"

Wanda showed him the badge. "It's about your daughter," she said evenly. "You'll be able to claim the body after the autopsy, and arrange a funeral."

"Police," he said distastefully. "I see."

"You'll be notified, you'll have to go to the coroner's office or arrange for a mortician to pick up the body. Don't you have any idea where your wife is?"

"None," he said stiffly. "She has chosen her own way and she must abide by it. She has no money, and after the way she has behaved and what she said to me she needn't come back asking for any. Thank you for the information." He shut the door in her face.

That poor damned soul, thought Wanda, where would she go? What would she do? Probably she'd never know. A piece of flotsam cast out to sink or swim. She went home and tried to settle down with the novel.

GONZALES CALLED HACKETT just as the end of shift was coming up. "We've got them for you. Frank and Geraldine Leeper."

"Good God, already?" said Hackett. "You're a miracle worker. We weren't even sure they were there. The Poole woman just vaguely remembered they'd said something about Ventura."

"Well, they were here," said Gonzales. "Once we had the right plate number it was just a question of hunting around town. It got spotted in the parking lot of a movie house about an hour ago and we staked it out. About fifteen minutes ago they came walking up to the car as big as life. They were damned annoyed to find cops waiting for them, and being fetched into the station. Naturally nobody here's said anything to them, it's your business. But you wouldn't turn to look at them in the street, ordinary young couple. To think of the baby—it's enough to make you wonder if we're making any progress at civilization at all.''

"As you ought to know, cops are always wondering about that," said Hackett. "We'll send somebody up to get them—"

"Oh, it's not much of a drive," said Gonzales. "We'll stash them in jail overnight and I'll ferry them down in the morning."

"Thanks very much, that's neighborly of you, we appreciate it."

"Probably get there about ten," said Gonzales. "I haven't seen your burg in a while. I nearly joined that force, but all my wife's family lives here and she doesn't like the big city. The only damned trouble is, you keep growing. My God, these days you start to hit the outskirts of L.A. as soon as you get through Oxnard, and before we know it you'll have swallowed us up lock, stock, and barrel."

Hackett laughed, but it was all too true. All the predictions about one big city complex taking in the whole coast up to San Francisco—well, he hoped it wouldn't happen in his time.

THEY WERE WAITING in Mendoza's office on Monday morning, Mendoza, Hackett, and Higgins, when Gonzales came in with the Leepers. Gonzales was medium-sized, with a thick moustache. He saluted them genially. "Here are your two birds, boys."

"And *muchas gracias, amigo*," said Mendoza with a rather wolfish grin. "You're welcome to sit in."

"What the hell is this all about, anyways?" asked Leeper. "Arrest us and bring us back here, what's it about?"

It was pure bluff; his eyes and the expression on the girl's face said they knew. As Gonzales had said, an ordinary-looking young couple. He might be in the early twenties; she was younger. They were both quite good-looking. "We haven't done nothing for cops to be after us," he said weakly.

The girl sat down in the chair Higgins pushed forward and crossed one leg over the other. "I guess they know, Frank," she said. She sounded merely annoyed. "I guess you weren't smart enough about hiding it somewhere."

"You're talking about the baby," said Mendoza. "Would you like to tell us which one of you it was cut the baby's throat?"

"Oh, Jesus, mister." She shuddered. "I couldn't have done a thing like that, I get sick at the sight of blood. He did."

Leeper didn't attempt to deny it. He gave them all an ingratiating grin. "Look, the way I figure it," he said, "it's just the same as if Geraldine had an abortion. See? It's really just the same. Only we couldn't afford an abortion. It was just a damned nuisance."

"That's right," she said quickly. She gave him a resentful glance. "If I'd had the sense to pick up with a guy could make decent money—but I never wanted any brats anyway, just a nuisance, yelling all the time."

"Where was the baby born?" asked Higgins. "Over in Dateland?"

"Yeah," said Leeper. "I'd been workin' there on a ranch outside town, but it wasn't much of a job—"

"I'll say it wasn't," she rejoined coldly. "I had to go to work at that damned café, have enough to keep a roof over our head, and then when I got so big with the brat they wouldn't let me work no more. It was a damn drag. My sister, she lives up in Ventura, she said she could get Frank a job at her boyfriend's uncle's gas station. So we come over."

"Stopping to murder the baby on the way?" said Hackett.

"Murder!" yelped Leeper. "Nobody did no murder, for Jesus' sake. It's just like I said, just like an abortion, only after instead of before. We didn't want no kids to take care of."

"Why didn't you think about that before?" asked Mendoza coldly.

He wriggled uneasily on the hard chair. "I guess you mean like birth control. It don't always work, and besides,

hell, you feel like it, you do it, who's goin' to be bothered
think about all that before?''

''If you had to have the damned babies you'd be bothered,'' she said petulantly.

''But I don't know what you're talkin' about, murder. It
wasn't anything like that, just like an abortion, that's all. I
suppose you found it.'' That was just resigned.

''If he'd done like I said and put it down a sewer or
something—but I might have known he wouldn't have sense
enough—''

He turned on her, goaded. ''You always tryin' to tell me
I'm so damned dumb! They never found the other one, did
they?''

''Shut up, Frank!'' she said sharply, but too late.

''Another one,'' said Mendoza interestedly. ''When and
where was that?''

''You got to open your big mouth,'' she said viciously.

He looked at them piteously, like a dog punished for some
unknown fault. ''Well, hell, we never wanted no kids at all.
When the first one come, about a year and a half ago, we
didn't know nobody in that town. I just took it outside town
and left it back from the road.'' Dimly he seemed to sense
some kind of disapproval in their expressions, and added
quickly, ''But it wasn't nothing like murder, either one of
them—I don't know why you'd try to say it was murder!''

EIGHT

ACCORDING TO THE ATLAS, Dateland, Arizona, had a population of four hundred and fifty souls. Would there be any police at all, wondered Hackett.

"Bound to be a town marshall or something," said Mendoza.

At random Hackett called the mayor's office—there had to be a mayor—and found that there was a chief of police. His name was Butterfield, and he sounded competent and brisk. He listened to what Hackett had to say and said, "God almighty, Sergeant, a year and a half ago? In this climate? Does the bastard say exactly where he left it?"

"He just says, outside of town, back from an old ruin of a ranch house."

"Oh, that'd likely be the old Ruiz place, hell, Sergeant, a newborn baby and that long ago, I don't figure it'd be much use even to look, but we will. Most likely the coyotes found it. My God, what a thing. We'll have a look around but I doubt if we find anything, even bones."

"That's about what we figured," said Hackett, "but we thought we'd pass it on. They'll both be up for murder one here, of course."

"And they won't have any money for a smart lawyer to spout the doubletalk," said Butterfield. "I seem to recall that fellow, he was working for Joe Nabors but according to Joe he did more sleeping than working, and Joe fired him a few weeks ago. What a hell of a thing. Well, we'll poke around and let you know if we come up with anything, but I doubt it."

Higgins and Calhoun had taken the Leepers off to jail, and Mendoza had applied for the warrant. The night watch had left them another heist, but by what they got on it it hadn't been Gibbons; the victim, the proprietor of a small independent market in Lincoln Heights, described the heister as young and thin, hadn't seen a gun—"He had it in his coat pocket, he pointed it at me through that."

"You know, Luis," said Hackett, "we've heard about this one before. In a general way. I wonder if he's got a gun at all, whether the victims just aren't taking any chances." In any case, there were no leads on him; none of the victims had said they would recognize a picture.

It was Palliser's day off. They had had R. and I. run off a lot of copies of the F.B.I. sheet on Gibbons and distributed them around to the squads, but it was a long shot that anything would come of that. Sporadically reports were drifting in from other forces about those Model A's elsewhere in the state, but so far they all seemed to have been at home during that crucial Friday. Another one came in before they went to lunch, from Sacramento; the car was owned by one of the city's councilmen, and hadn't been out of its garage in weeks. "It's a beautiful thought," said Mendoza, "even a minor politician getting drunk and pulling a hit-run resulting in a homicide, but evidently it didn't happen." He had already called San Luis Obispo again this morning, with no result, and again was fuming at delay.

Landers and Galeano brought in a new rape suspect to question. Grace had some new snapshots of his kids to show around before he and Calhoun went out again on the legwork. A piece of new and tiresome business came in, a rumble between a few members of rival gangs, leaving a couple of knifed bodies in the street. Hackett and Higgins went out to cover it. That would either dissolve into air, nobody knowing a thing about it, or result in a lot of tedious questioning if anybody claimed to. The patrolmen called to the scene had pulled in four gang members who hadn't been quick enough to disappear.

Mendoza sat dealing himself crooked poker hands, and at three o'clock, expecting another rebuff, tried San Luis Obispo again. This time he got his man.

"Oh, yes," said Lounsbury, "Adam told me you'd been calling, Lieutenant. I must confess I'm damned curious to know what the L.A. police want with me. What have I been up to? Of course, any way I can help you I'd be glad to." He had a pleasant deep voice and sounded friendly.

"It's just a matter of some information," said Mendoza. "You stayed at the Sheraton Plaza a week ago Thursday night. Apparently on Friday—we think it was that Friday—you had lunch at the restaurant with another man."

"Yes, that's so," said Lounsbury.

"Who was the man? We've been trying to trace him."

"What on earth for?" asked Lounsbury, astounded.

"Well, if he's the man we think he is, he met a woman in the hotel lobby around noon. It's her movements we've been trying to trace. Who was he? Do you know where he is now?"

"Presumably back home," said Lounsbury. "I can't imagine what all this is about, but of course I'll tell you anything I can. His name is Richard Pilkington. He's an attorney and his home is in Indianapolis. One of my clients here died about two months ago, a man named Archer, he'd retired and moved out here quite recently. Thought he had a good many years ahead, but we never do know, he was only sixty-four—dropped dead on the golf course. He'd moved here from Indianapolis, had a thriving furniture factory back there, he was quite a wealthy man. He'd intended to put all his affairs in my hands, and in fact he'd done so to all intents and purposes. I'm one of the executors of his will, and the other one is Pilkington, who'd been his attorney back there and an old friend."

"Pilkington was here about the will?" asked Mendoza.

"That's right. It wouldn't have been strictly necessary—we've accomplished a good deal by mail—but Archer had just bought some land as an investment in L.A. County, in the San Fernando Valley. I hadn't had a look at it, and Pilkington wanted to look at it, we had to decide whether it ought to be resold and the proceeds added to the estate, and it represents a healthy piece of change, around two hundred thousand. The principal legatee is Archer's niece, he was a widower without children, and she lives in Indianapolis."

"I see," said Mendoza. "So Pilkington came out?"

"He's a very nice chap," said Lounsbury. "We'd had a good deal of correspondence, of course. Yes, he flew out that Friday, or rather he got a night flight on Thursday, he had a layover in Denver and was getting into L.A. about eleven-thirty that Friday morning. I took the shuttle flight down from there on Thursday night."

"And arranged to meet him in the hotel lobby about noon?" said Mendoza.

"That's right. We didn't have to get the desk to page either of us," and Lounsbury chuckled. "I'd know him by his height, he's six-foot-six, and he'd know me by my missing arm. We joined up and had lunch. You said something about his meeting a woman—"

"Mrs. Louise Cannaday," said Mendoza. "Did Pilkington say anything about her?"

"I don't recall the name, but he did mention running into an acquaintance unexpectedly, a woman. While he was waiting for me to show."

"In the hotel lobby," said Mendoza.

"Yes, that's so. He said she was the wife of an old friend in Indianapolis, another attorney, he hadn't seen her since her husband's funeral."

Mendoza could foresee the end of this, but he persisted. "That's all he said about her? He didn't mention that he expected to see her again that day, perhaps take her to dinner?"

"Good heavens, no," said Lounsbury. "It was just a casual meeting. How could he? We had our plans all laid out. We had lunch, and took a cab out to the valley, had a look at the land, had some discussion with the realtor Archer had bought it from, and let me see, where did we have dinner? Oh, the Café Parisienne in Hollywood. Then we went back to the hotel. He'd checked his luggage there, and I'd already checked out. We got the seven-fifty shuttle flight back to San Luis and he stayed with me that weekend, at my place here. We got through the rest of the business, and he flew to L.A. and back to Indianapolis that Monday, at least that's what his plans were."

"That's all very clear," said Mendoza, "but not very helpful to us in tracing Mrs. Cannaday."

"I see, I'm sorry," said Lounsbury.

"To be frank, I was rather casting the man at the hotel as the villain of the piece," said Mendoza sadly, "but evidently he isn't. Mr. Pilkington sounds like an upright citizen."

Lounsbury was amused. "Very pleasant chap," he said. "Very sound attorney, Lieutenant. What happened to your Mrs. Cannaday, did she get waylaid by a villain?"

"She did indeed, but not, it appears, by Mr. Pilkington. Well, these setbacks occur. At least we know who he was now, and thanks so much."

"Sorry I couldn't be of more help."

Mendoza put the phone down and said to himself, "Hell." Now they knew, and the man at the hotel, such a potentially sinister figure, had dissolved into nothing. Or had he? By what they'd heard she hadn't talked with him long, but conceivably had she said something, anything, about her immediate plans? It was a very slim possibility, but it had to be tried. He called information, and after a delay he got Pilkington's number in Indianapolis and dialed. After another delay he got Pilkington, who was considerably annoyed at being called away from dinner, even by a high-ranking police officer. Mendoza was meek with him, explained the circumstances, and Pilkington calmed down.

"Well, I'm very sorry to hear about Mrs. Cannaday, but I'm afraid I can't help you at all. I didn't know her well, of course, just through her husband—as you know, he was an attorney here too. I was surprised to see her that day. We just said a few words. I'd already been looking around for Lounsbury, and spotted him and we joined up. Oh, so far as I remember she said she'd been in San Francisco visiting her daughter and was going home that Sunday. No, I don't recall that she said why she was in Los Angeles. I don't suppose we were talking five minutes."

So that was that. Mendoza put the phone down and swiveled around to stare out the window at a clear cold blue sky and a lot of cirrus clouds whipped by a strong wind.

When Hackett and Higgins came in at five o'clock he was still sitting there; he had gotten out the autopsy report on Louise Cannaday and the various statements they had taken from the son, Adele Mowbray, the Schultzes. Hackett and Higgins were feeling disgruntled about the gang members. Unfortunately, both the bodies and the gang members they had hauled in, all members of the Hellcat Gang, were over eighteen, so it couldn't be handed over to Juvenile. They hadn't gotten any identification of the possible knife wielders. The ones they had brought in had all been in possession of the reefers and one had been holding a deck of heroin; they could be held on that, but it didn't amount to anything. They had just growled aggrievedly at the Robbery-Homicide men. Well, these goddamned White Knights had come over into their *barrio*, hadn't any goddamned business there, they'd had to jump them first. Neither of the corpses had been carrying formal identification, but their pals had supplied names and one address. That one at least apparently had a set of parents; Higgins sat down at his desk to call them and break the news, and Hackett listened to the tale of Lounsbury and Pilkington.

"Dead end," he said. "We might have guessed it was something like that, Luis. Something casual. So the upright Pilkington couldn't have been the man with her at Maxime's. In the fancy red velvet vest."

"So who the hell was it, Art? Who could it have been?" Mendoza swiveled around restlessly in the desk chair. "Most of the people she knew here were women. There's Lemoyne, of course. Damn it, I still like him. He's really the likeliest. She'd taken the trouble to let him know she'd be here. She'd have liked to see him again, for a—mmhm—very feminine reason."

"How do you mean?" asked Hackett.

"Use your imagination," said Mendoza irritably. "She didn't look her age, she was still good-looking. She probably didn't have the slightest impulse toward renewing the romance, but she wouldn't have been at all averse to having him see her, see how young she looked after all those years."

"All right, I'll give you that," said Hackett.

"If she caught his call at six-thirty they might well have been at Maxime's at eight o'clock."

"Then why didn't they stay on and have dinner there?" asked Hackett. There hadn't been any point in asking at the restaurant; they knew she hadn't had dinner.

"They got into an argument," said Mendoza in a dissatisfied voice. "And he said, all right, I'll take you back to the hotel. And on the way—"

"You know," said Hackett, "I haven't met the man and it may be a little thing, but just from what you said I can't see this correct businessman Lemoyne wearing the fancy red velvet vest."

"Dios Mío," said Hackett, leaning back and shutting his eyes, "it wasn't Fred Schultz. George told me about that wild little idea of yours, and since you wanted to know I went and asked. Last Friday, I think—I forgot to mention it. The Schultzes were at that anniversary party. I asked the Beverly Hilton who gave it, and found this Mrs. Garstein. I didn't even have to make up a reason for questions—she's the kind who talks to anybody anytime and tells all she knows. They were there from beginning to end."

"I didn't really think they weren't," said Mendoza. He regarded the clutter of papers on his desk and at random picked up the address book. By now James Cannaday had gone back to Indianapolis, and the body had been flown back for burial there. He leafed through the book haphazardly. "Who the hell could that have been, if it wasn't Lemoyne? Granted, by Friday night she knew she'd have an extra day here, and if Lemoyne called she could have put him off to Sunday. *If* she already had a date, a meeting set up with someone else. But who was there here she might have wanted to see? Nobody we've heard of—" and then he stopped at one page, and sat up with a jerk and said, *"Por Dios.* What's in my mind now?"

"Well, what?"

"This poet," said Mendoza softly. "Bruce Mallory. Cannaday said, and the Mowbray woman said, she admired his poetry, wrote and told him so, had a nice letter back. Finished. As far as they knew. Then will you tell me why she had his home address in her address book? I presume she'd written him in care of the poetry magazine."

Hackett sat up and looked at him. "We both should have realized that, all right."

"It looks as if she might have been corresponding with him, doesn't it? Why? I think we go and ask him. It might be interesting to know."

"A poet," said Hackett thoughtfully. "I can't say I know much about the breed, but it strikes me that a poet might be a damned sight likelier to go in for the fancy red velvet vest. Well, he'll keep until tomorrow."

THE NIGHT WATCH didn't have a single call. It was Schenke's night off, and Conway and Piggott sat around talking desultorily, listening to the police calls on the radio in the background. There was a pile-up on the Harbor Freeway: Highway Patrol business.

"You still looking for a house?" asked Conway.

"It seems to be impossible unless you buy out in the sticks somewhere, or some chicken coop needs everything done to it," said Piggott gloomily. "The interest rates—Prudence keeps saying she could get a job to help out, but I don't see it. By the time you figure in transportation and her meals out, and a babysitter, it wouldn't work out to that much extra. Neither of us likes the idea of raising a family in an apartment, and we'd like at least one more. I just don't know."

They were both bored and sleepy by the time the shift came to an end, but it was a weekday night; the weekends usually made up for it in action.

HACKETT AND HIGGINS were still busy clearing up the paperwork on the gang fight, and it was Jason Grace's day off. Palliser and Galeano started out to try a rather long cast after Howard Gibbons, but it was the kind of thing that could pay off. From the F.B.I. bulletin they knew he was a billiard player, and a pretty good one. So far the heists pulled here had all been on the central beat, and that took in a good deal of territory but narrowed the area down from the whole county. They started out to cover all the billiard parlors in that area, armed with his mug shot. It was just possible that some of those proprietors, somewhere, would say, sure, that guy comes in here a lot. It was, of course, an even longer shot that he might go on to say, his name's Jack Robinson, he lives at the hotel up the street. But it was a chance. There was a lot of legwork on this job. And more rain was forecast.

Mendoza was out in North Hollywood by nine o'clock. Bruce Mallory's address proved to be a newish garden apartment building painted pink, with balconies and a pool at one side. Mallory-Hooper was listed on the second floor; there would only be about eight units in the building. He pushed the bell for five minutes without getting an answer, and then tried the apartment next door. A harassed-looking young woman opened the door to him, a fretful baby in her arms.

"Oh, they've gone up to Big Bear to ski," she told him. "They both like to ski. Which is fine if you can afford it and have the time, I guess. You a salesman or something?"

"I just want to see Mr. Mallory on a business matter," said Mendoza. "Do you know when they'll be back?"

"I don't suppose they'll be gone long—even with Ann's job they couldn't afford it, and she can't take off too long. Business, I don't know what that'd be with Bruce, he hasn't had a job since they've lived here, just sits around scribbling or listening to the stereo all day. She earns the living. She's a hostess in a restaurant somewhere. I don't really know them too good. I don't really approve of people living together without being married, and neither does my husband. And after some of the parties they've thrown— Once we had to call the cops and complain about the noise, and another time he got arrested. I saw the cops come after him. I don't know what that was about, I guess he didn't get in jail, but it just shows you what kind they are. You got any business with Bruce, mister, you better read the fine print, like my husband says. And I better go see about the laundry."

Mendoza went back to the Ferrari, thinking about that
with interest, and naturally made for the Valley station of
L.A.P.D. There he explained his business to the desk sergeant and was eventually ushered into the office of a Captain Batista, who sent a couple of minions hunting through
the files. The results came in about fifteen minutes later, and
he passed them over. "I couldn't tell you anything about
him personally," he said, "but as you can see, we've had
him in twice for possession. On information from one of
our street people. He's a customer, or has been, of one of
our known dealers. Just the pot, but we may have been unlucky in not catching him with anything else. We couldn't
hold him, he got probation both times and somebody paid
the bail." That was all Valley knew about him, but it was
interesting. What had been the relationship between one like
this and Louise Cannaday? There'd be no getting at him
until he came home from Big Bear, but Mendoza was now
violently curious about him.

He went back to base and sat ruminating it. It wouldn't
be any use to prod James Cannaday or Adele Mowbray
further; they had told what they knew.

ARNOLD SPANGLER came on duty at noon that Tuesday. He
had been a paramedic for eight years, and he liked the job,
was good at it, it was an interesting job and he liked the
feeling that he was helping people. For the last four years he
had been attached to the fire station at Seventh and Bur-
lington, downtown.

He came on at noon and settled down in the paramedics'
quarters on the second floor of the station, to wait for any
calls. The other men sat around reading or talking; some of
them had a pinochle game going. Spangler had brought one
of his birthday presents with him; yesterday had been his
birthday. In his off time he was a hiker and a rockhound,
and among his other birthday presents had been an expensive and very good pair of binoculars from his brother. He
fingered them lovingly, a really beautiful pair, and they'd be
useful on climbing expeditions. He sat at the big window
there trying them out, looking over the panorama of the

city. Of course there wasn't anything to see, just buildings and streets. About the only faint point of interest anywhere around was MacArthur Park, three or four blocks away. The binoculars brought it right up to his eyes in sharp detail, and he panned back and forth, looking at the park without any interest in it, just testing the glasses. Not a soul there, sitting on the benches or walking the paths. Well, it wasn't a very popular park, and these days in a rather run-down section of town. He went on looking idly. Then a woman walked into the park, from the Sixth Street side. She was pushing a stroller with a baby in it. She sat down on one of the benches. Spangler panned the binoculars again. When he came round to the woman the second time, a man had come to sit down beside her. They were talking, the woman gesturing. The rest of the park was still empty.

Suddenly Spangler said aloud, "Hey, what the hell does he think he's doing?" In sharp focus there at the other end of the binoculars, the man had grabbed the woman by the throat and seemed to be throttling her. For a second Spangler didn't believe what he was seeing. He kept the binoculars glued on the scene. The man let go of her and she fell off the bench and sprawled on the blacktop path. The man got up and walked away, out of the park, over at the Alvarado entrance. As far as Spangler could judge he was a medium-sized man, fairly young; he was wearing dark pants and a dark jacket. He mingled with the people on the street there and Spangler lost him. The woman was still sprawled on the blacktop, not moving.

Spangler put the binoculars down and said, "Hey, fellows, I don't believe it but I just saw a murder committed!" He made excitedly for the nearest phone. "The cops have got to hear about this."

WHEN THE CALL came in from the squad Wanda was alone in the office, but a minute later Pat Calhoun came in looking bored and said, "We let Flores go. His pedigree makes him look good for it but he's got a tentative alibi, he says he was at a party that night from about five on, gave us some names. Of course, the kind of pals he's got, the kind of party it probably was, it'll need some checking.''

"Yes," said Wanda. "Something funny just showed up, Pat. A paramedic says he saw a murder committed," and she told him about the binoculars. "Traffic sent a squad over, and there's a dead woman all right, apparently strangled. We'd better go and have a look."

"Now that's a damned funny one," said Calhoun, intrigued.

They took his car. On the way he asked her for a date and she turned him down, making a little joke of it. When Calhoun had first joined the team she had been, she admitted to herself, very much attracted—he was quite a man, Calhoun—but she had a good deal of common sense, and after a first date she had read him accurately. He didn't mean any harm, he was just so constituted that he'd flirt with anything in skirts automatically, and it was just skin-deep, he wasn't serious. He took the refusal noncommittally. Not holding a grudge, she thought with a small smile, admiring his handsome rugged profile.

When they got to the park Dave Turner was there by the squad. "Not a soul around when I got here," he said. "She's over there by the memorial."

It was a chilly day and this wasn't any longer the kind of park where people sat around feeding the pigeons. They looked at the body. There was a baby about a year old crying its head off in a Taylor Tot. The body was that of a young woman in the mid-twenties; thin and nondescript, with dark hair. She was wearing a dark-green pantsuit and a black wool jacket. A black plastic handbag was on the bench, and Wanda opened it gingerly, mindful of possible prints, and looked through it. No billfold, no identification: a coin purse containing slightly over fifteen dollars in cash, a prescription bottle in a small paper bag, a few cosmetics.

"She hasn't been dead long," said Calhoun, feeling her throat.

"No, evidently the paramedic saw it done, about half an hour ago. We'll have to try for some identification, Pat."

"And the first place to go is the pharmacy," said Calhoun. There was a slip of paper, tab from a register, stapled to the paper bag: People's Pharmacy, an address on Wilshire. They got Turner to call up the lab, and Horder came out to take some pictures. The morgue wagon came and took the body away; surprisingly, no curious crowd had collected at all. "What about the baby?" asked Calhoun. The baby was now yelling its head off. Pending identification there was only one answer to that; they got the Taylor Tot into Calhoun's car and took the baby down to Juvenile Hall. It was two-thirty before they got to the pharmacy.

There was, of course, a name on the prescription bottle, Julia Camacho, and a doctor's name, Ewing. The pharmacist disclaimed any knowledge of her. "It's just a simple antihistamine," he said. "She comes in here about once a month to get it refilled. I don't know where she lives." But he could tell them about the doctor, at a clinic on Olympic, and the doctor gave them an address, Maryland Avenue.

"Be damned if it isn't starting to rain again," said Calhoun as they got out of the car. "Talking about adding insult to injury."

It was the usual ancient apartment building, of about thirty units. They got no answer at the door labeled Camacho. There was a manageress on the premises, a fat dark woman named Echeverria, and she regarded them with interest.

"Now you're the second people today come asking after her. All I can tell you, like I told him, she's likely sitting over in the park. Wouldn't be my idea of how to spend an afternoon, unless it was a nice warm summer day, but she's a great one for what she calls fresh air." At the sight of the badges, the explanation, she was only slightly excited. "Mother of God, you say she's killed? Just sitting in the park? Such terrible things happen these days, you wouldn't believe it. And I don't know much about her to tell you, honest. She's lived here about four months, I know she's separated from her husband, I don't know nothing about him. He sends her money to live on, but she was always complaining it wasn't enough. I don't know nothing about any relatives.''

"Who was it who came asking after her today? When?" asked Calhoun.

"It was a fellow. I'd never seen him before. Just a young fellow. No, she didn't have a boyfriend far as I know. I just told him, like I told you, she'd gone walking up the street with the baby, I saw her leave, I was out on the step talking to Mrs. Espinosa from next door. She said she was going to the drugstore and then the park.''

There was a ring of keys in the handbag, and one of them unlocked the door of the cheap little apartment; they looked around. There didn't seem to be an address book, but on a pad beside the phone in the kitchen were several scrawls and numbers, *Mama, Sylvia, Lucia, Juana*. Wanda tried Mama first. It was a Santa Barbara number, and it produced an outburst of shock, grief, and indignation. Julia was dead, killed, murdered, and where was the baby? Who was taking care of the baby, her precious grandchild? It must have been that *piojo*, that bum, that no-good *hombre* she had married in an evil moment, never enough money he gave her, Julia had been brought up a lady, nice things she had to have, it was understood. Of course they would come for the baby, one took care of one's own. Mama did not drive but Juan would bring her to the city tomorrow, she would come to see the police and tell them about the villain, without doubt he had been the murderer. His name was Carlos Camacho, but she did not know where he lived. He had once, she knew, worked at a garage, but where, who knew?

"Well," said Wanda, putting the phone down in some relief, "at least that's something, a lead of sorts."

"These temperamental Latins," said Calhoun with a grin; he had been listening in. "When can we expect to see Mama, I wonder?"

"It's only about a hundred miles. I expect whenever she can get Juan to drive her down.''

AT ABOUT TWO-THIRTY that afternoon Patrolman Douglas Frawley had been sent to a complaint on Olympic Boulevard. It was an independent pharmacy on the corner there, and the owner was voluble and angry about neighborhood boys. "I don't suppose there's much you can do about it, but I've got fed up and I thought I'd register a complaint anyway. Time and again I've warned them, don't come in unless it's to buy something, but of course I might as well talk to the wind. They come in here, sprawl all over the magazine racks, read the magazines or at least paw through them, without buying a damn thing, and leave the magazines in a mess, all torn sometimes. They're big kids, eleven or twelve, old enough to know better. They won't pay me any attention, just keep coming back."

"Well, sir, there's not much we can do," said Frawley, "if you don't know any of their names." The pharmacist shook his head. "If you could get any of the names, we can send a Juvenile officer to talk to them."

"And a hell of a lot of good that would probably do," said the pharmacist, exasperated. "I am getting fed up. Spoil my stock, and I wouldn't put it past them to snitch the candy bars."

"You can see there isn't much we can do if you don't know any names, sir. I can see it's annoying."

"Annoying!" said the pharmacist. "They're nothing but a damned bunch of vandals. Well, I'll see what I can do. There's one of them, I could probably find out his name, he comes in sometimes with a woman who may be his mother, I've spoken to her about it. Thanks for nothing. I might have known you couldn't do anything."

Frawley was apologetic; you had to maintain the good relationship with the citizens. He came out to the street. He had parked the squad about half a block down.

"Hello," said somebody beside him.

He looked down and around. There was a kid there on the sidewalk beside him, a girl maybe eleven or twelve, a skinny kid with a lot of reddish-brown hair in two braids. "Hello, there," said Frawley. She had a thin face with a lot of freckles.

"My name's Rhoda May Flannery," she said.

"Well, hello again," said Frawley. He'd been an only child, and he wasn't married; he didn't know much about kids.

She started to walk alongside him. "My grandfather was a policeman on the L.A.P.D.," she told him. "For thirty years. He's retired now."

"Is that so?" said Frawley.

She nodded vigorously. "He says it's the best police force in the whole world."

"Well, we try to do a good job," said Frawley.

"I know you do. My daddy, he wanted to join the force too but they wouldn't let him. I don't see why not, but Grandpa says there have to be regulations. You see, he, my daddy, he was in a war a long time ago when he was only eighteen, and he got shot in the leg and they had to cut off part of it. So they wouldn't let him join the force. He can do anything with his artificial leg, run and jump and all, and he works real hard. He works at a Plymouth agency, he's real good at fixing engines."

"Well, that's fine," said Frawley inattentively. He came up to the squad. "I'd better get back to work now, Rhoda May. Nice to have met you."

"But I haven't told you yet," she said. "You see, I saw you go in the drugstore and I thought it might be better to tell a policeman. First I thought I'd tell Miss Fleming, she's my teacher. But she's not real interested in children and I thought she might not listen. So I was going to tell Mother, but she won't be home till four, she works part time at a bakery. And Daddy won't be home till six. I'm on my way home from school now. And I saw you go into the drugstore, so I thought best I tell you."

"Tell me what?" asked Frawley.

She looked up at him with bright, intelligent blue eyes. "Eddy Kruger's got Sandra's locket," she said.

"What?" said Frawley blankly.

She looked slightly impatient at his stupidity. "Eddy Kruger's got Sandra's garnet locket. He was showing it to some other boys, I saw him behind the cafeteria today. The police know about Sandra, an awful thing happened to her, she got raped and hurt real bad last week. She's in my homeroom at school, I know her pretty good. And she's just crazy about her locket, she'd sure be mad if she knew Eddy Kruger had it.''

"Sandra who?" asked Frawley.

"Sandra Dale. And Eddy was showing it to some other boys, I guess maybe trying to make them like him better, maybe because he stole it. Nobody likes Eddy. He's only been in school this semester, and he's a big dumb nothing,'' said Rhoda May dispassionately. ''He can't even hardly read, he's just dumb. So I thought he prob'ly stole the locket from Sandra and maybe he's the one did that to her too.''

Frawley stared at her. A rape—his shift ended at four o'clock but of course he'd heard something about the rape from the other men, the watch commander. It had been somewhere on this beat. He said, ''That's interesting, Rhoda May. Thanks for telling me.''

"You'll tell the detectives and they'll find out if it was him," she said brightly.

"I certainly will. Where do you live?" She rattled the address off glibly, Sunset Place. "And what school do you go to?"

"Washington Elementary. I won't be in junior high till next year.''

"Well, thanks very much," repeated Frawley. "You'd better chase along home now, it's going to rain again." He thought maybe this had better not wait for the end of shift, it might be important. In the squad, he got a dispatcher and asked for one of the detectives to meet him, he might have some needed information.

IT WAS GALEANO who took the call, and he thought what Rhoda May said was interesting enough, listening to Frawley, that he got back to Hackett in the office immediately from the nearest phone. "You know what Wanda said about this locket."

"Yes, indeedy," said Hackett, "we'd better get on it, Nick. But you realize the chances are this school kid picked it up on the street up there where it happened."

"Well, I don't know, Art. I suppose it could be. But the girl says her father looked around for it pretty carefully."

Hackett came out and they listened to Frawley in more detail. "I don't think she knows where this kid lives," said Frawley. "He's just a boy at school to her."

"An elementary school," said Hackett. "Hell, they get out of there at about twelve, don't they? A boy of twelve—of course there might be an older brother." But it was a lead, and they had better follow it up.

He and Galeano went over to the school. It looked deserted at this hour, the kids all gone; but there were several cars in the parking lot, and on investigation they found a vice-principal still there having a conference with some of the teachers. Hackett asked about Eddy Kruger.

The vice-principal, a middle-aged man, looked irritated, looked at the badges and said, "Police now. I've begun to feel like a policeman myself, all we seem to be good for, ride herd on these little savages. I seem to have heard that name before—"

One of the teachers spoke up, a thin woman with shrewd eyes and a hard mouth. "You certainly have," she said tartly. "We've only had that one this semester, and he's a troublemaker. A bully and a fighter, and he's so much bigger than all the other boys, he's got them terrified of him. I can't say I blame them, there's something not right about him. It's just not that he's backward, it's—oh, I don't know. Several of us think he belongs in a special school, but of course the foster mother wouldn't have anything to say about that, we'd have to deal with the Social Service people and all the red tape—" She shrugged. "I don't suppose it's worth it, he's really not educable anyway."

"He's in a foster home?" asked Hackett.

"That's about all we know about him. Except his evaluation tests, of course. He's in my homeroom, so of course I saw those. He's got a low-normal I.Q., but socially he's very backward. He reads at about a second-grade level. Of course it's ridiculous to have put him in fifth grade, he's fifteen, three years older than most of them in sixth. Why are the police interested in him? I'm not surprised, just curious.''

"We'd like his home address, that's all," said Hackett. They looked it up: Menlo Avenue. Outside, Hackett said, "Now what do you know, Nick, that's the next street over from Westmoreland.''

It was a big ramshackle old California bungalow, and the woman who answered the door was about sixty, fat and shapeless in an old cotton housedress, but her expression was pleasant and she looked kind. She asked them in, and her eyes grew anxious as she listened to them; she had introduced herself as Mrs. Rodman.

"That boy," she said. "That Eddy. Do the police think he might have done something as wicked as that? He's only fifteen, but—well, I just don't know. We've only had him since August. We started to take in the foster children a couple of years ago, we raised five of our own and we both like kids, thought it'd be a way to help out some of the kids who need a home and make a little money as well. My husband's still working, won't retire till next year. And mostly it's worked out all right. Most of them we've had. It'd make your heart sick, some of the poor things, not bad kids, just neglected and nobody caring about them. They're so grateful for a little attention and kindness. The social worker, she'd tell us about them before we took them, this one had got abandoned by the mother, that one caught in the middle of a divorce or some such. Some of them only stay with us a little while, until things get sorted out for them, the mother able to take them back or some relatives adopting them. We only had real trouble before with one of the girls, and the social worker said her mother was a prostitute and she'd lived with her, maybe you couldn't expect anything else. She was wild as a hawk, always running after the boys, you couldn't keep her at home, out all hours and we never knew where she was. We finally asked the social worker to take her away. But this boy, this Eddy." She looked troubled. "Both my husband and me have tried to talk to him, teach him this and that, but you can't reach him. They told us about him. He's illegitimate, his mother's feebleminded and in some sort of institution. One of her sisters tried to rear him, but she died and there aren't any other relatives. And they say he's not feebleminded like her, but he certainly hasn't much of a brain. Nobody's taught him any manners and he won't learn any. We had to send him to school, it's the law, but he certainly isn't getting anything out of it. I don't think he could even learn a decent trade. And he's an awful bully. We've got another boy here, Arnie, and he's a good boy, he'll be going back to his mother as soon as she's on her feet from a long sickness, and Eddy just torments him all the time. We asked the social worker last week to do something, make other arrangements for Eddy, we can't put up with him any longer."

"And where is he now?" asked Hackett.

"Oh, he'll be out in the garage playing with that old electric train set belonged to our youngest. The kind of thing a real little kid likes to do, and it's queer. He's queer. What you might call uncanny," said Mrs. Rodman uneasily. "Not right. He's fifteen, but to look at him you'd think he was a man."

They followed her out to find him, and they saw what she meant. When he stood up to face them from the miniature track laid out on the garage floor and the old cars and engines running round and round, they could estimate that Eddy was nearly six feet tall and heavily built. There was a fuzzy beard on his rather vacant face; he was more than physically mature. He looked at them without much expression. "Who are you?"

"We'd just like to talk to you, Eddy," said Galeano. "We understand you've got something pretty. A gold necklace."

His pale eyes turned sly but he didn't look frightened. "Has it got a red stone in it?" asked Hackett.

Eddy retired into thought for a long moment. Then he said, "I'll let you see it if you make her go away. It's all right to show it to you because you're boys, but she's a girl. You make her go away." Hackett nodded at Mrs. Rodman and she went out of the garage obediently.

"Now let's see it," said Galeano.

Eddy rummaged in his pants pocket and brought it out to display, a small heart-shaped gold locket with a garnet set in its center. The chain was broken where it had been wrenched away. "Where'd you get it, Eddy?" asked Hackett softly. "You can tell us, we're boys."

He laughed at them triumphantly. "I got if from that girl. Those boys at school, they can't do that to a girl, but I can. I did it before once with a dog and with a cat and I did it by myself but it was better doin' it to a girl, that was good. It was lucky I was there to see her come along. Everybody thought I was in the bedroom."

"Oh, my God," said Galeano under his breath. So now they knew, courtesy of Rhoda May Flannery. And after all the work they'd expended on it, it wasn't any of their business; he was fifteen.

They called in to Juvenile, and Sergeant Gleason came out to take him in. For the moment he was quite docile; he only balked when Hackett tried to take the locket from him. "He'll forget it when we get him settled in at Juvenile Hall," said Gleason. "I'll see it gets filed away as evidence."

There would be the psychiatric tests, the medical examinations, and he would probably end up in an institution like his mother, tucked away for other people's safety. Mrs. Rodman was crying softly to herself in her shabby living room, probably feeling sorry she hadn't been able to do more for Eddy, probably feeling sorry for Sandra Dale.

There wasn't much to discuss about it. It was raining again, and it was getting on for six o'clock.

"At least," said Galeano, "we can forget about all the rapists on file." By the time they dropped into the office briefly, only Higgins was there to hear about the case being broken; everybody else had taken off.

Hackett was tired as he started home, and here it was only the middle of the week. Maybe he needed some extra vitamins or something. He turned out of the lot onto San Pedro, heading for the Stack where all the freeways came together. At the second intersection down, Second Street, the light was against him and he put his foot on the brake. Then, as he came up to it, it changed to green and he stepped on the accelerator and eased into the intersection at about twenty-five. There was just one split second when he was just beginning to be aware of something off to his right, and then in one shocking blare of sound the world ended and everything fell away from him.

An unknown time later at least part of his mind came back to him and he tried to open his eyes. A great round face with glittering glasses as big as saucers was bent close above him, frighteningly. He tried to speak, but nothing came out.

"You take it easy," said a voice from nowhere. "We'll have you strung up in no time." Hackett's mind conveyed alarm and fright. Strung up? But we don't hang them in California, his mind told him. "I think he might as well go to sleep again until we've got this tended to," said the voice. "The concussion's nothing to worry about, very minor." A huge soft pad covered his face and his mind went away again.

It felt as if a very long time had passed when he came back again and opened his eyes. This time Angel was there, bending over him. She kissed him and said, "Welcome back, darling. You're going to be all right."

"What happened?" he asked fuzzily. His tongue felt too big for his mouth.

"Just a little accident, darling," said Angel. "I said you needed some rest. You're going to get it. About six weeks of it, and a lot of kind nurses waiting on you hand and foot. Especially foot. But you'll be fine. It's just a broken leg."

He tried to sit up and a firm hand from the other side pushed him down. "Take it easy," said Mendoza's voice. "They've got you strung up in traction, *chico*." He was grinning down at Hackett, looking pleased for some reason.

Hackett said faintly, "You needn't sound so damn happy about it."

Mendoza's grin broadened. "Well, if you had to run into an accident, Arturo, it might all have been for nothing. As it is, you've just broken another case. You got clobbered by the drunk in the Model A, and he's sleeping peacefully just down the hall."

NINE

HIS NAME WAS Ronald Obermeyer, and when he faced Mendoza and Higgins from the hospital bed next morning he wore a lugubrious expression. He had a broken ankle and a broken left arm, assorted bruises. He was a big heavy man in the forties with pendulous jowls and shaggy eyebrows. He said, "I sure hope that police officer isn't real bad hurt. I'm sure sorry about it."

"There was another accident a good deal more serious," said Mendoza.

Obermeyer's soft brown eyes filled with sudden weak tears. "I know," he said humbly. "I know. That was it. That little girl. I just felt so awful bad about that, saw about it in the paper, it was just a couple of lines on a back page. A little girl named Alice, and she was dead. It said where, and I knew it was me. I just felt terrible. I didn't tell Bill about it, he never knew until he came to see me last night and I figured I better tell him. It's just that I shouldn't ought to have come over here. I'm not used to driving in the city." They knew from the identification on him that he lived in Nevada. "Bill, he's my brother, I come over here to see him, we hadn't seen each other in a long while."

"And you no sooner got here than you got drunk and went for a joy ride in the antique car," said Higgins, "and killed the little girl."

"I just shouldn't ever try to drive in no city," said Obermeyer mournfully. "Over home, it don't make no never mind, there aren't any of these signals flash at you or nothing, maybe I'm carrying a little load but it don't matter I can't keep straight on the road home, there's nothin' to run into. Sure," he added proudly. "It's an antique all right. Fixed her up myself, engine and new paint and all, and she runs just fine, smooth and easy. They really built cars back then, not like they do now. But I been just awful sorry about the little girl. I don't know how it happened, I'd had maybe a couple more than I should have, I was at a bar somewhere. Bill, he works at night, at an eatery open all night for truckers, and there wasn't anything to do at his apartment. I was havin' a little trouble seein' the damn road, but I never saw that woman and little girl till I hit them, and I thought maybe I'd just knocked them down. I never knew the little girl was dead till I saw it in the paper.''

"You'll be up for voluntary manslaughter," said Higgins. "You're under arrest now. You'll be transferred to jail sometime this week."

He nodded sadly. "I figured. You know, I just felt so bad about it, every time I thought of that poor little girl I had to go out and tie one on again, try to forget about it.''

Outside in the corridor Mendoza laughed but Higgins just looked disgusted. "And we think people are getting smarter in every generation?" he said. "This damn stupid lout, killing the kid because he's drunk, so he has to get drunk again to forget it. My God, Luis, it's just fool luck he didn't kill Art.''

They had already applied for the warrant. Being privileged to bypass visiting hours, they dropped in to see Hackett and tell him about Obermeyer. Hackett was sitting propped up on pillows looking out at a drizzle or rain, and at the sight of him Higgins laughed. "They've got you hogtied, you're not going anywhere for a while," he said, surveying Hackett's leg elevated on pulleys.

"Nice you find it amusing, George," said Hackett coldly.

"Well, you've got to admit, Art, it makes a hell of a good story. Gallant L.A.P.D sergeant gets his man, even if he has to put himself into the hospital to do it.''

"I didn't know a damned thing about it until it happened," said Hackett with an unwilling grin. He heard about Obermeyer and just said, "Expectable. Just a lout.''

"One thing I will say," said Mendoza, "if it demonstrates anything it shows they don't build them like they used to. That Model A, I won't say it's in running condition, it'll need a new radiator, but it's in one hell of a lot better shape

than the Monte Carlo. He got you broadside and it's to-
taled, you'll have to junk it and use the insurance for a new
car."

"I know," said Hackett. "Angel was telling me. She says
she never did like that car and good riddance."

"You need anything?" asked Higgins. "Cigarettes,
something to read?"

"Oh, they're looking after me fine. Angel brought me
some clean pajamas, and she's getting me a lot of library
books this afternoon. I just hope to God they don't put
somebody in with me who wants the TV on all the time." At
the moment he was alone in the room. "I'm getting along
all right but I've got the feeling I'm going to be damned
bored before I'm on my feet again. And I'm sorry to leave
you shorthanded."

"Better bored than dead," said Mendoza. "You'll have
company, we'll all be around, Arturo."

THE OFFICE had taken the news about Eddy Kruger with
expectable resignation and satisfaction. "Of all the damned
flukes," said Calhoun, "after all the legwork we put into
it—" But it was gratifying to have that one cleared up,
however it had happened. Everybody was a good deal more
interested and concerned about Hackett.

Calhoun and Wanda, having caught the new homicide
first, Julia Camacho, would be working that. Grace and
Galeano, Palliser and Landers, freed of hunting the rapists, spread out on the hunt in the billiard parlors for Gibbons. That afternoon Higgins was just finishing up the
paperwork on the gang members—they'd never pin anybody down for those killings—when Butterfield called back,
the Chief of Police over in Dateland. Mendoza came to listen in and Higgins punched the amplifier.

"—Just as we figured," said Butterfield, "there's not a
sign. I even took a dog out there, I've got a redbone hound
could track a gnat on a cold trail to hell and back, but
there's nothing. The way I told you, I figure the coyotes
found the baby. Leeper said he just left it there, alive. The
coyotes would have found it inside a couple of hours, likely

before it was dead, and they wouldn't leave even the bones. Makes you sick to think of."

"Well, we didn't expect anything else," said Higgins grimly.

"Just thought I'd let you know we looked," said Butterfield.

Ten minutes later a lab report came down, the report on Leo Putzel's apartment, and Mendoza said, "About time." He looked it over, passed it on to Higgins. There was this and that in it that might be relevant. Chester Rieger's prints had been picked up on the coffee table and a straight chair. But he'd been in the apartment before, and there was no knowing when he might have left them. No other prints had been picked up at all except Putzel's own, on the used glass, most of the furniture, the TV set. All the bloodstains were type O. And that was all the lab had to say about the apartment; there was nothing remarkable about the place relevant to the crime. Ordinary clothes in the closet, ordinary belongings around, nothing else. The Bergens had called yesterday about getting in there; by this morning the lab would have finished and taken the seal off the door.

"Where the hell is the autopsy report?" asked Mendoza.

"They get backlogged sometimes," said Higgins. "It'll be in eventually."

About noon, as they were thinking of going out for lunch, the office was invaded by a mountainous female with an incredible amount of black hair arranged in a high pompadour, a lavish amount of makeup, arrayed in a voluminous purple dress and stilt-heeled shoes. She was trailed by a thin young man, and was spouting alternate Spanish and English. "Who in God's name is that?" asked Mendoza, eyeing her progress fascinatedly.

Calhoun got up from his desk and said, "It's got to be Mama, of course. On the Camacho woman."

"I won't even offer to translate," said Mendoza, regarding her with awe. "You and Wanda are on your own." He took Higgins by the arm and fled.

ARNOLD SPANGLER had come in about ten o'clock to make a statement as requested. He had been frank. "I'd be telling a lie to say I could recognize the man. Those are damned good binoculars but they can't perform miracles. I never got a look at his face, he had his back to me. She was facing me. And as for size, my God, I was looking down at him, I couldn't begin to estimate his height. The best I can do for you, he was medium built, not fat or thin, and he wasn't wearing a hat, he had dark hair."

"And he hadn't been with the woman long before he grabbed her by the throat?" asked Calhoun.

"He couldn't have been. I'd been panning the glasses around, and when I came back to that bench the first time he was sitting there with her. I panned around some more, it couldn't have been over a minute, and when I got back there again he had her by the throat. Damndest thing I ever saw," said Spangler. "But of course as far as he could see there wasn't a soul around, he wouldn't have had any idea that anybody could see him."

"No, it was a funny kind of coincidence," said Calhoun. "It's just bad luck you never saw his face."

"What more do you want?" asked Wanda reasonably. "If it wasn't for Mr. Spangler's binoculars she might not have been found for a couple of days. Not many people go wandering around MacArthur Park."

"Well, that's true enough," said Calhoun. "Praise heaven for small mercies."

"I think he was wearing navy pants and jacket," said Spangler, "but I couldn't swear they weren't black."

Wanda had typed up a statement and he had signed it. And now they had Mama. Mama had turned out to be Mrs. Inez Ortiz, and she spoke good enough English, if accented, when she wanted to. She poured a flood of repetitious information at them. They heard how Julia, certainly the best daughter a woman ever had—"and Juan can tell you too, he is my youngest, Julia's brother—"had been raised like a lady, a good virtuous girl, used to nice things, and she was ambitious, she wished to make something better of herself, she had come to the city, this was five years ago when she was twenty, she had taken a course at a beauty school, to be a lady's hairdresser. But it was a hard world for virtuous beautiful girls, and all the positions she had found—¡ay de mí!—the way she was put upon! Standing on her feet for long hours, and the continual demands and orders from the cruel shop owners, such terrible women, always angry at the girls who worked for them because they did not work harder, no sympathy, no kindness. It was Julia do this and Julia do that every hour, it was insupportable. Every place Julia had worked it was the same, orders, orders, they expected her to work until she dropped exhausted, and she had worked at five, six, seven places but it was all the same. And naturally, being such a beautiful girl Julia had had many admirers, many young men had wanted to marry her.

Mama took a breath and Juan said from the chair beside her, "She was too choosy. Wasn't so many, what I heard."

She admonished him with a glance. But everyone knew that such girls as Julia were too trusting, knew little of the world, and that was as it should be. In the end she had married this Camacho, this cheapskate, this bum, who told her he had a good position and earned fine money, and how did that turn out? Mama paused dramatically and proceeded to tell them. Imagine, he worked in a garage, dirty all the time from fixing cars, and he expected Julia to live in a very tiny, cheap apartment with poor old furniture, to wash his filthy clothes, and he complained that she did not cook better, did not scrub and clean and polish like a housemaid. And then the baby had come, the precious grandson, and Carlos grew even worse. He said she did not take proper care of the baby, as if Julia was a bad mother, imagine. And so Julia had left him and his incessant orders, and a lawyer had got for her a paper which said Carlos must pay her money every month. But he did not always pay, and in any case it was not enough for her to live on properly. He was always calling, coming to see her, to say he could not afford even that much money, it was again unsupportable. Julia had had such bad luck in life, it was terrible to think.

Mama took another breath and Juan said, "Made her own bad luck, ask me."

Mama quelled him again. And now without doubt it was this monster who had murdered her, the mother of his son, so that he might stop paying her any money at all. It was villainous, it was beyond wickedness, the good virtuous Julia who had never harmed a soul and who without any doubt was now enjoying the delights of heaven in the company of all the good saints.

Wanda had made several efforts to stem the flow, and now she said loudly, cutting across the flood of words, "Do you know where he works?"

How indeed should Mama know that, she had seen the villain but once, at the wedding, and had thought then he looked like a bad man and not a proper husband for the sweet Julia, but girls would go their own way. And where, where was the precious grandson? He must be given to her at once, dear Julia's little son, to be given a good bringing up—it was not to be supposed that his wicked father should wish to take him, but if he tried to do so Mama would do battle until she drew her last breath. Where had the police taken him, where?

Calhoun wrote down the address of Juvenile Hall and handed it to Juan. "If you have the papers to prove the relationship, they'll let you have the baby."

Juan nodded at them and began to urge her to her feet. She panted heavily, hoisting herself out of the chair. She was still talking volubly when she got to the door. Juan paused in the doorway, looked back, and said, "Last I heard, it was the Acme Garage on Vermont." He went out after her.

Wanda and Calhoun looked at each other and started to laugh.

MENDOZA AND HIGGINS came back from lunch at two o'clock and there was a Manila envelope on Higgins' desk. He looked at the typewritten label on it and said, "Finally, the autopsy on Putzel. Now maybe we can get somewhere." He slit it open and took out the stapled sheets. "If you ask me, that Rieger is all ready to crack. He's running scared. He's the only one had a reason to have a fight with Putzel, he was there that night, and—" He had been running an eye down the report, and now he said blankly, "What the hell. What the hell do they mean, natural causes?" He let Mendoza take the report, snatched up the phone. "Rory, get me the Coroner's office!" Put through, he demanded the doctor who had signed the report, Cox. After some delay he got him. He punched the amplifier for Mendoza's benefit. "Listen, what the hell are you talking about, that autopsy report on Putzel? Natural causes hell, he had a fight with somebody and got knocked on the head—"

"Sorry to have got delayed on that," said Cox. "We've had quite a few stiffs in lately from all over the county. Well, that's the story. The man died of a heart attack, in lay language."

"Don't give me that," said Higgins. "The place was a shambles, anybody could see there'd been a violent struggle, furniture knocked over, blood on the rug—"

"Yes, that would be natural," said Cox.

Mendoza said from Higgins' other side, "He puts it sometime on Wednesday. A week ago today."

"Wednesday!" said Higgins. "But we know Rieger was there on Tuesday night. What the hell, a heart attack? With the place obviously showing there'd been a fight—"

"I can't help what your deductions may have been," said Cox. "That's what happened. Any time between nine A.M. and nine P.M. last Wednesday, I can't pin it down closer because we didn't see him for four days or so. It was a heart attack. Unless the man was a heavy drinker and apt to be drinking in the morning—and I doubt that, there was no sign of it—I'd say it was in the evening. There was a small amount of whiskey in the stomach, and he'd had a meal about three hours before he died. It'd be my guess that he was sitting peacefully having a little drink when it hit him. It would have caused sudden intense pain at first, he'd have realized there was something wrong with him and probably tried to get up and call for help. He'd have felt dizzy, and in trying to reach the phone or whatever it's very likely he'd have knocked over some furniture, fallen against something and got that gash in his scalp."

"Well, I will be damned," said Higgins. "The phone was in the kitchen and he was in the middle of the living room."

"Yes, I can see that happening," said Cox. "He may have found it impossible to reach the phone, tried to make for the front door and call for help instead." And Higgins remembered suddenly that Griggs had found the body because the apartment door had been open. Putzel staggering around, getting the door open, finding nobody around, maybe making another try for the phone and collapsing finally on the way.

"Well, I will be damned," he said again. "We thought we had a murder all figured out."

Cox laughed. "Sorry to disrupt your ideas, but there it is."

Mendoza began to laugh as Higgins cut the connection. "We can't even say it's one for the books, George. We've both seen corpses before who died like that. Preconceived notions, both Griggs and the daughter handed us Rieger on a plate. So we can write that one off, and Mr. Rieger can stop worrying."

Bruce Mallory hadn't returned to the North Hollywood apartment yet.

WANDA AND CALHOUN found the Acme garage on Vermont after lunch. Carlos Camacho worked there but he had called in sick today.

The owner was a phlegmatic middle-aged man named Pete Barnes. After studying the badges, he said, "Ask me, Carlos don't have the flu, he's probably got a hangover. Not that he's a lush, and I hope he won't turn into one, but he's been having a few lately—which he never did before, but sometimes a couple of drinks helps a fellow." He spat on the garage floor. "It beats all, what hell a female can play with a man. Now me and my old lady, we had a look at each other and all that while back and I liked the look of her and I guess she thought I was a fairly good bet too, and we been married twenty-eight years come January and get along just about all right. Raised three good kids. But some people are just unlucky, I guess. That girl Carlos married, I only saw her once but I heard all about her. Carlos is a good guy, not exactly the kind to set the world on fire like they say but a good steady worker, reliable, and a nice guy. He sure let himself in for trouble when he married that one." Unexpectedly, after a moment's thought, he asked, "Either of you ever read a fairy story called The Fisherman's Wife?" Wanda nodded. "Well, she was one like that. Never satisfied. She could have married a millionaire and still complained she didn't have everything she wanted. And she kept their place like a pigsty, couldn't be bothered to clean up, dirty dishes all over, even the baby not taken decent care of. Listen," said Barnes, "I'll tell you something." They had, of course, told him why they were asking questions. "I sure as hell don't approve of murder, I don't figure there could ever be a really good enough reason for killing anybody, but if that girl got herself murdered like that and it was Carlos did it, I could understand it. She was driving the poor guy crazy, what she'd done to him. About four months ago she up and left him, and she got a lawyer to fix it—it was something about a legal separation—so he had to pay her money every month. It was more than he could afford, three-quarters of his salary, and he had to live himself, you can see that. He's been feeling kind of desperate about it and you can see why." It wasn't any news to them; they had gotten the picture of Julia from Mama. "It's a funny thing in a way but natural to a man," said Barnes. "He was in love with her all right when he married her, she was a pretty enough girl, but after a while that kind of goes away from a man, just being in love, and it's more important that it's comfortable at home and a decent hot dinner on the table. A man's tired, he comes home from work, and you can't eat a pretty face." He rubbed his nose thoughtfully. "My wife never held a job outside, neither of us wanted her to and I make enough, we get along. But I always figure, it's a kind of mutual bargain. You each got something to put into a partnership. If she don't want an outside job, she's got a regular job at home. Take care of the house, the meals, the kids—though that's part of the partnership too, and how Audrey'd have managed those three hell-raisin' boys without me, God knows." He chuckled.

"Do you have an address for him?" asked Calhoun.

Barnes spat again. "Yeah, but it won't do you any good. He's moved. Couple days ago. He told me he couldn't afford the rent even for the one room he had, where he could make coffee and warm stuff up on a hot plate. He was moving into some boarding house where he could get a room and two meals a day for about the same price. It's a damned shame. He couldn't even afford to have his hair cut when he needed to. He'd had to give up smoking, he's been bringing just a hot dog for lunch, eating it cold."

"Well, I suppose he'll show up at work sometime," said Calhoun. "We'd be obliged if you'd let us know."

"Sure," said Barnes. "There has to be a law, and there has to be police, and I don't approve of murder. I'll let you know. But I feel damned sorry for Carlos."

Back in the car Calhoun said, "And damn it, so do I, Wanda. These rapacious females."

"The Fisherman's Wife," said Wanda, and laughed. "I hadn't thought of that one in years. She got her comeuppance all right. But if it was Carlos—"

"Oh, yes, we'll have to pull him and charge him," said Calhoun.

WHILE THE BUSINESS of the office went on, necessarily, all of them would make occasion to visit Hackett; he wasn't going to lack for cigarettes, snacks, reading matter, or company. But he felt rather lackadaisical that afternoon and abandoned one of the books Angel had brought, an interesting true-life adventure about photographing wildlife in India, and lazily drifted off to sleep. He had heard about Leo Putzel from Higgins, and something about Camacho from Wanda, who had dropped in on her way to lunch with a carton of cigarettes, and he had a long and vivid dream in which he divined the answer to the mystery of Louise Cannaday. It was all beautifully clear in the dream. She had foiled The Fisherman's Wife of her last wish, the rulership of the world, and had been struck down herself by inscrutable fate. It was all perfectly clear, and there could never be any charge, the case would have to be filed away and forgotten, and he must remember to tell Luis so he could stop worrying about it.

But just as he had gotten it all straightened out in his mind, a hand as inexorable as God's took hold of his arm, and a voice said briskly, "Now here's a nice warm eggnog for you, Sergeant, mid-afternoon snack," and he woke up fully to see Nurse Ellsworth's long plain horse-face looking down at him. On reflection he decided that the dream was something less than a revelation.

ABOUT ONE O'CLOCK on Thursday morning Bill Moss, cruising down Glendale Boulevard on regular tour, spotted a body in the glare of the headlights. He stopped, got out and looked at it to decide whether it was a hit-run, a derelict dead of probably natural causes, or what. It was the body of a man looking to be in the thirties, quite nattily dressed in a navy-blue suit, white shirt, and flashily colored tie. There didn't seem to be a mark on him. He was lying on the sidewalk in front of a large store plastered with signs advertising a carpet sale. Moss logged it in his report and called for the morgue wagon, all he could do. He wasn't very curious about it; leave it to the detectives. He went on with the tour, and about an hour later one of the dispatchers sent him to an address on Sixth.

It was an old building, three stories high, and there were two men waiting for him on the sidewalk outside. They were both young.

"You can't do anything about it," said one of them as Moss came up from the squad. "He's long gone, but I says report it anyway," and that was to Moss. "Barry here, he's fit to be tied, and man, who's to blame him? A hundred and ten bucks is a hundred and ten bucks." He was a long, tall, thin man with straggly blond hair, and he was dressed in western sports clothes: tan pants and shirt and boots and Stetson. The other one was a small man, only about five-three, rather good-looking, with regular features and sleek black hair; he was wearing the cowboy dress too: nail-studded blue shirt, tight black pants, and a big Stetson. He was exhibiting a colorful vocabulary.

"Calm down, Barry, there's nothing you can do about it now, for God's sake, just tell the cop what happened." All around them on the sidewalk here were boxes and cases, as well as a bass drum in a canvas case and what looked like a folding card table with a row of wooden bars on top of it.

"All right, for God's sake," said the little one. He was pressing a bandanna to one temple. "We finished playing the gig at two A.M., as per usual. There's some kind of ordinance, shut down the playing at two A.M."

"Up there," said the other one helpfully, nodding at the building. "Top floor, dance hall. It gets rented by private clubs, fraternal organizations, that kind of thing. It's one of our regular gigs, Wednesdays once a month, the Moose Lodge. Their hall isn't big enough for a dance. We're Greg Young's Country-Western Cowboys. I'm the piano player, name of Iverson."

"All right," said Moss. "What happened?"

Iverson said doubtfully, "I don't know if you know anything about combos. It's a funny thing, kind of a fact of life you might say. The piano player, he's usually pretty big, he hasn't got a thing to carry, the piano's already there. The drummer, he's got all the traps to carry, he's always a little guy, like Barry here. Barry O'Leary. You can see it all. Bass, case for the snare and traps, bells, cymbals, the portable marimba."

"So?" said Moss.

"Well, like usual I'm going to give Barry a hand to carry all the stuff down to his car. After we finish the gig. Everybody was leaving, rest of the guys, and Barry went down with the bass. And I got into a little discussion with Greg, he's our arranger of course, over the treatment of *Stormy Weather*. I wanted a stronger lead into the vocal, I showed him what I meant at the piano and we kicked it back and forth some. We talked it over with Retta, she's one of the vocalists, and guitar, and she agreed with me, so then I picked up the snare and trap case and went downstairs to the street and here's Barry out cold in the gutter. He got jumped by a mugger.''

"And a goddamned miracle nobody put a foot through the bass," said Barry furiously. "The goddamned black bastard—I saw him all right, the entrance lights were still on—he jumped me from behind, but I got a look at him before he whammed me over the head the second time—He was black as the ace of spades and about six feet high, and that time he knocked me out cold—I came to and first I checked the bass, and Iverson comes up and says am I all right, and then I find about five bucks on me, the hell with that, but my new boots! A hundred and ten bucks, and that was wholesale, they'd be double that retail—they were a custom job. And why the hell I can't begin to figure out—" Barry was nearly inarticulate with fury. "He was a big bastard like I say, six feet anyway, he must take a size eleven or twelve. And I wear a custom size five, he couldn't get his big toe in them! And I'd only had them two weeks!"

That offbeat mugger again, thought Moss. If he hadn't felt especially curious about the dead man, he was curious about this, but he wasn't about to try to figure it out.

MENDOZA WAS ANNOYED on Thursday morning by a long-winded deputy D.A. who wanted to discuss Eddy Kruger at length. There wasn't any point in that until the psychiatric evaluation had been done, and after that let the lawyers thrash it out; the police job was over. When he finally got rid of the man he felt he'd wasted most of the morning.

Nearly everybody else in the office had switched over to the hunt through the billiard parlors for Gibbons, armed and dangerous and on the most-wanted list; Gibbons they'd like to locate.

But before he went out to early lunch he tried that apartment in North Hollywood, and this time the phone was picked up at the other end, and a carefully modulated voice said, "Bruce Mallory speaking." Mendoza replaced the phone gently.

It had stopped raining, if temporarily. He had a sandwich at the nearest coffee shop and headed for the Valley.

At the pink-painted door of the apartment he faced a startlingly handsome young man: Mallory was tall and willowy, with beautifully chiseled Greek features and a head of golden-blond hair just touching the open collar of his elegantly cut sport shirt. The rest was a poem in matching colors: the shirt beige, the slacks chestnut brown, the shoes polished dark-brown moccasins.

"And what can we do for you, friend?" asked Mallory genially, beaming down at Mendoza. He had a beautiful voice too, deep and soft.

Mendoza did no beating around the bush. Shock tactics, he had decided, might be the best way to go. He thrust out the badge. "I'd like to ask you a few questions," he said brusquely, "about Mrs. Louise Cannaday. May I come in?"

Mallory looked only slightly taken aback. He stepped back from the door and Mendoza followed him in, to a square open living room furnished in Danish modern but with overtones of simple shambles. There were LP records spread over the floor on all sides of a huge blond stereo, a card table with cards scattered on it in the middle of the room; the only wall decoration was a huge poster, unframed, illustrating a circus scene. "Do I seem to recognize that name?" wondered Mallory vaguely.

"Well, do you? Mrs. Louise Cannaday. Did you by any chance see her a week ago Friday? Were you at Maxime's restaurant with her that night?" Mendoza rather agreed with Hackett that Mallory might be the likely owner of that red velvet vest, but surely Delfino couldn't have missed the movie-star looks, or could he? The disparity in age, even as nice-looking as she had been? Mallory wouldn't be over thirty.

"Oh, I don't think so," said Mallory. "I really don't think so. Ann, we haven't been at Maxime's lately, have we?"

She came in from the kitchen, a brisk dark young woman with a leggy figure and a face like a model's, all angles and planes rather than pretty. She was wearing skin-tight black pants and a leopard-skin printed shirt. "Not likely, darling, with their prices. Why? And who's the natty Latin gent?"

Mendoza showed her the badge. "He seems to think I was," said Mallory. "With some woman—I don't take other women out, do I?"

"You'd better not," she said pleasantly.

"Mrs. Louise Cannaday," said Mendoza, watching them. Enlightenment came into her eyes but she was silent.

"I do seem to know the name." Mallory gave him a sudden sunny smile. "Oh, of course, she is on the list, isn't she? One of those dear generous appreciative fans." Ann sat down, watching Mendoza. Her eyes were surprisingly intelligent. "How much had she pledged, darling? I know you have it all at your finger's end, efficient as you are."

"I think it was two hundred dollars," she said placidly.

"The dear creature," said Mallory. "Not a very great sum, but something." He bent a dreamy smile on Mendoza. "You see, my dear policeman, publishers are a crass lot of materialists. They are only interested in publishing the kind of veritable trash which will sell to those readers unable to appreciate anything else. Poetry is quite beyond the pale, they simply will not look at it. We are planning to bring out an anthology of my best work, but with the state of the arts as it is, I'm afraid it is hardly a commercial prospect."

"In other words," said Ann, "we have to pay to have it printed. It's called subsidy publishing."

"And several generous admirers have already agreed to contribute," said Mallory complacently.

"And Mrs. Cannaday was one of them?" asked Mendoza.

"Yes, that's right," said Ann.

"As I recall, if I place her correctly, a rather young and undeveloped soul," said Mallory. "Well-meaning, of course. She had sent me several of her own efforts. Quite impossible, of course, but showing some slight sensitivity." He had very long slender hands which he used effectively on gesture.

"Had you been corresponding with her, Mr. Mallory?" asked Mendoza.

He looked at Mendoza through folded hands resting on his brow. "Oh, I believe we had exchanged a few letters. As was the case with several other admirers. Alas, not too many. There are so few souls capable of appreciating the true effort to grasp the impossible dream. I always answer fan mail, it is only courteous."

"And potentially profitable?" asked Mendoza. "That is, concerning the anthology?"

He laughed musically. "Oh, come now, I don't batten off admirers like that. It is simply that it is important to me, to my career, to have my work put before that portion of the public who may appreciate it. It's no use doing things by halves, the format and binding must be of top quality, and that will cost quite a bit of money. Naturally anyone who is interested in the project we encourage to make themselves part of it by contributing. I'm sure even a policeman can appreciate that."

"And by the way," said Ann, "why is a policeman asking questions about this woman?"

"You see, she's dead," said Mendoza. "Probably murdered. We're looking at the people she knew."

Mallory shut his eyes and shuddered. "Death," he said. "So very crude and irrevocable. I don't like to discuss it."

"But my dear good man," said Ann, "we didn't know her. She doesn't live here—some place in the midwest. I'd have to look up her letters—I act as Bruce's secretary, you know. She simply liked his poetry. She'd written four or five times, I think, it was mostly about the anthology. She was going to contribute two hundred dollars."

"And I expect we'll never see that now," he said. "What a pity."

"Neither of us had ever laid eyes on the woman."

"Didn't you?" said Mendoza. "A week ago Friday? Perhaps she called and said she was here unexpectedly, would like to meet Mr. Mallory?"

She shook her head. "Nothing like that. We never met her. Was she here?" Her gaze was limpid and clear. "A week ago Friday? I think that was the day we went to a party at Linda and Tom's."

Mendoza's opinion of Mrs. Louise Cannaday had gone down slightly in the last few minutes. Mallory was so obviously the conceited poseur on the face of it. But his business was supposed to be words, doubtless he could be charming and persuasive on paper, and if he'd sent her a portrait of himself—any woman might have succumbed to that handsome boyish facade. For all Mendoza knew he might even be a good poet. But when he came to think of it, having met Mallory, why should she have gone out of her way to meet him while she was here? If she had had more time, possibly; but she'd had only that Friday night, the Saturday to be spent with Adele Mowbray, the Sunday, as far as she knew. It was much likelier that she had agreed to meet Lemoyne. And come to that, why should Mallory have gone out of the way to meet her, even if she had called him, if he knew she was here? She had not really been a foolish woman, though her son and Adele Mowbray would probably think she had been in subsidizing the poet even with such a modest amount. It had without doubt been clear enough to Mallory and Ann that they wouldn't get any more from her. For a fleeting moment Mendoza wondered just how much had been pledged by how many foolish women who were convinced that Mallory was a new Keats or Swinburne. And suppose they had met? Suppose, and now he didn't think it was at all likely, that Mallory had been the man with her at Maxime's? It took a wild flight of imagination to envision any reason for a quarrel between them, for a physical struggle. It just wouldn't make sense. Damn it, the more he thought round the thing, the more he came back to Lemoyne. That felt right emotionally, and nothing else did.

He looked at the pair with distaste. They were no help to him, and he didn't like either of them. His interest in Mallory had begun to evaporate almost as soon as he saw the man. From a distance Mallory might be persuasive, but Mendoza had the sudden irrational conviction that if Louise Cannaday ever had met him, she would have seen through the arrogant empty front too.

WANDA LARSEN was typing a second report on Julia Camacho on Friday morning when she had a phone call. It was
Pete Barnes, the garage owner. He said, "I've got something here I guess you and your partner ought to see. It's a
letter from Carlos."

"We'll be right over," said Wanda and collected Calhoun from an argument with Rory Farrell over football
teams.

When they got to the garage on Vermont, Barnes met
them at the door to the office. The garage was a thriving
place; he had three other employees. He said soberly, "I
found this Scotch-taped to the door when I came to open up.
I don't so much like the sound of it."

Neither, when they had read it, did Wanda or Calhoun.
It had been enclosed in a cheap envelope with nothing written on it. Inside was a single sheet of paper torn from a tablet, with a few lines in ballpoint. Carlos Camacho had
surprisingly neat and literate handwriting.

"Dear Pete, things are just too much for me now. You
know how it's been with Julia and me. She has made all my
trouble. Of course I would always want to see the boy was
taken care of, but she is not a good mother to him, and I
can't see how I can do that now. The money is running out
and I don't know which way to turn. I have tried to talk to
her but she won't listen. She doesn't seem to understand that
you can't get blood out of a stone and I don't have any more
to give her. Now about Julia, I want to tell you that I did a
very bad thing yesterday, something I should not have done
no way, but I just got too mad all of a sudden and the next
thing I knew it was done and there's no help for it, it's done
and nobody can change that. I am not sorry for it either, I
know I ought to be but I'm not. So I am getting out of this.
I don't know where I might go or what I might do, I haven't
got much money, but maybe I can find a place where I can
make a better go of things. And if I can't, I guess there's
nobody to care much if I get out of things all the way.
You've been good to me and been a friend while I worked
here, and I just wanted to say good-bye. Carlos."

"It kind of sounds as if he's admitting it," said Barnes. "Killing Julia. If he does just say, a bad thing."

"Yes," said Wanda. "Do you have any idea where he might go?"

"I couldn't have a guess," said Barnes. "I know he was raised right here, his father got killed in some accident when he was just a kid, and he and his mother had some hard times while he was growing up. He thought a lot of his mother, he talked about her sometimes, she seems to have been a fine woman, did her best by him. But she got this leukemia and died, it was just before he came to work for me, about four years ago. You know, he's only twenty-six. Good steady reliable worker." Barnes looked away suddenly and blinked hard. "You know, it's a fool thing, but I can't help but think of that cat."

"What cat?" asked Wanda.

"Well, she's our cat now. I like a nice cat and so does Audrey. Named her Emily, she's kind of a pretty calico. She was just a stray, just a little kitten, she first started to hang around here, and Carlos used to feed her pieces of his lunch. Well, of course I fed her too. But when he was having it so tough with Julia, the money and all, he couldn't afford a decent lunch, like I said, and he'd apologize to her because he didn't have anything for her. *Gatita*, he called her, I guess that means little cat in Spanish. He was mighty glad when I took her home to Audrey, so she'd have a home and somebody to take care of her."

"There aren't any other relatives?" asked Wanda.

"No. His mother's sister, she's a nun somewhere, but I don't think he knew where."

"Does he have a car?" asked Calhoun.

"You'd find out from the D.M.V.," said Barnes. "It's an old two-door Chevy, light tan, the D.M.V.'ll give you the plate number."

"You know, Barnes," said Calhoun, "if he killed her it was murder, and he really doesn't deserve much sympathy. You said yourself, there can't be any reason good enough for murder."

"And I guess that's right," said Barnes. "All I say is, the Good Man had something to say about mercy too. If Carlos killed that bitch of a girl I could understand it."

Back at headquarters Calhoun got the plate number from Sacramento and put out an eight-state A.P.B. for Carlos Camacho and his car.

So far none of the legwork at the billiard parlors had turned up a smell of Howard Gibbons.

THE NIGHT WATCH were all on. They sat around waiting for calls, and the police frequency muttered in the background. There was a pile-up on the Ventura Freeway. At seven-thirty a dispatcher sent up a call: missing child, suspected kidnapping.

Technically they didn't have to go out on that right away, until the suspicion was confirmed. But with Sandra Dale in mind, and possible other things, Conway and Schenke rolled on it, just in case. At an address on Vendome they found Gibson beside the squad looking disgusted, and a woman in floods of tears on the sidewalk outside the apartment building. "I'm sorry as hell I routed you out," said Gibson, "I'd just started to listen to her."

"Oh-oh-oh," she was sobbing. "I just know he's been kidnapped, he's been gone over two hours and he said he'd be right back, he knows how I worry—Oh-oh-oh, my little boy, I just know something's happened to him—"

"Now try to calm down, ma'am," said Conway. "Try to give us a description of him. How old is he?"

The tears flooded anew. "Oh, he's tw-tw-twenty-nine," she panted. "And he never even told his wife where he was going—"

"Oh, for God's sake," said Conway.

"I thought I'd let you walk into it," said Gibson.

Two minutes later a young man came walking up and told her not to be more of a fool than she could help. "I was just talking with the neighbors down the street," he apologized. "Sorry she turned in a false alarm."

It was slightly funny when they thought about it. An hour later they got another call, to a heist, and Piggott and Conway took it. It was a small shopping mall close in on Hoover, a cluster of shops around a good-sized parking lot. Evidently most of the shops had just closed or were closing, only a few cars left in the lot, presumably belonging to the shop owners. The place that had been held up was one of the largest, a liquor store with a glittering display behind a big plate-glass window. The owner, a man about forty with a long nose and a high voice, was excited.

"It's the first time I ever got held up—he came in just as I was starting to close—a big guy, and he had the hell of a big gun, and he took all the money from the register and he took two fifths of Scotch off the shelf there—"

"Oh, he did," said Conway, and hauled out the mug shot of Gibbons. "Does this look like him?"

"That's *him*," said the owner, astonished and impressed. "You already know him? That's him, I'd swear on a stack of Bibles—and he was drunk as a lord, I was afraid he'd let the gun go off without meaning to—"

They calmed him down. They didn't tell him he was lucky, that Gibbons could be hair-trigger. He agreed to come in and make a statement in the morning. It was about thirty minutes later when Piggott and Conway came out to the parking lot, deserted now except for Conway's car and another in the next aisle over. There was a full moon sailing a clear sky, and the arc lights in the lot were still on.

"Damn it," said Conway. "I wish we had a better lead on this bastard. What are you looking at?"

"I suppose that's the store owner's car," said Piggott. He started over toward it, and he had a hand on the gun in the shoulder holster. "There are a lot of gray cars around. Light blue too."

"So what?" said Conway.

"Just curious," said Piggott. The driver's door was hanging all the way open. Piggott bent and looked into the middle-aged gray sedan, and then he started to laugh. Conway came to look over his shoulder. "I don't think we'll need the cuffs, Rich."

Sprawled behind the wheel of the car, Howard Gibbons was passed out cold, a fifth of Scotch still halfway clutched in one hand, dribbling liquor all over his shirt and pants. He was wearing a faint smile.

"For the love of almighty God," said Conway.

Piggott was still laughing. "'Wine is a mocker, strong drink is raging,'" he gasped. "Isn't it the truth. Let's take him in before he wakes up. Not that I think he will any time in the next eight hours."

TEN

MENDOZA AND PALLISER met Fothergill at the police garage on Saturday morning. Fothergill was still saying, "I don't believe it, damndest thing I ever heard of, but thank God we picked him up." The old car Gibbons had been driving was an arsenal: there were four .38 revolvers and a sawed-off shotgun in the trunk, and there had been two more .38's on him. There was also a couple of hundred dollars in cash in the glove compartment. In the breast pocket of his shirt had been a receipt for rent at an address on Bronson Avenue, which proved to be a small apartment building.

"Good Lord," said the apartment manager, looking at the mug shot, "he's a dangerous crook? I'll be damned, I'd never have suspected it. He took the apartment last month, said he'd just come out to California and was looking for a job. Nice quiet tenant. This is one for the books."

Reportedly Gibbons was being a nice quiet prisoner, waking up with a hangover in jail. The F.B.I. had first jurisdiction on him, and he'd be transferred to a Federal prison when the red tape was wound up. It had been an anticlimax, but they were glad to have him under lock and key.

There would be arraignments coming up next week—the Leepers, Edna Bacon—for somebody to cover in court. It would be some time before Eddy Kruger saw the inside of a court room; he'd been taken out to the Norwalk psychiatric facility for examination. Frances Doolittle might be up for arraignment next week too. The courts were backlogged; it would be another while before those trials came up, after the indictments.

Mendoza got back to the office around mid-morning. He glanced over the night report and found another one just sent up from Traffic at the change of shift about the body

found on Glendale Boulevard. It might be nothing or
something. Palliser went over to the morgue to have a look
at it and reported that there might be something faintly interesting about it. "Wait for the autopsy report, find out
what killed him. He's just a young fellow, well dressed,
anonymous. Nothing on him but a couple of bucks, a pack
of cigarettes, and a bunch of keys. He didn't smell of
drink."

"More flotsam and jetsam," said Mendoza, uninterested.

"His prints are down at R. and I. If we've got him on file
we'll find out who he was anyway."

Mendoza was slightly more interested in the mugger.
"Now that one is offbeat, stealing boots and shoes yet,"
agreed Palliser, looking at the report, "and no way in God's
world to catch up to him. You don't suppose he's got a fe-
tish about shoes?"

"Who knows?" said Mendoza. "Even a street mugger
might be entitled to a sex phobia."

But with everything peaceful at the office, all the cases
demanding legwork and long hours cleaned up, they might
have expected something else to break. Things seldom
stayed peaceful around Robbery-Homicide. Late that afternoon reports began to come in thick and fast from
Traffic, some kind of major gang rumble up by Lincoln
Heights Reservoir, and Higgins, Palliser, and Grace went
out on that. They ended up doing the overtime, and all of
the night watch joined them. When the smoke was cleared
away there were four bodies, seven wounded carted off to
Emergency, and six assorted gang members in custody to
question. Nobody involved had any love for the cops, not
even the victims, and it would be like pulling teeth to get any
names, any facts. They would be days getting through the
paperwork on this, and in the end probably with very little
result; even if they came up with some definite evidence on
the actual killers, it would amount to charges of voluntary
manslaughter, if they were over eighteen. Two of the dead
ones and three of the wounded were minors, so a Juvenile
officer came out on it too.

Higgins got home that night dog-tired, and Mary brought him a drink. "Have you had anything to eat?"

"Snatched a sandwich about an hour ago. I just want to relax. These damned kids, just bands of savages. The whole thing was likely a fight over the dope, you should have seen what they were holding. Hard stuff as well as the pot, coke, and H."

"Did you get a chance to see Art today?"

Higgins yawned and laughed. "He's doing fine, sitting up in bed with nothing to do but read and look out the window. I could almost envy him, in for a nice long rest out of the rat race."

LATE SATURDAY AFTERNOON the word had come up from R. and I. The dead man's prints had been on file; he was Joseph Finlay, and had done a short stretch for burglary some years ago. On Sunday morning Mendoza sent a note about that down to Lieutenant Navarro in Burglary in case they knew any more about him, and just before noon Navarro showed up in Mendoza's office. "You don't mean to say little Joe's lying over in the morgue? That's kind of a shame, Mendoza. We'll miss him."

"So who was he?" asked Mendoza. "We don't know what he died of yet."

Navarro sat down and accepted a cigarette. "He wasn't a bad little guy. Did that stretch for one job, and as far as we know stayed straight ever since. He had a job as night security guard at an office building on Beverly. Of course he wasn't regular security, he couldn't have got clearance on account of his record, but they'd had some vandalism and wanted somebody there, kind of a night watchman. I recommended him myself when he asked me. It left him part of the day free and he used to roam around and pick up pieces of information for us."

"Oh, an informer," said Mendoza.

"Pretty useful one," said Navarro. "He didn't often drop in with something, or rather call it in, but when he did he usually got something accurate. I know he got quite a lot of stuff for Narco too."

"So maybe that's why he got taken off," said Mendoza.

"You don't know he was taken off," Navarro pointed out, "yet. But it might look that way. He was only about thirty-three, and he didn't drink much or dope—he was death on the dope, a real fanatic. Unless he had a heart attack or a stroke, which doesn't seem likely, it could be he was quietly taken off. You'll find out in due course."

"Did he have any relatives?" asked Mendoza.

"Sister. Perfectly respectable woman," said Navarro. "I can't give you an address for him, but she's unmarried and works for a big department store. Maybe she knows where he lived. Or his employers."

Landers and Galeano had drifted in to listen, and Landers said, "I'd take a bet on murder. Word always gets around about the informers."

"Well, I'll be interested in what you find out," said Navarro.

It was Landers who started out to follow it up; everybody else was out on the gang rumble, talking to all the gang members they could lay hands on, getting through the paperwork. The sister, Miss Amelia Finlay, was a decent homely woman about thirty who was genuinely grieved for her brother. "I know he got into that trouble that time, but he'd never done anything wrong since and he was always good to me. I don't know what to do about a funeral, I don't have much money saved, but maybe he had some." She could tell him where Finlay had lived, an apartment on Yucca Street in Hollywood, and Landers got to it late on Sunday. One of the keys found on Finlay unlocked the door, and Landers prowled around the place, went through the drawers. He didn't come up with anything. Finlay had evidently been too wise a bird to write down any of the information he collected for the police. There was a bank book; he had a savings account of nearly a thousand dollars. And he'd owned quite a few books, of surprising variety: anthropology, astronomy, history, and, curiously, palmistry and predictions. There was a modest collection of good clothes in the closet in the bedroom, and Landers went through all the pockets but came up with nothing more helpful than twenty-seven cents in change and the receipt for a library fine. There was a row of carports at one side of the building, and the sister had told him about Finlay's car, a two-door Plymouth. He looked, and it was there. Another of the keys unlocked it. Discouragingly, the car was very clean, and there was nothing in it but, correctly, the registration in the glove compartment together with a county map and a pocket flashlight. Nothing in the trunk but the spare tire.

Landers was annoyed. Well, if the man had been murdered—wait for the autopsy report—they could find out from Navarro and Goldberg about the latest pieces of information Finlay had passed on. Possibly somebody had wanted vengeance, if not an apprehended one sitting in jail, one of his pals. Thinking of Putzel, he decided to call it a day, wait to find out what had killed the man.

HIGGINS, STRUGGLING with the paperwork, was somewhat annoyed at Mendoza perched on one corner of his desk talking about Mallory and Lemoyne. From what he'd heard he didn't like either of them on Cannaday, and there just wasn't anywhere else to go on that one anyway. He typed, "Statement by Antonio Garcia, witness states he and Eduardo Feliz on—"

"And damn it," said Mendoza, "I would have thought she'd have seen through that bag of wind even by his letters, but even so, why should she have called him? Besides, when you think of it, she didn't have time. Did she?"

Higgins grunted and discovered he had typed, "Thirty-ninth of November, were on way to meet—" and reached for the eraser tape. "Go away and brood in private, Luis," he said, and the phone rang on his desk. He picked it up and said his name.

"I want to speak to Sergeant Hackett," said a male voice at the other end.

"I'm sorry, Sergeant Hackett's out of the office, I can take any message."

"The other one then, a guy named Mendoza, it's important, this is Delfino, I'm the bartender at Maxime's, if I could talk to him—" Higgins handed over the phone. He was close enough, and Delfino excited enough, that he could hear. "Listen, this is Delfino, you know I told you about the woman being here, the one got murdered? Well, I couldn't tell you much about the guy she was with, but he's back again! He's in here right now. I recognized him by that funny red vest. He's sitting right across from the bar with this other guy, I know it's the same one and I thought you'd want to know—"

"Thanks very much," said Mendoza, and slammed the phone down. "Don't tell me we're going to get a break at last? Come on, George, let's go and find out. I just hope he stays put until we get there." At that hour, with rush hour traffic starting to build, they made better time on surface streets; Mendoza got them out there in thirty minutes. They went into the bar. Delfino had been waiting for them and came up right away.

"He's been here about forty minutes, with the other guy. They came in just after we opened at four. I knew him right off, since you were here and told me about that dame got killed. They're right over there by the wall, they're both drinking margaritas. He doesn't look like a murderer, but I knew you'd want to know he was here."

Mendoza just nodded and started across the room, Higgins after him. The two men sitting at the banquette against the wall had the vague appearance of professional men. Both were dressed in conventional business suits. The smaller one looked to be in the fifties, gray-haired with a genial expression and gold-framed glasses. The other one was wearing the vest. He was younger, a tall man with a rather handsome face, a thick head of silver-gray hair. The vest, sounding so garish in description, was actually a rather austere affair of tapestry pattern, dark crimson predominating, and worn with a dark-gray suit, looked more distinguished than odd. Mendoza stood at the table between them and took out the badge.

"Excuse me, gentlemen," he said suavely, "but we'd like to ask you a few questions."

They both looked up. "Police," said the older one, sounding interested. "Questions? What about?"

"Would you mind giving us your names, please?"

"Not at all," and his nose was all but twitching with curiosity. "I'm Paul Blanchard," and he handed over a card. Below his name was a flowing script, Omega Films, Incorporated.

The man with the vest said stiffly, "Andrew Trulock. What's this all about?"

"Two weeks ago Friday night," said Mendoza, "you were here about eight o'clock with a woman, Mr. Trulock. With Mrs. Louise Cannaday. We'd like to ask you about your relationship with her."

Blanchard began to laugh. "Nemesis at last, Andy. I always suspected there was something under all that Puritan morality. How long have you been two-timing Joyce? Don't tell me it's one of your ingenue starlets, you've got better taste than that."

"Don't be a fool, Paul," said Trulock stiffly. "I'm afraid I don't know what you mean, Officers. Cannaday? I never heard of the woman."

"You were here with her," said Mendoza. "She was identified, and the bartender has just recognized you as the man who was with her."

"I still don't know her," said Trulock. "I don't know what you're talking about. What day did you say?"

Mendoza repeated that. "You see, Mr. Trulock, Mrs. Cannaday died later that night, and she was probably murdered. We'd like to know how you met her and where you went when you left here."

"My God," said Trulock, losing some of his austerity, "murder? I never heard of the woman, I don't know anything about her!"

"You're not serious," said Blanchard, "suspecting old Andy of murder? Not but what it might be good publicity, if nothing ever came of it. Make good headlines. Producer of new dramatic series arrested on suspicion."

"Oh, for God's sake, don't be an idiot," said Trulock. "This is ridiculous. That Friday night? That was the night

Joyce flew up to Sacramento. We did meet here for dinner. You remember I told you, Paul—her mother—''

"Oh, yes, I remember. You told me about it. Damn shame," said Blanchard perfunctorily.

Trulock looked back to Mendoza. "I was here with a woman that night, that's true enough. My wife. She got me at the studio about six-thirty, I'd been tied up there all day, we're just starting to shoot the episodes for the second season of *Ransome's Folly*." Both Mendoza and Higgins recognized that vaguely as one of the TV soaps. "She'd just gotten a wire from her sister, her mother had had a stroke and wasn't expected to live. Naturally she wanted to go up there to be with the family. She'd already got a reservation on the ten o'clock flight. So I suggested we meet here, and we did, she came in a cab with her luggage, we put it in my car, had a drink and dinner and then I took her to the airport and saw her off."

"I see," said Mendoza. "That's a rather specious story, Mr. Trulock, seeing that Mrs. Cannaday was identified as being here with you. At about the same time?"

"How would I know?" said Trulock. "Joyce met me here just before eight, and we left about nine for the airport. I don't know how you come up with this bullshit, I never heard of that woman, I didn't know her, she wasn't here with me that day or any day."

Blanchard was watching them with bright amused eyes. He said, "Just to put my two cents' worth in, I've known Andy for twenty years and he's a very moral fellow, wouldn't dream of cheating on his wife. I know the public, probably including the police, think of all us show business people as sex-mad dope addicts given to the orgies, and some of the young ones, maybe it's justified, but we're not all like that. Nothing would ever get done if we were all hopped up on coke all the time, you know."

"Look, for God's sake," said Trulock. "You can go and talk to my wife. She's at home now. She'll confirm all that." He wrote down an address on one of the cocktail napkins, pushed it over. "Go and ask her, she'll tell you."

"I just hope they'll be convinced," said Blanchard. "God, what headlines—but come to think of it, would it be good publicity? That's a pretty damned moral show, so far—slow. I've been telling you, you ought to get more sex into it."

As the next step on, Mendoza and Higgins went to see the wife, and Delfino looked disappointed as they left without arresting anybody. The address was in Beverly Hills, and turned out to be a palatial big stucco house on about half an acre on Summit Drive. A gardener was running a riding lawnmower over an expanse of lawn in front. Mendoza pushed the bell and a minute later the door opened. They took one look at the woman facing them and both began to laugh.

She looked back at them uncomprehendingly and annoyed. "May I ask what's so funny?"

Mendoza pulled himself together. "Mrs. Joyce Trulock?"

"Yes, that's me, what is it you want?"

"Nothing much," said Higgins. "Just a little confirmation." Joyce Trulock was younger than Louise Cannaday—she might be in the early forties—but otherwise she resembled her strongly. She was medium height and slim, a very handsome woman, and she had black hair with a striking streak of natural white up the side of a wide wave on the side where her hair was parted. She certainly bore a great resemblance to that photograph in the *Times*, and it wasn't surprising that Delfino had thought he recognized it.

"What are you talking about?" she asked in a bewildered voice. "Who are you?"

They told her, they got confirmation of exactly what Trulock had said. "And that," said Higgins on the way back downtown long after the end of shift, "is really the dead end, Luis. We might as well file the thing away and forget it. Whatever happened, whether your favorite Lemoyne was concerned or not, we'll never find out."

"I don't like things left up in the air," said Mendoza.

"Neither do I, but sometimes that's the way it works out," said Higgins.

On Monday, about the middle of the afternoon, the autopsy report came in on Finlay. He had died of an overdose
of chloral hydrate. Landers had just come in from more of
the legwork on the gang thing, and looked it over with
Mendoza.

"Well, there you are," he said. "Somebody slipped him
a lethal Mickey Finn." There had been a small amount of
alcohol in the stomach, equivalent to about one drink.
"Somebody was annoyed about his stooling to the cops
about this or that."

"It might look like two plus two," agreed Mendoza,
stroking his moustache, "but it was somebody he trusted,
Tom. Sitting with somebody over a congenial drink. Well,
you can go and ask who he'd been talking about lately."

Landers went up to Narco to see Goldberg, who listened
to the tale and said, "I don't know that we can help you.
Finlay—hell, I think the last time we heard from him was on
that Cardoza thing. He gave us the word that broke that,
and very nice too, a ring of dealers we'd been after for a
while. It's so often like a logjam, one little thing holding it
up from breaking. We knew who we wanted, but there
wasn't any usable evidence until Finlay gave us one key bit
to break the jam. Cardoza's girlfriend. He'd been stepping
out on her with a couple of other girls and she was mad at
him, and she knew about most of his business. Once we had
the word from Finlay, it all came apart. She told the tale on
him and we got the evidence. He got sent away for three-to-
five, and half a dozen of his sellers went up too. But hell,
Landers, that's six months ago and I can't think of anybody who was a close enough pal of any of those to want to
get back at Finlay for that. I don't think anybody realized
it was Finlay who blew the whistle on them."

Navarro in Burglary wasn't any more help. "The last time
we saw Joe he had a little to tell us about a burglary ring
operating in Hollywood, but it wasn't much. We passed it
on to Hollywood for what it was worth. He said he'd try to
get some more on it, it was a pretty slick ring, and he hinted
that it might involve some important people in business cir-

cles. I couldn't say how much that meant. Sometimes Joe liked to sound important. That was about two months ago.

It all sounded fairly nebulous, and it gave them nowhere to go on it.

UP TO THAT TUESDAY the A.P.B. on Carlos Camacho and his car had produced nothing. The autopsy report had come in on Julia, and it contained no surprises; she had died of manual strangulation. Then, late on Tuesday, Calhoun got a call from headquarters in Oxnard. It was brief and stark. Camacho's car had been spotted just outside Port Hueneme, and on being approached by the patrolman he had driven the car off a cliff over a high drop to the beach. He was, of course, dead. Further particulars would be forthcoming, for the necessary red tape.

"So that's that," said Calhoun to Wanda. "You could say, tacit admittal of the murder. Poor devil. You want to do the final report?"

"I might as well," said Wanda with a sigh.

ON THURSDAY Higgins went out for lunch early, dropped into the hospital to see Hackett, and got back to the office at two o'clock. Mendoza was down in Narco talking to somebody about Finlay. There was a note from Scarne on Higgins' desk, which said simply, "This cluttering up office—Where belongs?" Draped over his desk chair was a coat, a woman's coat, and he looked at it twice before he identified it: that coat of Louise Cannaday's, left in her rented car. He scowled at it. It would have to be returned to the son. Mendoza had packed up the address book and sent it back. Higgins, not much interested, rummaged in Mendoza's desk box, failed to find James Cannaday's address, and swore. He could, of course, call the man to get the address; he could call Adele Mowbray. But it would be a hell of a nuisance to parcel the thing up, it would be easier to let the Mowbray woman do that. There was still paperwork to get through, and a new homicide had gone down late yesterday which might pose a little mystery: the owner of a tailoring shop bludgeoned to death, cash undisturbed, no evidence of a struggle.

He bundled up the coat, annoyed at the waste of time, and drove out to the Mowbray condominium to hand it over. There he was foiled; there was no answer to the bell, and as he waited the neighbors across the hall came out and said, "Oh, she's away, up in Lancaster visiting her sister, and the husband's out of town again on business."

Higgins was more annoyed. He had several pieces of business he wanted to get through this afternoon. He decided the only thing to do with the damned coat was to hand it over to those Schultzes and be rid of it, they would have the address in Indianapolis. He was carrying Hackett's notebook and looked up the address. Of course he had never seen the house before, or the Schultzes.

He parked in front of the big handsome house. There was a nearly new Chrysler parked just ahead of him. He put the coat over his arm and started up the front walk. A man had just stepped off the front porch, and a woman was at the half-open door. The man cast Higgins a glance as they passed, a nondescript man in the forties, very well dressed. The woman had been closing the door, opened it again as Higgins appeared on the porch. He explained and handed over the coat. She was a thin woman with dyed blond hair and too much make-up on a rather raddled face, and he thought her eyes looked like those of a skittish horse, too much white showing. "Oh, we'll take care of it," she said, and shut the door abruptly.

Higgins went back to his car and found the other man apparently waiting for him at the curb. "Excuse me," he said, "you're a police officer, aren't you?"

Might as well have *COP* tattooed on the forehead, thought Higgins. "Yes, sir, is there anything I can do for you?"

"Well, I don't know," said the other man. He produced a card. It bore the legend Duncan Culbertson, Dean, Curtis, and Brock, Investments, with an address on Spring Street downtown. "May I talk to you a few minutes? I'm not sure, but I think there may be something wrong. In there,'' and he nodded back at the house.

"What's on your mind?'' asked Higgins.

Culbertson got into the passenger's seat beside him. "I don't know why you're here,'' he said, "what the police are interested in here. But I think maybe there's something wrong in there. I don't feel right about it, it's just an uneasy feeling. You know who lives here, who's supposed to live here?''

"Mr. and Mrs. Schultz,'' said Higgins.

"And Dr. and Mrs. Lorne,'' said Culbertson. "Mrs. Schultz's parents. It's them I'm concerned about. The Schultzes moved in here about a year ago, I gather to look after the old people. I was old Lorne's broker for twenty years, he was a damned shrewd investor, he really didn't need much advice but I acted for him, selling and buying. But he's been going downhill the last year or so, he's way up in the eighties, and he was getting senile. About six months ago the daughter got a power of attorney to take care of his affairs, he was beyond understanding anything, all the way gone, just tottering around. Well, there hasn't been any business to do for him since then. He's got a solid portfolio of very sound stuff, there wasn't anything I wanted to change around. It's the rest of it's been worrying me.''

"How do you mean?'' asked Higgins.

"Well, he'd put quite a sizable amount in his wife's name, thinking to avoid the inheritance tax. There are several big parcels of preferred stock, mutual funds, and on one parcel there's this merger coming up, it's quite a good deal. I've got to get the old lady's signature for it, and I can't seem to get at her. I've been here five times in the last two weeks and Mrs. Schultz keeps putting me off. She doesn't seem to understand anything about business. The last time I saw Mrs. Lorne was about six months ago, and she was bright as a button, a nice old lady, as sharp mentally as she'd ever been. Of course old people can deteriorate suddenly, but if she has, why doesn't the daughter say so? First the old lady isn't feeling well, come back another time, and then she's taking a nap, can't see you now, and just now—'' Culbertson was looking very uneasy ''—she says the old lady isn't there and she doesn't know where she is, and that's just ridiculous. She must know, her own mother, an old lady in a wheelchair. I tell you, I've got a feeling there's something wrong in there.''

"The old couple are in a convalescent home," said Higgins.

"Oh, really, since when? Mrs. Schultz hasn't said a word to me about that. I think there's something wrong."

"You know, Mr. Culbertson, just possibly you could be right," said Higgins. "Let's have a look." He got out of the car and went back up the walk, Culbertson trailing him uncertainly. He pushed the bell and they waited a long time before the door was opened halfway. He got out the badge. "We'd like to see Mrs. Lorne," he said to the woman.

Mrs. Schultz's eyes were suddenly terrified. "You can't come in, I'm busy. You can't see her, she's taking a nap right now—"

"Even so," said Higgins, "I think we'll take a look at her, Mrs. Schultz. Is she here? You just told Mr. Culbertson she wasn't." There was a strange hollow thudding sound from somewhere up the hall. "No!" she said wildly. "No—you go away, you can't come in!" And she turned and ran up the hall away from them. She stopped and leaned on a door there and began to scream thinly. "Stop it—stop it—stop it—I can't stand any more, I can't stand it—" As Higgins came up behind her she tried to scream at him, "Go away!" but it was only a breathy gasp. Higgins pulled her away from the door. It was locked but the key was there, and he unlocked it and opened the door. Mrs. Schultz was prostrate on the hall floor, moaning. For one moment Higgins and Culbertson stood motionless, looking into the room.

It was a large square room, the master bedroom of the house, and had its own bathroom, visible off to one side. The old woman in the wheelchair was just inside the door and the wheelchair had just missed hitting Higgins at knee level where she had evidently been ramming it against the door. The room was a filthy shambles, clothes draped over the twin beds and other furniture, trays with dirty dishes littering the floor, nearly every inch of the carpet covered with dark stains, and there was a fetid cloying odor over everything. The old woman stared up at them with wild eyes; her thin white hair was uncombed and tangled, the nylon housecoat she wore covered with stains. "Please—help—" she croaked painfully. There was an old man lying halfway off one of the beds. He was unconscious, gaunt and emaciated, in dirty pajamas and an even dirtier dressing gown. There was a straggly growth of sparse white beard on his face, and his feet were bare.

"Please help John," she croaked. "Tried—when heard voices—make noise—but never any good—"

"Oh, my God," said Culbertson. "What's wrong with them?—have to get an ambulance—"

Her eyes fixed on Higgins imploringly. "Louise came—she was going help—"

Higgins took another look at the room. First things first. Culbertson was no use, shocked and incoherent. "Take it easy, ma'am," said Higgins. "We'll get help right away." He found the phone in the hall and called an ambulance. Mrs. Schultz had dragged herself up and was crouching in a chair crying. She looked up at Higgins with dull eyes and said, "I couldn't help it, I couldn't stand any more, any more. I told him—have to do something—he kept putting it off. I said what would happen if they died—he'd come to see we'd have to do something, more nurses—but I couldn't help it, when you came I just couldn't stand any more—"

The ambulance came and took the two old people away. Higgins picked up the phone again and called the office. "You'd better chase out here pronto, Luis," he said grimly. "I think we're going to hear the answers to a lot of questions."

THEY DIDN'T LOCATE Fred Schultz right away; she was vague as to where he might be. One of the hardware stores—"Business has been so bad, he's been worried about it, that was another reason—"and they could have wasted a little time taking her in to question, but everything was all ready to flood out of her right now, she was utterly demoralized and seemed, in a queer way, eager to talk, and they thought they had better listen.

"So Dr. and Mrs. Lorne never were in the nice convalescent home?" said Mendoza, standing over her.

She sipped at the glass of water they had given her, gasped and sobbed. "They're so terribly expensive—and there was all the money, all Daddy's money, he has a lot—and Medicare doesn't pay, it's the state pays for that but not until you've spent all your own money and there's nothing left. Fred found out about it. It was that nurse started it, we had her coming to take care of them since before Mother had the stroke—she said she couldn't go on unless we got two other nurses to help, but they really ought to be in a convalescent home, Daddy was senile and it was too much for one nurse—but they'd have had to use up all the money before the state would pay for it and I'd never get anything—all the money left to me—and first we were going to put them in one, we told the nurse so, and she left, and then Fred found out what they cost and he said it was highway robbery. And the doctor they'd had, he was old too and he died and we never bothered to get another—and Fred said I could take care of them, save the money—the nurse was expensive too and if we'd have gotten two more—"

"And then," said Mendoza, "your cousin Louise was going to show up. She wanted to see them, be sure you were looking after them properly." His face was granite.

She flapped her hands wildly. "I couldn't do it! It wasn't fair of Fred to expect it—I just can't stand old sick people like that—I'd bring them TV dinners, they wouldn't eat and they'd drop food all over the floor, and he has to wear diapers like a baby, it was disgusting and horrible, I couldn't do it! They got so dirty and horrible and I said at least get a nurse back, but they cost a lot too and Fred wouldn't, he said we'd have to spend every cent they had before they died—people ought to die when they get like that, they ought to die!" cried Eleanor Schultz wildly.

"Your cousin Louise," said Mendoza.

"She was coming, and if she saw them like that—we couldn't let her, and Fred thought up the story about the convalescent home not letting visitors in right away. With any luck she'd just have gone back east like she was supposed to." Eleanor was feeling bitterly sorry for herself now. "But she didn't, she called the hotel and she changed her flight reservations, and she expected to see them that Monday, and I was terrified—I didn't see how—and she went down the hall to the bathroom and I said to Fred, Oh, God, what'll we do—but Fred said don't worry, we'd get them into some rest home over the weekend and it wouldn't matter if Mother said anything about us, we'd say she didn't know what she was talking about, old people always get ideas about being persecuted, don't they? We might have managed, only Mother kept bumping her wheelchair against the door, and Louise asked about it and before I could stop her she got the door open—"

"And raised a row about what she found," said Mendoza.

She was bent over like an old woman, and her voice was muffled. "Oh, it was awful, it was awful—she kept saying how could you, your own parents, but they're just dirty disgusting old people—and she was shouting at Fred, she was going right to the police, and he took hold of her and shook her hard and her head went back against the door and she fell down—"

"So that's how it happened," said Higgins under his breath. "Earlier than the doctor thought, maybe about four that afternoon, when they said she left."

"And what did Fred do then?" asked Mendoza.

"Ask him—I was so scared, I just did what he said! He felt her head and said she was going to die pretty soon—we'd have to cover up—" and however Fred had known about depressed skull fractures, he would probably have known that with prompt treatment she could have been saved; but then she'd have told about the treatment of the old people, which wouldn't have suited him at all. In for a penny, in for a pound, and might as well be hanged for a sheep as a lamb. "And he made me go to the hotel—"

"Oh, yes," said Mendoza. "I see." They could read that now. It hadn't been Louise Cannaday who went back to the hotel but Eleanor Schultz, probably wearing a hat to cover her hair. The desk clerk had been busy, taken notice only of the room number, and the Schultzes would have known that by the card in her bag.

"I just did what he said, you can't do anything to me for that," she muttered weakly. "He said she was going to die—so I went out and put her car in the garage, and we put her in it. And I went to the hotel, and I sent that telegram. And I left the key on the desk, and then we went to the Garsteins' anniversary party, and when we got home Louise was dead. So Fred drove her car down there, I followed him in ours—he said the police would just think it was an accident—"

That answered most of the questions. "And how right Mrs. Mowbray was," said Higgins grimly. "So simple when you know."

Fred Schultz was a different proposition from his wife. They located him and brought him into headquarters late that afternoon, and when he heard what they had to say he shut up like a clam. He just said, "I might have known better than to trust that goddamned fool woman not to talk." Besides that he had only one bitter communication. "It's all the goddamned government's fault. Think they'll give you something for nothing, fat chance. We'd have had to spend all the old man's money, pay to have them taken care of, the damn government wouldn't start to pay until it was all spent, every last dime. A goddamned waste of money, they're just worthless old zombies, no good to anybody. He must have a couple million, and it'll all come to Eleanor. A goddamned waste, pay it all out to a nursing home. And if that damned woman hadn't shown up, poking her nose in—" He shut up then, refusing to answer questions, but they could fill in a lot of gaps.

Higgins went home and told Mary about it, and she was silent and then said, "The great Mendoza says simple. It is simple, George. Just the one simple thing that prevents the world from being perfect."

"And what's the magic formula?" asked Higgins.

"Why, what's called empathy. If everybody in the world could really put themselves in another person's place, and really understand—how would I feel if that was done to me. Hasn't it ever come into that woman's mind, maybe some-day she'll be old and ill and incompetent?"

"You're talking about the millennium," said Higgins wryly.

HACKETT HEARD about it from Mendoza, and told Angel when she came to the hospital that night. She said things about empathy too, sitting on the bed beside him with his arms around her. "It's frightening to think your own chil-dren could turn against you like that."

"Luis said they've figured out it must have started about four months ago, after their regular doctor died and the nurse said she couldn't go on with the case, they needed more care than she could give, ought to be in a nursing home. Evidently they'd intended to find one, and then the miserly Fred found out what those places cost and decided to save the money. Well, my Angel, we'll just hope that the kids grow up thinking enough of us they'd at least see we were taken care of decently."

AT ABOUT TWO O'CLOCK on Friday afternoon a stranger came into the communal detective office and looked around hesitantly. He was a very young man with pink cheeks and blond hair, tall and slim, neatly dressed in tan slacks and tan jacket. Palliser got up from his desk and asked, "Can we help you?"

"I'm supposed to see Detective Larsen or Detective Cal-houn," said the boy. "I'm from the Oxnard force. My name's Eaton, Eugene Eaton."

Calhoun was out somewhere. Palliser took him over to Wanda's desk and introduced him. He looked surprised to see a good-looking blond female. "The captain said I should come in and tell you about it, you'll need the facts to close the case. It's about that fellow named Camacho. I was the one who spotted him. I've been on the Oxnard force for nearly a year."

A rookie, and he must be over twenty-one but he didn't look it. Wanda smiled at him. "We'd like to hear about it, Mr. Eaton," she said.

And because she was a girl and sympathetic, he lost some of his wistful dignity and said, "It shook me, it really did, Miss Larsen. We all had that A.P.B. posted in the squads, we'd been on the lookout. Of course nobody knew what he was wanted for, probably nothing serious. I was on tour, it was about the end of shift, when I spotted the plate. The car was parked way out at the top of the palisades, and there was this guy sitting in it, behind the wheel, just looking out at the ocean. I got out of the squad and went up to the driver's door, you know how we're supposed to. And I said to him, are you Carlos Camacho, and he said he was. He was kind of a nice-looking fellow. And he said, you're going to arrest me, aren't you. And I said there was a want out on him from L.A., and he'd have to come in with me to the station. He didn't look as if he'd give any trouble, but being alone on tour I was figuring to go by the book, put the cuffs on him. I was just about to tell him to get out of the car when he said something funny. I didn't understand what he meant."

"Yes?" said Wanda.

"He looked at me in a funny kind of way and he said, it'll be all right if I can find Mother. She'll intercede for me, and she was the best woman I ever knew so I don't think God would refuse her a favor. It'll be all right then. And then— my God, Miss Larsen, he got the engine started before I knew he was going to do it, and he just put his foot down and drove straight over the edge—must be six hundred feet down to the beach, and it's all rock right there—the car was all smashed to hell and so was he. Just a young guy."

Wanda was silent. And for murder there was no valid reason, but she hoped Carlos had found his mother and found some peace. "Thanks for coming in," she said. "I'll get the statement typed up and you can sign it."

THE SCHULTZES were lodged in jail and would come up for arraignment sometime next week or the week after. Nothing more at all had shown up on Finlay; they were now talking to his known friends, and there weren't many of them.

But when Mendoza came in on Sunday morning, a little late, he was still thinking about Louise Cannaday. They could fill in a lot of gaps from what Eleanor Schultz had said, but there were a few loose ends.

"You know, George, I'll always wonder what the hell Schultz might have intended to do when and if the old people died? Bury them in the backyard? But there'd have been the will to prove, to get all the nice money. There'd have had to be death certificates. And any doctor who saw them would know they'd been maltreated."

"Just doing what comes naturally," said Higgins. "Playing it by ear. Not looking ahead."

Mendoza laughed. "I saw the old lady in the hospital yesterday. She's a spunky old lady. Sitting up and talking sensible as you please, once they'd cleaned her up and begun to feed her. She's mostly concerned about her husband. He's about on his last legs, can't last long. Of course he's senile and doesn't know what's going on, but of course it didn't help much that he's apparently had practically no food for weeks or months. She says she tried to feed him—the Schultz woman just dumped the TV dinners in front of them—but her right arm's paralyzed, she could hardly feed herself with the other hand. People—I suppose it never occurred to Mrs. Schultz that she might end up in the same condition, and appreciate the nice kind attention."

Higgins grunted. "What Mary said."

"And something else rather peculiar. If Art hadn't got broad-sided by that irresponsible drunk, we might never have broken that case. Has that occurred to you? You hadn't had much to do with it directly. If Art hadn't been in the hospital, he'd have taken that coat out there, and Culbertson would have glanced at him, put him down for a salesman or lawyer or exterminator, and passed on his way. But one look at you and he knew you for a cop, so he spoke up."

"I thought about it," said Higgins seriously. "I guess there is something managing things."

Mendoza picked up the night report and looked it over, and the next moment sat up and said, "*¡Diez millónes de demonios desde infierno!* This damned mugger—"

"I saw it," said Higgins.

The night watch had been called out at nearly the end of the shift to find Moss waiting beside a dead man on the sidewalk along Rampart Boulevard. There was identification on him for a Harold Brady, an address on Ocean View. His billfold had been left beside him, but whatever money it had contained was missing. So were his shoes.

"*¡Por Dios!*" said Mendoza. "Now the damned mugger has killed somebody, and there's no possible way to go looking for him. Hell and damnation—"

"What can be cured," said Higgins. "We might as well file it away as unsolved right now and forget it." But of course they couldn't do that.

For once Mendoza didn't hang around the office long. Sunday was supposed to be his day off. Unfortunately, when he got home he found no peace and quiet waiting for him. It had started to rain again, and the twins were prevented from riding the ponies or playing outside. Luisa was under everyone's feet, still towing the imaginary kite and making a loud humming noise. Cedric was sound asleep in front of the fire with three cats curled up between his forepaws; El Señor was brooding on top of the credenza. Alison was in her armchair nursing the new one.

Mairí had followed Mendoza down the hall to say, "I was thinking of a nice chicken pot pie, and the apple cobbler you like."

"Fine," said Alison. Mendoza bent to kiss her.

"Not fine," said Johnny. "I want fried chicken. And cake."

"I want spaghetti," said Terry.

"Now you two, you'll take what the rest of us have and be thankful for it."

They came to hang on Mendoza. "Sissy's been real good today, she hasn't cried once," said Terry.

"But I wish she'd grow faster," complained Johnny. "She hasn't growed hardly at all since you got her at the hospital."

"She will, darling," said Alison.

"But it'll be a long time before she's anything but little Sissy," said Johnny. "When's it going to stop raining? I'm tired of reading."

Mendoza decided he needed a small drink and went back to the kitchen, hotly pursued by El Señor. When he came back the twins were whining loudly about the rain. "Oh, for heaven's sake, settle down," said Alison. "Go and play with your building set."

"That's Johnny's, it's a boy's thing," said Terry. "I haven't got anything to do. When's it going to stop raining?"

"I don't want to do that," said Johnny. "When's it going to stop raining?"

"Now look," said Alison, "see how nice and quiet Sissy's being, such a good little girl—"

"Oooh, you said it!" said the twins in unison. "You said Sissy!"

"I was just starting to say Cecelia," said Alison hastily.

Mendoza sat down in his own armchair and laughed at all of them.

"A superlative whodunit from the popular author of *No Escape* and *The Lure of Sweet Death*."

—*Mystery News*

SARAH KEMP

What Dread Hand

A Dr. Tina May Mystery.

Something very strange—and very deadly—was happening in the quiet little town of Trepoll Haven. Two women were suddenly dead, and Dr. Tina May, celebrity pathologist, finds herself deeply implicated in both murders as either killer or intended victim!

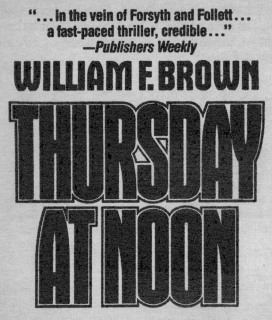

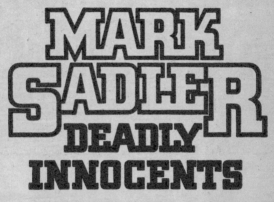

Take 2 books & a surprise gift FREE

SPECIAL LIMITED-TIME OFFER

Mail to: The Mystery Library
           901 Fuhrmann Blvd.
           P.O. Box 1867
           Buffalo, N.Y. 14269-1867

YES! Please send me 2 free books from the Mystery Library and my free surprise gift. Then send me 2 mystery books, first time in paperback, every month. Bill me only $3.50 per book. There is no extra charge for shipping and handling. There is no minimum number of books I must purchase. I can always return a shipment and cancel at any time. Even if I never buy another book from The Mystery Library, the 2 free books and the surprise gift are mine to keep forever.

414-FBA8

Name	(PLEASE PRINT)	

Address		Apt. No.

City	State	Zip

This offer is limited to one order per household and not valid to present subscribers. Price and terms subject to change.   MYS-BPA3